RED RUNS THE RIVER

Life of the Dead Book 5

TONY URBAN

PACKANACK
publishing

The life of the dead is placed in the memory of the living.

— CICERO

Long is the way and hard, that out of Hell leads up to light.
John Milton, Paradise Lost

INTRODUCTION

It's nearly impossible to believe that, after 3 years, 300,000 words, and 5 books, my *Life of the Dead* series has reached its conclusion.

Thank you to all of the readers who kept clamoring for more and for sticking with me every step of the way.

And now, let's get on with the getting on.

—TU

CHAPTER ONE

THE GROUND WAS HARD FOR DIGGING. BETWEEN THE ROCKY SOIL and the cold half-frozen Earth, Wim had been working all morning and part of the afternoon and only made it down three and a half feet. He reckoned that might be deep enough but knew tradition was six feet, and he was determined to dig a proper grave, even if it took him the entire week.

Such slow progress gave him time to think. Too much time. He tried to push all thoughts out of his head, to think about nothing but shoveling out scoop after scoop of dirt, but no matter how hard he tried, he couldn't keep his mind from working. From reeling. From reminding himself over and over again that this hole - this burial plot - was for Ramey, and that, soon enough, it wouldn't be him standing inside this half-dug grave, it would be his wife laying inside it.

Wim still struggled to accept the truth of it. He'd known the day might come - would come - since her father spilled the secret at the Ark over three years earlier. Ramey wasn't immune. She'd been vaccinated, but that vaccine was only temporary, and the reality was, sooner or later, she'd fall prey to the virus her demented, homicidal father had created. From the moment they'd heard that news, they both knew it was only a matter of time before Ramey became a zombie.

Each of them had tried to ignore the coming fate, but the truth hung over their heads like an anvil suspended by a frayed rope, waiting to fall on them when they least expected it. After fleeing the Ark, they made their way to North Carolina, where they found a small but perfect log cabin all the way at the top of the mountain on which they still lived. It had already been stocked with more canned goods than they could eat in half a year, and cautious trips into the nearby town of West Jefferson kept them more than well stocked.

Over the years, they added some livestock which they came across while scouting the surrounding areas. It started with a brown and white spotted cow that was mostly skin stretched over bone. She was far past her milking days, but Wim was eager to take her in. Eventually, a couple of chickens were added, and once a rooster came along, their flock expanded so quickly that they could barely keep up with the eggs.

Two goats, a blue pig, and a half-wild stallion Ramey had taken to calling Gypsy rounded out their poor excuse for a farm. Wim built a coop for the chickens and a stable for the rest, and even though he wasn't much of a carpenter, it sufficed, and life seemed almost normal again.

Except for the anvil.

The shovel glanced off a particularly large rock, and orange sparks flew. Wim muttered a swear under his breath as the reverberations of the blow tingled all the way up his arms and into his shoulders. He crouched down in the hole and pushed away some of the dense wet dirt with his hands. It was a big rock and was going to take some work. He set the shovel aside and grabbed the pickaxe.

While alone on his family farm, after his Mama's death, Wim had never thought much about love, at least not the romantic kind. He was happy there, alone and mostly cut off from human contact, and he'd never been apt to daydream about meeting a woman, let alone getting married.

If Ramey hadn't stumbled onto his farm in the early days of the apocalypse, he reckoned he'd still be living there, alone. In some ways, especially now while he stood in a damp hole over halfway past his waist, he wished that was still the situation. That Ramey would have taken a different route south and bypassed him entirely. Then he wouldn't have met her and fallen in love. Then he wouldn't have lost friends like Emory and Bundy. Then he wouldn't have seen the evil men - men like Ramey's father - were capable of. An ignorant life might have been preferable to all of that. And most of all, he wouldn't have had to do so much killing.

Yet, as he worked to free the stone which had revealed itself to be more than two feet across and almost ten inches thick, he knew he would trade all that pain for the good time with Ramey six days a week and twice on Sunday. And there were so many good times that, while he struggled to fall asleep at night, he wondered what he'd done to be deserving of such happiness.

In Ramey, he'd found a woman he not only loved, but with whom he felt so comfortable that it seemed like he was a pair of old, broken-in gloves, and she was the set of hands on which they fit perfectly. Where every crinkle and wrinkle and worn-down part was the mirror match for the delicate fingers inside. She wasn't only his wife, she was his best friend, and it was near impossible to imagine his life without her.

He remembered a few months after his Pa died, a morning when Mama sat at the kitchen table. She'd been drinking her coffee when tears began to trickle down her cheeks, splashing onto her saucer. He hadn't said anything. A woman's tears had always caused him considerable duress and confusion, but he reached across the table and laid his hand on top of hers.

She looked at him and worked up a wan smile and said, "Wim, I looked at myself in the mirror this morning, and I didn't know who I was. It's like half of me has up and disappeared."

Wim was a teenager and didn't understand that much at the time, but now it made sense. He supposed that's the way life worked. You only understood large parts of it in hindsight. And no matter how hard you tried, you couldn't truly appreciate what you had until it floated out of your life like dandelion seeds in the wind.

Wim had worked the rock free of the dirt. He grabbed it in his blistered and dirt-stained hands, hoisted it up, and tossed it aside with a tired *oof*. Then he returned to digging.

CHAPTER TWO

THE HOLE WAS ALMOST AS TALL AS WIM. IT WASN'T PERFECTLY level at the bottom, but he supposed that didn't matter. It would serve its purpose just as well either way.

As he stood in the grave, he thought he might be better served staying there permanently, and his hand instinctively dropped to the butt of the revolver he kept holstered at his waist. He couldn't imagine a life after this. A life without Ramey. But he knew the animals needed tending to. He'd already been responsible for too much death, and he wouldn't leave them without any provisions.

He hadn't given much thought to getting out of the grave, and a full day of digging had left his arms feeling like overcooked noodles. He struggled, clawing at the ground above and digging his feet into the dirt walls for a full five minutes before managing to extricate himself. Once he was out, he flopped down onto the earth, which was covered with a soft blanket of golden yellow pine needles, and caught his breath.

It was nearing dark. He'd long ago given up wearing a watch but knew it must be closing in on 8 p.m. He realized he'd been at this task the entire day and guilt washed over him for daring to leave Ramey alone for so long when they already had such little time remaining.

It was five days earlier that she got sick. It started with sneezing and a nose that dripped like a faucet. But before that day was up, the sickness filled her lungs and the coughing started. She'd gone downhill rapidly after that.

She'd been bedridden for the last two days. Even sitting up left her weak and exhausted. She tried to talk occasionally, but it wasn't long before delirium overtook her and all she did was moan. One-time, her feverish eyes locked on him, and her mouth opened, and he thought he heard her say, "Please, do it," but he told himself that was nothing but his imagination. At least, he tried to tell himself that. That was the last time he saw her conscious. In some ways, that was easier. Maybe it made him a chicken, but he didn't want to hear that kind of talking.

It all seemed unfair. Wim knew that very idea, that this was unfair, made little sense in a world where barely one in a million people had survived the plague and many, maybe even most of the initial survivors, had died in the weeks and months after. They'd been given almost four more years than most, but that wasn't nearly enough.

The years in the cabin were the happiest since Wim's childhood. Maybe his entire life even. They'd had their evenings on the swing. Their cold winter nights in front of the fireplace. As he'd predicted, it wasn't always an easy life, but it was always a good one. Every day was a good one with Ramey at his side. He'd grown to love her more than he thought possible.

Ramey was self-conscious about the scar on her face which she'd sustained when the Ark was collapsing, but Wim thought it gave her face character and showed some of the toughness a stranger might not otherwise have known she possessed just by looking at her. He loved the way her chocolate-colored hair felt when it spilled into his face when they were in bed and how she would cuddle with the chickens when she thought he wasn't looking, and maybe above all, her strength. He couldn't imagine many people could have dealt with that anvil hanging over their head with so much courage and acceptance.

When he left that morning, the fever had taken hold, and her clothes were so wet it was like she'd just gone for a dip in the lake fully dressed. And when Wim held her in his arms before going off to dig her grave, he felt like he was holding onto someone who was burning from the inside out. In a way, he supposed that's what was happening.

When he left, she'd been so sound asleep that he thought she might have slipped into a coma. He wasn't sure how to check whether that was the case, so he tried giving her a gentle shake. She responded with a pained groan but didn't come awake. He thought letting her sleep would be the kindest decision.

The grave he'd dug, Ramey's grave, was a hundred yards from the cabin, down the road a piece and in a little clearing where wild black-eyed Susan's grew in the summer. He thought it would be a pretty spot for her, but it was also far enough away that she wouldn't know what he was up to if she did make it out of bed and look out the window. As he returned to the cabin, he worried he'd been gone too long. That the sickness might have ended her and all that remained behind was her body, now reanimated and hungry. Without thought, he doubled his pace.

The pig greeted him as he rounded the corner, and the cabin was revealed. It waddled up to him and pressed its wet nose against his leg. He gave its head a hurried scratch and felt bad when he pushed past without any further acknowledgement, but there'd be more time to be kind to the pig. There might not be more time for Ramey.

Wim climbed the four stairs to the cabin porch in two galloping steps, then pushed the front door open. Everything inside appeared normal enough. No broken lanterns or tipped over end tables. Nothing that would indicate a zombie had been staggering around. His breath spilled out on something between a relieved and tired sigh.

"Ramey?" His voice trembled as he stared at the closed bedroom door. "I'm back. Sorry I was out so long."

No response came, and Wim supposed that news could go either way. He moved to the door, took the cold knob in his hand, and gave it a quarter turn. He stopped to listen, heard nothing, then spun it the rest of the way.

There was no sense in dragging it out further, so Wim pushed the door open.

The bed, their bed, was empty. No Ramey, just sopping wet, disheveled sheets and a pillow discarded onto the floor.

He opened his mouth to say something, maybe call her name again, but no words came. The sight so surprised him that he was speechless.

He turned away from the empty room, back to the cabin, and tried to find something that could tip him off to what was going on.

It took him a full minute before he saw the note on the coffee table. The table that sat across from the fireplace where the two of them had spent so many nights in each other's arms. He crossed the room, sat on the couch, and took the paper in his hands. It was filled top to bottom with Ramey's looping handwriting.

Wim, I know I'm a total shit for doing this. For leaving you again with only a letter in my wake. But it's the way it has to be. We both know I'm dying and that it'll happen soon. I tried to talk about it, but you won't, and I understand, but I know what you're doing in the meadow today. I knew when I saw you take the shovel. I probably shouldn't have been spying on you like I was, but when you get quiet, my mind works too hard and curiosity gets the best of me.

I wish I never had to leave you. I wish we could have grown old and fat and gray together. Nothing would have made me happier. But thanks to my asshole father, that isn't possible. I'm a dead woman walking. I'm sorry I asked you to kill me. I know the toll the killing has taken on you, and the very least I can do is save you from doling out one more death.

So, forgive me for leaving without a goodbye. For leaving you alone again. I really do believe it's for the best. I don't want to die, but even more than that, I don't want you to see what I'll become. I took one of your pistols. I think it was the one you always complained about having to clean, so hopefully you won't miss it. I'm going as far as I can walk, and then I'm saying Sayonara. I can't beat my father's disease, but I can stop it from turning me into some kind of awful husk. Don't come looking for me. I don't need to be buried. Let nature reclaim me. Dust to dust and all that.

I want you to know that I loved you more than I could ever put down on paper. You're the best man I've ever known, and you have more strength and compassion than a hundred others. Yet I know your heart is half broken from the things you've had to do the last few years. I wanted to be able to fix that, but in the end, I just piled on. I hope you won't hold it against me.

Don't get too caught up in mourning me. This is part of life. Stay here and take care of our animals. Give Miss Piggy the second my portion of food tonight and give Gypsy some sugar and tell her it's from me.

You've been my hero and my savior. My rock and my soft place to fall. I love you, love you, love you.

It ended with an uneven heart and the letter 'R'.

Wim read it all the way through four times. He knew she must have been gone for hours and cursed himself for leaving her alone in the first place. He thought about leaving. About trying to find her, but in the end, he followed her wishes. He figured he owed her that.

He took to staring out the window, where he could see nothing but the stars poking through the black emptiness of the night. He remembered, years earlier, having a discussion with Emory about the stars and the correlation between them and the dwindling state of humanity. It seemed like everyone and everything he let himself care about died or left him. And he felt cursed for being the one who survived it all.

CHAPTER THREE

A LITTLE OVER SIX MONTHS HAD PASSED SINCE RAMEY LEFT HIM to die alone, and Wim had managed to go on. In many ways, it was like life on the farm after Mama died, only the hole in his heart was bigger now. He didn't talk much to the animals anymore but did his best to care for them through what was a particularly harsh winter on the mountain. He lost a few chickens to a fox or maybe a bobcat, and the old cow didn't make it through the season, but the rest trudged on. Just like him.

He'd given the cabin several deep cleanings, but her smell remained behind. That was the worst of it. Her clothes, her trinkets, those could be tucked away in closets. The photos of them together were hidden in drawers. But he couldn't erase her scent, no matter how hard he tried, and every time he breathed in her aroma, the synapses in his head fired too quickly and he thought she was still there, or that she'd come back to him. And then the rest of his brain caught up, and he realized it was nothing but the leftovers of what had once been a happy life.

One late June morning, the sunlight and blue sky worked together to turn the surface of the water trough into a mirror, and

Wim was shocked when he caught his reflection. He hadn't bothered to cut his hair or shave since Ramey left, but even through all that fur, he could tell he'd lost a considerable amount of weight. His eyes looked like dull marbles in their sockets, and his face had taken on deep etchings, especially around his eyes. He looked like a tired, old bum, and he supposed that wasn't too far off from the truth.

It had been a few months since he'd made a trip to town to restock, and he was running low on everything. As much as he didn't care about himself, he knew there wasn't enough feed for the livestock to make it through another week, and he needed to remedy that, so he pulled the wagon out of the barn and rolled it to Gypsy.

She shimmied side to side as he hitched it up. "Come on, now. Behave yourself."

The horse settled a bit, but its nostrils flared as it huffed. She was a contemptible beast.

The trip to West Jefferson took almost two hours by horse and wagon and would take twice that long going back, loaded down and mostly uphill. Before, when he made these trips with Ramey, they were events to be enjoyed. Long, dusty versions of Sunday rides. Miniature adventures. Now, he found the journey downright miserable.

The mountain road seemed even bumpier and ragged than before, and a few times, he thought a wheel might break on the wagon, but it survived, and riding became smoother once he got to paved roads.

He'd cleared the town of zombies when they first arrived years earlier, disposing of a hundred or so. Over the years, he found and killed a few dozen more that trickled in in dribs and drabs. He supposed they were probably residents who lived in the houses and farms outside of town and had managed to find their way back to the place they once frequented through some vestiges of memory that remained inside their rotting heads. There were never more than a few on any given trip and, as far as he could recall, it had been a year or more since there'd been any at all.

That's why he was surprised when he saw movement through the plate glass window of the grocery store. He pulled the reigns, and Gypsy gave an annoyed nicker before slowing to a stop.

He tied her off to a Stop sign, double knotting the rope. "You stay now." As if she had a choice in the matter.

Wim grabbed his rifle from the wagon and moved toward the store without bothering to exhibit much stealth. The door was open, but, although he was certain he'd closed it the last time he was there, that didn't concern him much. It was a rickety door, after all.

The bright midday light lit up the store as well as the overhead fluorescents once had, if not better, and Wim had no trouble spotting the mostly bald head that bobbed up and down as the body it belonged to moved through the canned goods aisle. To Wim, it looked a little like a brown egg rising up and dipping down. Up and down. If it was a zombie, it was an active one.

He flicked off the rifle's safety and stepped to the end of the aisle. When he arrived, he saw the figure from behind and quickly realized the up and down motion was occurring because it was removing cans from the shelves and depositing them into an olive-green duffle bag that looked about big enough to hold a body.

Wim thought about announcing his presence but decided that waiting and watching was more interesting. For the next four minutes, the man with the bald head emptied the shelves of every can of soup and then all the vegetables with the exception of green beans. Upon completion, he made an attempt to pick up the bag. An attempt that ended in failure and a pained grunt.

"That's a good way to give yourself a hernia," Wim said.

The man spun around so fast that his foot got caught in the strap of the bag and his arms flailed as he tried unsuccessfully to get his balance before he fell on top of his bounty with a pained *urgh*.

"Aw, darn it now." Wim hadn't meant to make the old fellow fall. He set his rifle against the shelf and moved toward him as the man tried to climb back to his feet. "Let me help you out there." He was a few feet away when the man looked up.

His face was the color and texture of old leather, and one eye was clouded over by a cataract. He sneered as he saw Wim, revealing a set of teeth that was at thirty percent capacity tops. He wore clothing that reminded Wim of a WWII Army uniform and which was too large, sagging off his thin frame.

Wim didn't even realize the man had pulled a knife until he spoke.

"Stay back from me! I'll gut you, you get any closer!"

Wim's eyes went to the man's hand, and he saw a rusty Swiss Army knife clutched in his boney fist. But the can opener tool was open rather than the blade, and Wim couldn't hold back a smirk.

"I reckon you could if I stood still long enough. But you'd be better off using that on some of the food you just took."

The man looked down at his arthritis-swollen hand, and his good eye grew wide. He fumbled with the knife, his hands shaking like he had the palsy while he tried with no success to pull out the correct blade.

Wim gave him a whole minute before deciding it had gone on long enough. "I'm not gonna hurt you, fella, so why don't you save us both the trouble of trying to put an end to me?"

The man peered up at Wim, squinting his good eye. "You trustworthy?"

"If I wasn't, I doubt there'd be much you could do about it."

That seemed to be good enough, and the man stopped fiddling with the knife. He turned his attention back to the bag. "This is mine, though. I got here first. Fair's fair."

"Whatever you say. But from the looks of it, and the looks of you for that matter, you wouldn't make it a mile with all that loot before your ticker blew right up."

The man seemed offended at the slight and redoubled his efforts to lift the bag. That time, he succeeded, but his body tipped heavy to the side like the leaning tower of Pisa. "There. Shows how much you know."

Wim raised his eyebrow and nodded. The old man was already

out of breath and beads of sweat had risen on his forehead. "Uh huh. You showed me."

The man wobbled back and forth as he pushed by Wim and toward the exit. Wim watched him go and examined the shelves to see what he left behind.

"What do you have against green beans?"

"I don't..." the man huffed, puffed, "Appreciate the texture."

Wim didn't care about the texture and grabbed a few cans for himself. He was moving on to the baked beans when he heard a crash. When he looked toward the noise, he found the man sprawled on the floor, half the bag on top of him, and looking like he'd just gone ten rounds with Mike Tyson.

"You need some help up there?"

The man waved him away. "I decided to rest a spell."

"As you wish."

THE OLD MAN's name was Zeke. He didn't tender a surname, and Wim didn't bother asking—Zeke was good enough. He said he was sixty-two years old, and while Wim suspected he was off a good decade, he didn't call him on that either. He said he'd been on the move for the duration of the apocalypse, and from the looks of him and his worn-out loafers, Wim believed him that time.

The two of them sat on the sidewalk and ate cold peas and corn straight from the cans. Zeke wanted to follow that up with some Vienna sausages, but when he popped the can, Wim thought the vaguely gray meat looked well beyond its expiration date.

"Think I'll take a pass on those."

Zeke grunted. "More for me."

The old man wasn't much for talking and certainly didn't display any of the wisdom or eloquence of Wim's last elderly friend, Emory. But that was quite a high bar.

Wim noticed that Zeke kept eyeing his boots, so when the man commented, it wasn't a shock.

"Nice boots you got there."

"Uh huh."

"Wishum I had me a pair like that."

"They're heavy. Not the best for walking."

Zeke scratched at his groin for a while, then spoke again. "You got a woman?"

"I do not."

"Wishum I had me a woman."

Wim tried to push thoughts of Ramey from his mind. "You've been alone for the duration?"

"I traveled with a man, bout your age, and a boy not quite in his teens early on. Back when the cars still worked. We met up outside of St. Louis."

"Why'd that come to an end?"

Zeke gave another grunt. It seemed to be his fallback response when he didn't want to provide information. "How bout you? You alone?"

"Yup."

"Too quiet. Gives your head too much time to think. Too much thinking ain't good."

Wim thought that to be the most profound statement the man had made.

"That's why I wishum I had me a woman. You got a woman, there ain't never no quiet. No time for thinking."

That was less profound, and as much as Wim agreed silence wasn't good, he was tiring of this character. "It'll be nearing dark before long. I better get back."

He stood, and when he did, Zeke scrambled to his feet too. "You got a place round here?"

Wim nodded.

"An extra bed too maybe?"

It was Wim's turn to grunt.

AFTER SHOWING Zeke his way around the cabin, Wim unloaded the wagon and fed the animals. He'd brought back enough food to last the livestock a few months, and, despite the addition of the old timer, he felt more accomplished than he had in a while.

When he returned to the cabin, he found Zeke sprawled on the couch with sounds that reminded him of an out-of-tune chainsaw exploding from his open mouth. The snoring kept Wim awake most of the night. When he finally passed out, he slept like a stone, and when his eyes opened, it was well past dawn.

He sat up in bed, alarmed at the quiet. The roosters should have been cock a doodle doing by now. He remembered the first day of the plague when their silence was what tipped him that something was very wrong. He was in a near panic as he rushed outside and was expecting the worst.

What he found was Zeke sitting in the dirt and feeding the chickens out of the palms of his hands. The birds pecked at him, fluttering their wings and giving gleeful chirps. Wim smiled at the sight.

With each day that passed, Wim expected Zeke to say it was time to move on. Even if he hadn't meant it, making the offer would have been the polite thing to do. Only Zeke didn't mention leaving, and, if anything, he seemed to make himself more at home.

He wasn't a bad man, quite the opposite really. He'd shown himself to be a great hand with the animals, and he was good about cleaning up inside the cabin. But every time Wim saw Zeke sitting on the swing or on the couch or at the kitchen table, it only made him remember seeing Ramey in those same places, and Wim found the sight almost obscene. Like a pig inside a church. It wasn't Zeke's fault, and Wim knew that, but by the time two weeks had gone by, the very sight of the man only irritated him and made him recall what he'd lost.

One day, while watching Zeke shovel manure out of the pen,

Wim realized what needed to happen. He waited a few days before mentioning it, letting the idea stew inside his head to make certain he wasn't being rash, but time didn't change his mind.

Zeke sat at the edge of the coop and held a chick that was a couple weeks old in one hand and let it peck food from the other. When Wim's shadow fell over him, he swiveled his bald head around to see.

"Afternoon, Wim."

"Zeke." Wim didn't say anything else, and Zeke watched him, curious.

"You look like a man with something on his mind."

Wim nodded. "Umm hmm."

Zeke set the chick down and rose to his feet, brushing dust off his pants. "I'm listening. Don't have to hold back on me."

Wim thought the old man looked scared. That he seemed to know Wim wanted to be done with him. His fearful gaze was so pathetic that Wim looked away. "I'm taking the wagon to town to stock up."

Zeke gushed out a relieved exhale. "Oh. Okay. We ain't running too low, though, are we?"

We, Wim thought. *Friend, you and I aren't we.* "Not yet, but it goes quicker than you'd think."

"All right. You'd know better than me."

"I would."

Wim didn't say another word to the man before hitching the wagon to Gypsy and leaving.

He thought his mind might change on the ride to and from town, but it did not. He had so much feed on the wagon that he wasn't sure the nag would be able to make it back up the mountain, but she did. When they got back, he found Zeke had cleaned out Gypsy's stall, going so far as to shovel away the built-up mud from around the base. If he'd had any doubt about his decision, that dispelled it.

Zeke appeared at the cabin door and waved when he saw Wim hopping down from the wagon. "Made good time. I was going to mix up an omelette, but your arrival caught me off guard."

"I can go and come again if you prefer."

"Not at all. You'll just have to wait a spell for dinner."

"That's never been a problem."

By the time Wim was finished unloading the day's haul, he'd worked up enough of an appetite that waiting did indeed seem like an inconvenience. To take his mind off eating, he busied himself by surveying the area around the cabin.

Zeke had it all fixed up to the point where the buildings looked almost new and were cleaner than they'd been in months. The small vegetable patch Wim had often struggled to maintain in this rocky soil was doing better than it ever had previously. Even the blue pig which had always been on the scrawny side seemed to have fattened up since the old man's arrival.

"If we had a bell, now's the time I'd ring it."

Wim turned to see Zeke standing on the porch. "I hope you made enough for seconds."

"Thirds and fourths even."

The omelettes weren't anything special. Zeke put in too many canned mushrooms for Wim's liking, but he was hungry and cleaned two platefuls nonetheless. When they finished, Zeke moved to gather the dirty dishes but Wim stopped him.

"I've made a decision."

That panicked, fearful look washed over the old timer's face again, and Wim wanted to be done with this business as quickly as possible, so he spit out the rest of the words as fast as his mouth would move. "I'm leaving this place. It's not home anymore. I wanted to leave months ago, but I couldn't up and abandon the animals. Now that you're here, I don't have that worry."

Zeke only stared at him, his hazy eyes wide.

"I'll take the horse, and the wagon too for that matter, since it won't do you no good without an animal to pull it. I've got you stocked up for the better part of the year. After that, it's on you. So that's that. This is your place now. Think you can handle it?"

The old man continued to stare. He opened his mouth as if to speak, then closed it and swallowed hard.

"I'll take that as a yes, I'll head out in the morning." Wim stood, pushing his chair backward, the legs scratching at the wood floor. He'd miss that sound.

Zeke still hadn't spoken by the time Wim went into the bedroom, closed the door, and packed.

WIM WAS ready to ride out at dawn, but Zeke insisted he stay for breakfast. Wim agreed, but when he saw Zeke had put stewed tomatoes into the eggs, he regretted that decision.

The old man didn't have much to say, and that was just as well. After they ate, Wim loaded the few possessions he'd decided to take onto the wagon. Aside from his clothing, it was limited to a few rifles, one shotgun, enough food to last a few days, and the meager amount of photographs he had of Ramey, including one from their wedding.

As Wim climbed into the wagon and took the reins in his hand, Zeke stood a few feet away and watched.

"You change your mind, anytime, you come back okay?"

"I don't reckon that'll happen." And he meant it. Since he'd made the decision to leave, he felt more comfortable and less stressed than he had in months. He wouldn't go as far as to say he was happy, but he was better. He needed away from this place. Away from the ghosts that lingered.

"Well then, I don't know what you're looking for out there, but if it's other people, I came across a little settlement in Arkansas about ten or fourteen months ago. Wouldn't know how to tell you how to get there, but it was a little west of Prescott, and if you hunt and peck around long enough, you might just find it." He spat onto the ground. "Nice enough folks they was."

"Then why didn't you stay there?"

"Well, they had the place sealed up about as tight as a sardine canister. For protection, of course, and I couldn't blame 'em. Way the world is now, you need all the protection you can get. But I spent a good patch of time in the clink back when I was a younger man. After that, I don't much care for being cooped up."

"Fair enough."

Wim didn't know what he was looking for either, or if he had any use for other people, but he appreciated the information. He gave the reins a little shake, but Gypsy didn't take the hint. He stomped his boot against the wagon to get her attention, and she perked up.

"Wishum I had me a pair of boots like those," Zeke said.

Wim glanced his way as he rode off. "I already gave you my cabin. I imagine that's enough."

CHAPTER FOUR

THEY'D TAKEN TO CALLING THIS PLACE SHARD END AFTER THE neighborhood where Saw grew up. It wasn't really a town. It was a collection of campers, mobile homes, and shacks that were cobbled together in the flat like some white trash post-apocalyptic encampment, and the way Mitch viewed it, that's all it was.

When he threw in with Saw years earlier, back when he was sixteen and thought he knew it all, he believed Saw was a man with a vision. A man who could dominate in this bloodthirsty, lawless world.

The passage of time had revealed that the opposite was true. Starting with the events where Saw came up with the plan to take over the Ark, maiming Mitch for life and turning him into some stereotypical double-crossing bad guy, only to tuck tail and run when a few bullets flew his way, Mitch realized that Solomon Baldwin was every bit the blowhard his father, Senator SOB, had been.

Shard End had become a sort of Mecca for lowlifes and losers. There were no plans to build an army and conquer what was left of the world. No attempts to restore civilization. All these assholes cared about was getting drunk or high or laid, and none of the three presented much of a challenge.

Three times a day, Mitch made the trek along the dirt paths that passed for streets, checking to make sure no one was killing or getting killed, that no one was on the verge of dying and reanimating, and keeping his finger on the pulse of the camp. The task was mind-numbing in its monotony, but there wasn't much else to do.

"They wiggle, and they dance." The words rolled through the dry air, and Mitch looked to the source. A man who Mitch and everyone else knew only as Lumpy stood under a tattered canvas awning. "They wiggle, and they dance!" The words were empty and emotionless, but Lumpy's eyes watched all passersby like a carnival barker beckoning his next mark.

The man was on the downhill side of fifty with a pendulous gut that hung so low that the bottom few inches sagged out from under his stained shirt. His face was even less attractive, with small eyes that looked like black peppercorns and a roadmap of red spider veins crisscrossing his cheeks and nose. A feces-colored growth the size of a large cockroach clung to his lip, and every time Mitch was subjected to it, he wanted to slice it off so he'd never have to see it again.

At Lumpy's side were two female zombies. One more than usual, Mitch thought. Both had ropes tied around their necks with the opposite ends staked into the ground.

The new arrival was clad in only a silver Dallas Cowboys bikini top and short shorts. She had a good figure, but her mottled, gray skin and dead eyes didn't cause a reaction in Mitch's jeans. Beside her, an older, equally dead woman, whose spare tire sagged down over her crotch like she was smuggling a flounder under her skin, gave a thousand-yard stare into the empty landscape ahead. She was motionless, not wiggling or dancing, and as Mitch stared, Lumpy must have caught on.

"No slackers on my watch." He poked her with a sharp stick, the tip sinking into her pallid flesh. No blood came, just a thick dollop of black ooze. Spurred into action, the dead woman strained at her tethers, swaying slowly side to side. It still wasn't wiggling or dancing, but Mitch supposed it was close enough.

A younger man, Mitch thought his name was Heath or Keith, watched the dead women with desperate, rape-y eyes.

"No free looks, boy!" Lumpy said.

"What are you gonna do about it, Lardass?"

Without a hint of warning, Lumpy swung the stick, striking the onlooker on the cheek. An angry, pink welt rose up almost immediately.

"Fucker!"

"Now pony up some pay or scoot!"

The man scooted, and a satisfied grin spread across Lumpy's face. He shared it with Mitch, then beckoned him with a clumsy wave. "Come over, Mitch."

A morning chat with Lumpy wasn't high on Mitch's priority list, but keeping the peace was easier when he had their respect, and he obliged.

"Got me a new girl," Lumpy said as Mitch arrived on the scene.

"I noticed."

"I call her Debbie. Like *Debbie Does Dallas*." He leered at Mitch expecting a response, but Mitch was visibly clueless. "Before your time, I guess. Anyhow, ain't she a looker?"

Mitch gave her a cursory examination. Nodded.

"You took her teeth out, right?"

"Of course. Of course." He flashed a broad wink. "Tell you what, buddy, you gimme a bottle, and you can feel her up. And if you care to share any of that white powder you hoard, you can take the both of 'em in my camper and do whatever you please. No questions asked. No sir-ee bob."

Mitch regretted joining this man and tried to avoid his stare. "Sorry, Lumpy. Dead pussy doesn't do much for me."

Lumpy wasn't offended. "Maybe not for you. But the rest of this lot..." He looked toward the town, licked his lips. "Hell, I bet they'd fuck a wood knot if you greased it up for em."

"That wouldn't surprise me."

"How's Saw anyway? Haven't seen him out and about in a while."

"Saw's fine. If you want, I'll pass along your concern."

Lumpy's eyes grew wide, revealing a vaguely yellow color where they should have been white. "Hell, no! Less he thinks about me, the better."

"I doubt he gives you much of a thought."

"And thank God for that."

Mitch finally met his gaze. "You believe in God, Lumpy?"

Lumpy licked his lips, his tongue brushing across the obscene growth, lingering as it dragged against the roughness.

Shit, he's tasting it, Mitch thought.

"It's just an expression, ain't it?" Lumpy said.

"I don't know. That's why I'm asking."

Lumpy stammered, trying to get out an answer, then gave up. Mitch decided he'd grown bored of this conversation and moved on. As he progressed, he passed a drunk passed out in the middle of the street. The man's shirt was off, and he still clutched a bottle of whisky in his hand. Not much further, a boy in his early teens sat on the metal steps leading to a trailer and cooked heroin on a spoon.

As Mitch approached, the kid looked his way with narrowed eyes. "What are you looking at?"

"A piece of shit."

The kid set his drugs and spoon aside and moved to stand but stopped when he saw Mitch's hand on the grip of a pistol.

"Where'd you get the smack?"

"None of your business, freak."

This was a new arrival, and Mitch realized he'd been slacking on his introductions. When he reached the kid, he kicked the drugs into the dirt, causing the teen to jump to his feet, his body pulsing with rage.

"The fuck was that for? You think you're ugly now, you wait till I get done with you!"

A few years ago, Mitch was about the same size as this kid, but he'd had his growth spurt and stood a full six feet tall now. His baby fat had given way to lean, ropey muscle, and he used that strength to grab the kid by the throat and shove him against the trailer wall.

His arms swung, fists flailing, but that didn't deter Mitch.

"I asked you a question, kid. Where'd you get the heroin?"

"Fuck off!" The words came out in raspy hitches as he struggled for breath. He had balls, and Mitch had to respect that. He still didn't like him, though.

Mitch squeezed harder, his fingers digging into the teen's neck. His nails ripped the flesh and drew blood. The teen's frantic movements waned. Mitch leaned in, so their faces were only inches apart.

"I don't know where you think you landed, kid, but it's no place good. You might have thought life was hard out there, but out there, all you had to be scared of were zombies. In here, everyone would kill you. Every single one. And no one's going to save you because no one gives a shit."

The teen tried to speak, but Mitch wouldn't lessen the pressure he had on his windpipe to allow him to do so.

"The only thing separating this place from hell itself is me. So, I'm gonna ask you again, and I expect an answer. Where'd you get the heroin?"

Mitch didn't fully release the teen, but he let him breathe. After gulping down a few mouthfuls of air, he spoke. "Don't know his name. Skinny guy with a yellow mohawk."

Mitch understood immediately. "What'd you pay him with?"

The teen looked from Mitch to the ground, and Mitch understood this too. He could have let the matter drop but wasn't going to let the kid off that easy.

"Answer me."

The teen still wouldn't look, but he answered. "I sucked him off, okay? You happy now?"

"Definitely not." Mitch slapped the kid across the mouth hard enough to break his upper lip. The boy fell onto the steps, spitting blood.

"Heroin's off limits here. Any type of opiate. I catch you again, it'll be the last mistake you make."

The teen looked up. "You'll kill me?"

"No. I'll take you to the pit."

The kid spit a mouthful of blood onto Mitch's shoe. Mitch decided he'd earned that much and left him.

CHAPTER FIVE

THE TOWN BAR WAS TWO FORTY-FOOT-LONG TRAILER HOMES butted end to end. Above the doorway, someone had painted "Dry Snatch," and since there was no real owner to choose an alternate moniker, that stuck.

On a day like this one, it was a metal sweatbox, and even worse than the oppressive damp heat was the combined aroma of a dozen and a half men and women who hadn't bathed in months trying to get drunk as fast as possible. For flavor, a pile of vomit festered on the floor beside the entrance. A man named Tully was passed out beside the puke, and flies buzzed, landed, and ate off both the barf and the man who'd vomited it up.

Mitch stepped over both as he entered.

Diesel, the forty-something bartender, noticed him first. He whispered something to one of the drunks and soon murmurs filled the Snatch.

Mitch ignored their whispers as he surveyed the crowd. It was the usual bunch, and he didn't so much as give them a cursory glance as he stepped to the bar.

Diesel approached him, an empty glass in hand. The man's skin had the consistency of worn leather and his left eye was missing. He didn't have the decency to cover the wound with a patch or bandana, leaving the gaping, eggplant-colored hole exposed for the world to see. Mitch tried to avoid it.

"Morning, Mitch. What's your poison?"

"Little early, isn't it?"

Diesel looked around the bar as if that was answer enough.

"I'm looking for Boyd," Mitch said.

Diesel's eye skirted to the left, toward the restroom. Mitch didn't wait for a verbal answer.

The smell in the main part of the bar was a summer bouquet compared to the odor in the bathroom where piss, puke, and shit melded together to form a fragrance strong enough to make you question your reason for living. Mitch tried to block it out as he moved to a stall door under which he could see two sets of feet, both of which were partially covered by dropped pants and both faced the direction of the toilet.

Groans and grunts seeped from the stall. Sometimes Mitch really hated being in charge.

He pushed the door with his foot. It was unlocked and swung free, revealing one man bent over the shitter while another pounded him from behind.

"Play time's up, Boyd."

Boyd, he of the yellow mohawk, spun sideways at the sound of the voice, and Mitch got a brief but still too good look at his narrow cock, which was covered in blood and dotted with feces. The sight of it reminded Mitch of a banana split doused in strawberry sauce and chocolate sprinkles, and he thought that might have been the worst thing he'd ever seen. He looked away as fast as his head could swivel. "Fuck me, Boyd. Cover that up."

He then motioned to the receiver. "And you, get the hell out of here."

Boyd grabbed for his discarded pants. The other man ran, jeans still around his ankles, forcing him to duck-walk away. The door banged behind him as he fled.

"What's the problem, Mitch? Can't blame a man for fulfilling his needs."

"Are you dressed yet?"

"Sure am."

Mitch glanced his way, half-scared he was still naked from the waist down and he'd be subjected to his horrible cock again, but Boyd was indeed clothed. "What were you gonna give that man in return for tearing up his asshole?"

Boyd grinned, revealing jagged, brown teeth that made Mitch think of some sort of wild animal, maybe a badger or wolverine. "Why, he simply couldn't resist my masculine charm, that's all."

Mitch felt the only worthwhile response to such a quip was a hard punch to the jaw, and doing just that sent Boyd to the filthy floor. Mitch took the opportunity to grab him by his yellow mohawk and drag him from the room. When they emerged into what passed for a bar, the few drunks who were still alert enough to realize something was happening (and that was very few) looked toward them.

Mitch glared at them. "Boyd's been dealing H, and I bet more than a few of you knew about it."

The onlookers returned their attention to their spirits, whether in disinterest or guilt Mitch couldn't be certain. "He'll pay. And none of you better think about taking over his business, or you will too." He set his gaze on Diesel, the one-eyed bartender. "That includes you."

Diesel held up his hands in a not-guilty motion.

"Anyone wants to see what happens when you break the rules, go to the pit after sundown."

That got their attention, and the murmurs returned. The message had been sent, and Mitch didn't see any sense in prolonging the spectacle.

BOYD STAYED unconscious long enough for Mitch to drag him about halfway to the pit. His hair had started to come loose in handfuls that included not only the roots but also bloody bits and pieces of his scalp.

Maybe it was the pain that brought him back around. Whatever it was, Mitch was glad of that because he was tired of doing all the work.

Trickles of red ran down Boyd's face, making a detour into his eyes, and he wiped at them while he came back to the land of the living.

"The fuck, man? You scalp me or something?"

"Some of your hair decided to extricate itself from your head."

"Extra-what?"

"Never mind. Get on your feet."

Boyd did, but his legs looked like limp noodles, and Mitch had to steady him. "Thanks," he said, and Mitch thought there was genuine gratitude in the voice. If he only knew.

"What are you gonna do to me? Put me in the stocks?"

They'd passed the stockades while Boyd was enjoying his siesta. Mitch hadn't given them any consideration. They were for minor offenses. What Boyd had been doing was as major as it got. To Mitch, even killing a man wasn't as bad as getting him hooked on heroin because a man on heroin wasn't only a danger to himself, he was a scourge on the entire settlement and put them all at risk.

"No, Boyd. You knew the rules and you know the punishment for breaking them."

Boyd's disposition changed fast. He tried to spin and run, but he was still not all there, and Mitch grabbed onto what hair he had remaining.

"Come on, man. You can't do that. I'll do whatever you want. You want to know what goes on around here when you ain't around? I'll tell you if you give me another chance. Shit, I'll go undercover for you."

Mitch considered this. But it didn't take him long to realize the word of a rat was of little use, especially when said rat knew his life was on the line.

"Save your breath, Boyd."

The man struggled and protested the remaining two hundred yards to the pit, but he saved the best for last. When they were at the edge of the fifteen-foot-deep, fifty-foot-wide circle that had been dug into the hard caliche two years ago, Boyd was crying so hard that snot seeped from both nostrils, and he slobbered like a rabid dog.

"Take me to Saw, Mitch. It's my right."

"Right? This isn't even America, but no one's got rights anymore, Boyd. You know that as well as anyone."

"You stupid shit. You don't get it. Saw knows!"

Mitch kicked him in the leg, and Boyd fell to his knees. "Shut your mouth you damned liar."

"I'm not lying, Mitch. You think anything goes on here that he don't know about? You're smarter than that."

Doubt seeped into Mitch's mind, and he had to keep reminding himself that Boyd was scum and that he was doing whatever he could to buy time. "Saw hasn't even been out of his house in over three weeks. He's not God. He isn't all seeing."

"How can you be so fucking stupid? Saw knows I deal because he gets first dibs."

Mitch looked down at the blubbering, pleading wreck of a man, into his eyes. And in them, he saw the truth. He stood there, thinking, taking it in, and some semblance of hope came back into Boyd's face.

"You believe me now, don't you?"

He did. He didn't want to, but he did. It was like finding a central piece to a jigsaw puzzle, the one where, once you have it in place, everything else comes together around it.

"Yeah, I do."

Boyd managed a smile, revealing those brown fang-ish teeth. Teeth Mitch never wanted to look at again.

Mitch kicked him square in the chest, hard enough that he heard a rib snap and hard enough to sent Boyd tumbling backward ass over head. He'd been on the precipice of the pit, and the blow sent him careening into it.

The man squawked in pain as he fell, but those cries changed to screams of desperation, fear, and anger when he hit the bottom.

"Get me out of here, you shit! You can't do this to me!"

Mitch was tired of his voice. He turned and left the pit and Boyd behind. Apparently, he had bigger trouble to deal with.

CHAPTER SIX

SAW'S HOUSE STOOD ALMOST HALF A MILE FROM WHAT PASSED for a town. It was a mansion almost as big as the one Mitch had grown up in and lived in before Senator SOB shipped him off to boarding school. It had a decidedly Texan feel with plenty of wood and iron and gigantic windows that stood two stories tall. The house was the reason Saw and Mitch and Mina had stopped in this area in the first place. It was isolated and luxurious and situated on land so flat that it had an almost never-ending view.

"Won't be no one sneaking up on us here, Mitchy," Saw assured him. As if there was anyone left to sneak. They'd found the house over three years earlier, late in the fall when the oppressive Texas heat was held at bay by the coming winter. It had seemed a good climate then. Nothing like what it was now, of course. But by the time fall turned to winter and winter to spring, which brought with it that horrible, dry heat, they were settled in. Or Saw was, anyway, and his opinion was the only one that mattered.

As Mitch approached, he tried to peer into the windows that looked like black eyes peering out onto the land before them, but they were coated with a layer of dust so thick he couldn't see anything behind the glass. Anyone passing by would have thought the mansion abandoned.

The only slight clue that it might contain residents came from the trash bags that filled the left side of the porch and were stacked four feet high. When Mitch reached them, he kicked one over and heard the telltale rattles and clangs of cans and bottles.

He pounded his fist against the wooden door, not to convey the anger which was brewing inside him, but because he knew from too much experience that the man and woman who lived in that house were almost certainly asleep and wouldn't hear him unless he made a racket.

He hit the door again. Four hard raps. After which he gave up and tried the knob. It turned, and he pushed the door open, shaking his head. Solomon Baldwin, the man a sixteen-year-old Mitch had thought capable of taking over the world, was too damn lazy or stupid or drunk or all three to lock his front door.

The garbage bags on the porch were a few grains of rice compared to the buffet of trash that littered the first floor of Saw's mansion. About a third of it was bagged up, but the other 67 percent was strewn across the floor, stacked on tables, piled atop furniture. Mitch hadn't been in the house in a month or more and thought it seemed a much more disgusting sight now than then.

Fat flies buzzed and zoomed about, giddy over this goldmine they'd found to call home. One landed on Mitch's bicep and gave him a stinging bite before he could swat it away.

"Fucker!" He smashed it against his skin, smearing a red skid mark along his upper arm. A pink welt rose where the insect had left its mark, and Mitch wished he'd have worn long sleeves.

"Saw!" Mitch aimed the word at the staircase that split the first floor in half. "Mina!"

Nothing.

He knew he could ascend the twenty or so stairs that led to the second story before anyone was likely to respond, but as much as he thought Saw had grown sloppy and worthless over the last few years, he knew the man was always armed, and if he was to go storming into his bedroom, the old bastard might be apt to blow his pretty head off without bothering to take a glance to see who had come a knocking.

"Fucking assholes," he muttered. He shouldn't have wasted his time walking out here in hundred-degree heat. Now, instead of answers, all he had to look forward to was a half-mile walk back and an arm that was itching like poison oak from the fly's bite.

He scanned the rooms, trying to find something that might lend credence to what Boyd had said. Baggies or needles or syringes. But in this jumble of garbage, it was almost impossible to discern one bit of trash from the next. It was like Saw was going for the Guinness World Record of hoarding or something. And what was up with Mina? How could she let what had been one of the most beautiful homes Mitch had ever seen descend into this mess? He didn't expect Saw to have any pride but thought she might. Apparently, she was just as much of a pig as the man she'd shacked up with.

Mitch retreated through the maze of mess, careful not to step on anything hazardous and had almost made it to the door when a soft, barely-there voice broke through the buzzing of the flies.

"Thought I heard your mouth. What do you want?"

Mitch turned and saw Mina leaning against the handrail, halfway down the staircase. She was as skinny as ever, black flesh stretched taut against her bones. A breathing skeleton. Mitch had often thought, when looking at her, that you could stand her outside during Halloween and people would think she was one hell of a creepy decoration.

"Is Saw around?"

Mina looked from Mitch to the top of the stairs, then back again. "Course he is."

"Can he come down? I need to talk to him."

"Sleeping now."

Mitch thought she looked half-asleep too. Or half drunk, more likely. He was surprised she'd made it this far down the staircase without falling. "And you won't wake him?"

The woman's tight, angular face twisted into something resembling a maniac's grin. "I won't. You're welcome to, though."

Mitch wasn't about to do that, and he knew she knew that too, and that pissed him off all the more. "Fine. If he wakes up, you tell him I caught Boyd Yates dealing heroin."

"Oh yeah?" There was no surprise in her voice, just flat matter of factness.

"Yeah. And when he realized I was taking him to the pit, he couldn't stop his lips from moving."

That brought some genuine emotion to her face. Not exactly shock or worry, but maybe curiosity. Mitch couldn't tell for certain, but he was glad to see there was something left inside her head that could still put two and two together.

"He got anything interesting to say?"

"Bits and pieces."

Mina made it down the remaining stairs and came within a couple yards of Mitch. He could smell alcohol seeping from her pores.

"I'm sure. He always tended to blather." She stared at Mitch who kept his face purposely blank. "Thing is, a man walking to his death don't got no reason to tell the truth."

"I see it the other way."

"How's that?"

"I doubt a man with nothing to gain sees much use in lying."

Mina pushed a bowl full of mold-covered pasta aside with her foot as she leaned against a wall. "You set it off yet, Mitch?"

"Not yet. It's too damn hot out there. I'm waiting till dusk when it's cooler, so everyone can come and get a good look."

She nodded.

"You're invited. Saw too, of course. I think it would be good for the town actually, if you both showed up. It's been a while. More than a month by my count."

Mina looked away from him. "Has it?"

"It has."

Mitch turned back to the door and was in the threshold when she spoke again.

"You send someone out here to gather that garbage off the porch, Mitch, 'less you want to do it yourself."

Mitch didn't answer. He knew that if he did, she'd hear the anger in his voice and know she'd gotten a rise out of him. He wasn't about to give her that small pleasure.

CHAPTER SEVEN

THE SUN HAD SET HALF AN HOUR AGO, BUT IT WAS STILL HOT enough to work up a sweat without any great exertion. A mild breeze had kicked up, which gave a slight reprieve from the baking hot temperatures, but it also kicked up the dry dirt which then hit Mitch's sweaty skin and formed a kind of paste. He thought, with grim irony, that rich people like his mother probably paid for such things before the civilized world had ended.

"Well, when this gonna git happening?" a voice that sounded like rocks in a blender asked.

Mitch turned toward Horace, a middle-aged drunk whose bulbous nose was the only thing of interest on his wide, pasty face. "Soon enough, Horace. You act like you got better things to do."

Horace's hand went to a bulge in his pocket, a bulge that was shaped like a flask, and Mitch saw him lick his narrow, pinched lips.

"Go ahead and drink. No one's stopping you," Mitch said.

Horace scanned the crowd, a rough bunch if there ever was, and decided to keep his stash hidden. Mitch thought it looked like two thirds of the town had come to watch Boyd's end. Among them were all the new arrivals from the last eight months because anyone in town less than that amount of time had never seen what happened in the pit. Mitch knew they'd heard stories. He'd spread plenty himself. But seeing it in person was another matter entirely, and he aimed to give them a show they couldn't forget.

Absent from onlookers, not that Mitch was surprised, were Saw and Mina. He knew the chance of Saw being drawn out of his trash mansion was slim, but he'd held onto a small sliver of hope. That was gone now, and the murmurs in the crowd were transforming into annoyed grumbles.

In Horace's words, it was time for the show to git happening.

Mitch separated himself from the rest of the men and women, moving toward a truck trailer that stood at the far end of the pit. The tires at the rear end - the end facing the pit - had been flattened, so the trailer sloped downward at a twenty-degree angle.

As he grabbed hold of the latch to open the double doors, he took a look down at Boyd, who stood at the far end, his body so tight against the earthen wall that he might as well have been glued to it.

"You got anything to say for yourself?" Mitch shouted the words so that Boyd and everyone else in attendance heard them.

Boyd sneered at him. "Fuck yourself, Mitch!"

"Is that all?"

Boyd turned his gaze away from Mitch's face and toward the trailer doors, waiting.

"So be it then."

"What about me?" the voice carried across the crowd. Mitch couldn't see the source, but he knew. The voice hadn't really said 'what'. He'd said, 'wot.'

Everyone turned and gawked as Saw strolled toward the pit. The men and women separated, like some instinctual force had taken hold of them, to allow the man a clear path. With them out of the way, Mitch could watch Solomon Baldwin's grand entrance.

The man, Mitch's onetime idol, had never been tall. He was five and a half feet at the most but wide as a linebacker and carried himself in a way that made him seem twice his actual size. His girth had diminished since Mitch last saw him. He wondered if the man even broke a buck fifty now. But the swagger, the aura, was as bright and bold as ever.

Saw grinned, revealing the rotten teeth that made him look like he'd just chomped down a mouthful of shit, and Mitch wondered how those choppers hadn't fallen out. He wondered if teeth could somehow become petrified.

The people who had come to watch Boyd Yates die greeted Saw like he was the world's biggest rock star. They clutched and grabbed at him as he passed through them, desperate to get a touch, a feel, of the man they considered their leader, even though he'd never spoken so much as a single word to the majority of them.

Mitch found Mina following Saw. No one paid her much attention, let alone gave her the superstar treatment, but she didn't seem to mind. She trailed behind Saw like his shadow, unnoticed by most but always there.

"I didn't think you'd come," Mitch said.

Saw didn't look at him. He looked at the crowd. At his people. "And miss the ado? Wot kind of arsehole do you take me for, Mitchy?"

One no better than an absentee landlord, Mitch thought, but he kept his mouth shut as Saw reached the edge of the pit and came to him.

Even in the half-light of dusk, Mitch thought Saw looked haggard, his skin so loose that it quivered when he moved.

"Looks like you've been doing a fine job of holding down the fort, Mitchy. Such a good lad, you are."

When they first met, Mitch had looked up to Saw, physically and emotionally. Now he stood half a foot taller than the man and thought he looked almost insignificant in his current state.

"Did ya get even bigger than before?" Saw asked.

"Don't know. I don't make a habit of measuring myself."

Saw grinned again and gave Mitch a jab in the crotch, hard

enough to send a light wave of nausea into his belly. "That's aw right. I'll always be bigger where it counts."

The hole in Saw's forehead, which had always wavered between being scabbed over and an oozing divot, was at the present open. The skin around it looked raw, like he'd been picking at the wound. A black fly landed on the hole and ducked inside, exploring the recesses of the interior of Saw's skull. That, coupled with the ball-tap, made Mitch feel like he might barf.

Two things hadn't changed. Saw's eyes. They were as alert and as piercing as ever, and as he looked Mitch up and down, Mitch felt like he wasn't simply examining his face but instead peering into his soul.

Saw turned back to the crowd. "Ain't this just the dog's bollocks?" He raised his arms, and the people cheered.

Christ, Mitch thought, *he could disappear for a year, and they'd still worship him.*

"I see some familiar faces out there but a lot that I don't recognize just yet. That's aw right, though. I'll learn your names soon enough, and if you don't know mine, it's Solomon Baldwin, but you can call me Saw. All me friends do."

The crowd roared. And even though Mitch had heard variations of this a hundred times over the years, the man's perverse kind of charm was impossible to ignore.

"We don't have a lot of rules here in Shard End. Drink what you want. Fuck who you want. Hell, you can even kill who you want if you got a right good reason to do so, and no one's gonna bother you about it. But one rule we do have is no opiates. No heroin. You're all told that when you arrive, and if you don't like it, won't be no one stopping you from leaving. There's a reason for that. Opiates slow a man down. Make him careless and weak. And someone who's careless and weak puts us all at risk."

Saw stepped to the edge of the pit and looked down at Boyd, who had come in for a closer look. Mitch realized the condemned man was smiling.

"You got anything to say for yourself, you tosser?" Saw asked.

Boyd's smile faltered. "Saw. I was only doing--"

Mitch caught Saw's fist clenching. Boyd must have seen it too because the smile totally vanished, and his mouth sagged open and wordless.

"What are you waffling on about?"

Boyd looked at the ground. "Just get on with it."

Saw turned his attention back to the crowd. "It don't matter anyway. Rules are rules. Mitchy, open 'er up."

Mitch jerked the lever, and the double doors at the rear of the trailer burst open. As they swung free, nine zombies spilled through the opening and tumbled downward, into the pit.

Boyd raced to the opposite end, clawing at the walls with his hands. Kicking his feet into the dirt. Trying to find some way up and out. Once, he made it a few feet up before the earth gave way and he tumbled back to the bottom.

Mitch heard Saw bark out a laugh at that and turned toward him. The man's face was lit up with glee. Behind him, Mina stared at the ground. Mitch wondered what life was like in that mansion, then realized he probably didn't want to know.

The zombies were within arm's reach of Boyd. One grabbed his stringy hair, snapping his head backward. Another caught his arm and pulled it to its mouth, where it took a heaping bite. Boyd squealed, and the sound seemed to work the zombies into a frenzy. They'd been locked in that trailer for over four months with nothing to eat, and they were ready to remedy that.

They descended on the man, tearing away hunks of flesh, biting off fingers. One of the creatures went for his face and chomped off his nose in one bite. Boyd stared up, blood gushing from the hole in the center of his face, and Mitch realized he was looking at Saw. Saw looked back and smiled.

The dying man opened his mouth to scream, and when he did, one of the zombies reached out and grabbed, hooking its fingers into his mouth, pulling at his cheek. Another zombie took hold of him from the opposite side, and, together, the two monsters stretched the skin as far as it would go, then it ripped into ragged tendrils of flesh that they shoved into their own mouths.

Boyd deserved this, but now that Mitch knew some of the underlying story, he'd lost his bloodlust and turned away from the carnage. What he couldn't block out were Boyd's miserable moans.

As Mitch moved away from the pit, Saw grabbed his wrist. The man might have lost a third of his body weight, but he was still strong, and Mitch felt like his arm was trapped in a vise as Saw pulled him in close and spoke into his ear. His breath was hot and pungent.

"Don't know what you heard, Mitchy, but it's probably true. Now take a good look around."

Mitch did. The crowd was every bit as frenzied as the zombies.

"The truth don't mean nothing to them. *You* don't mean nothing to them. All that matters 'round here is me."

Mitch tried to pull his hand away but failed. That made Saw's smile even more avid.

"We got ourselves a good deal here. This isn't my place. It's ours. So, you don't got no good reason to upset the applecart, okay?"

Saw leaned in close, his moist fetid breath assaulting Mitch's nostrils. Mitch turned his face away from it, but that did nothing to deter the man who had control over him.

"I know I've been missing in action of late, but I'm gonna be around a lot more from now on. I promise you that. And that's the best thing for the both of us."

Saw released him, and Mitch wasted no time in fleeing. Behind him, he heard Saw's voice even above the roaring crowd.

"What do you fine people say? Do you think Boyd's suffered enough?"

"No!" came the immediate cry. It was joined by a chorus calling for the man to suffer. To die slowly. Mitch was disgusted but not surprised by their demands.

What did surprise him was Saw's response.

"You all are a bloodthirsty bunch. But I do believe Boyd's learned his lesson. Anything more is just pain for pain's sake."

A gunshot echoed through the night air, and that sound was immediately replaced by cheers. Mitch left it all behind.

MITCH WAS TEMPTED to duck into the Dry Snatch and grab a bottle of whatever would get him drunk the fastest, but he wanted to keep his head clear. That was also why he avoided his own home, a high-end RV that probably cost a few hundred grand before the plague but was now nothing more than a glorified mobile home that wasn't moving so much as an inch, unless a tornado happened along. Because in his home, there was cocaine. It had always been Mitch's drug of choice, even predating the Marsten Academy, but if he dared snort a line or two now, in this frame of mind, he'd be likely to do something foolish. And now was not the time to act the fool.

Instead, he walked until he came to an Airstream trailer that was more rust red than sparkling silver. It was covered with dents and holes of various sizes and looked a little like a beer can someone had smashed then tried to pull back into shape again.

He gave two quick taps against the door and only had to wait a moment before it opened.

"Mitch! How's it going, handsome?"

Sally Rose always called him handsome. From anyone else, Mitch would have thought it an insult. A sarcastic quip at his expense. But he'd never seen a cruel bone in this woman's body, and he'd been privy to almost every inch of it over the last few years.

She'd come to Shard End with a man in a wilted Cowboy hat who was three or four decades her senior. If he'd ever offered up his name, Mitch had long forgotten it, but that didn't matter because he was only in town for a few weeks before he ended up getting snake bit.

Sally Rose was there when it happened, and she was there when he turned into a zombie a few minutes later. The dead man tried to eat her, but one of the regulars drew his pistol and put a fast end to that. Sometimes, Mitch wished he'd have been there, so he could have been the one to save her. He thought that might have changed things for the better for both of them. But he wasn't, and those thoughts were nothing but unfulfilled daydreams and conjecture anyway.

While she was much younger than the now long dead man in the wilted cowboy hat, she still had almost two decades on Mitch. He had the good sense not to ask her actual age, but he could see it in her face, in the way her skin crinkled up around her eyes and mouth. And the way her breasts sagged down to the bottom of her rib cage. He suspected she was only a few years younger than his mother but tried not to think about that much as it only made their relationship feel weird.

Relationship, he thought. That was a serious word for something that didn't amount to much more than a good fuck once or twice a week. And he knew he wasn't the only man who came calling at Sally Rose's stoop. She wasn't exactly a prostitute, but she wasn't likely to turn away a fellow who turned up with some hard to find item of food or good booze or maybe even a little coke.

Still, Mitch thought he might be special to her. The smile she gave when she saw him reached all the way up to her eyes, and she never turned him away, even when he didn't come bearing gifts. Like tonight.

"It's been a long day."

Sally Rose grabbed his hand between her own and pulled him inside. Her skin felt so tender, like silk, that it almost gave him goosebumps. "I heard about Boyd. That bastard. How'd he think he'd get away with that?"

Mitch didn't want to talk about Boyd. Didn't want to rehash any of the day's events. Instead, he took his free hand, gripped her belt, and drew her in close to him. She fell into him and giggled, a sound that seemed too young for her age, yet perfect at the same time. The feel of her soft body against him made him hard, and she giggled again. Mitch would have said Sally Rose was plain, with her fair skin and freckles, a generic oval face and drab brown eyes, but when she smiled, he thought she was on the verge of beautiful. He thought that now as he looked at her.

Mitch didn't think he was capable of loving anyone except maybe himself, but this woman had a way of making everything better, and she was exactly what he needed.

CHAPTER EIGHT

Mead had just witnessed the impossible and the insane. A pastor proclaiming himself to have God on his speed dial had allowed himself to be bit by a zombie and survived with no ill effects. Then the man told all the onlookers that God had created the zombies to save mankind. The scene was so unbelievable that every man and woman in attendance at this tent revival got down on their knees and prayed with him.

Everyone except himself. Mead had never been the praying kind. Wasn't even sure whether he believed in the big man upstairs with the bushy white beard or not. He wouldn't have called himself an atheist or agnostic, mostly because he wasn't really sure what either term actually meant, but he knew what he'd never believe. If there was a God, he wasn't going to be spreading his word via a crazy, little man like Grady O'Baker. Healed up bite wounds or not.

After the spectacle, Mead grabbed the shoulder of Owen, the man with whom he'd travelled all the way from Brimley, Arkansas, to this Alabama shithole in search of this traveling sideshow.

"I don't know about you, but I've seen enough crazy for one day," Mead said.

Owen stared at him, eyes glassy, like a man who'd just taken a hit of a particularly strong marijuana. "What do you mean?"

"I mean I want to hit the fucking road, Owen. This guy's loonier than Yosemite Sam and less than half as charming,"

"What are you talking about, Mead?"

What the fuck do you think I'm talking about, Mead thought. He stared at the man who he'd known for a few years and had always seemed normal and practical and sane, albeit a bit of a bore. But his face was blank, or he was wrapped up in some kind of awe. Mead couldn't tell which it was. "This is a trick or something, Owen. No different than those preachers who juggled rattlesnakes in the old black and white documentaries."

Owen stared at him, clueless and stupid.

"For all we know, they pulled all of that zombies' teeth."

"But he bled, Mead."

"Blood capsules. Or strawberry jam even. Hell, if they could pull it off in professional wrestling, why not here? The point is, we don't know what we saw."

"I saw him get bit and not turn into a zombie like every other person I've seen get bit over the last four years. I saw all his scars too. But it's more than that."

Now it was Mead's turn to be confused and silent.

"That man. Pastor O'Baker. He talks to God, Mead. I know that as sure as I know my date of birth."

"You just got caught up in the spectacle of it. That's what they count on. Do a few tricks. Sing a couple songs. Work everyone up into a frenzy and next thing you know, you're signing over your IRA. That's how it always works, man. Now come on. Let's head home."

Owen shook his head. "This is my home now."

Mead was tired of this. He'd never taken Owen to be such a rube. "Jesus Christ, Owen. Don't be so fucking naive."

"This was real. Pastor O'Baker is real. And Mead, I've been needing something like this."

"Like what? A post-apocalyptic carnival barker and his band of merry idiots?"

Owen's eyes blazed, and Mead knew he was lost.

"So that's it then? After all these years of me taking care of you, you're trading in Brimley and safety for a bunch of whackadoos who keep zombies around like they're house cats?"

The man looked away, toward the sight of the revival, where a few dozen workers were folding up the chairs and tearing down the tent.

"Have it your way then. But keep these crazies away from Arkansas. Go spread your insane gospel somewhere else." Mead didn't know if Owen reacted because he turned his back on the man and stomped away. Their bicycles rested against trees at the edge of the road. Mead grabbed one, climbed on board, and pedaled away.

As far as dramatic exits go, it wasn't much, but it was the best he could do under the circumstances.

Mead was less than twenty yards away when he realized the bike he'd taken in such a hurry was the one Owen had ridden, and it was a girl's bike at that. But turning around and riding back would have been even more embarrassing, so he continued away from Owen, away from the religious zealots.

He was annoyed by the whole series of events and pissed that he'd ever biked all the way to Alabama. It had taken them almost two weeks of riding and searching for the damned traveling tent revival before they found it. Hundreds of miles and one very sore ass.

What bothered him more than all of that, though, was that he realized he was scared. Not scared of Grady. Not directly. If push came to shove, Mead knew he could out-push and out-shove the man with one arm tied behind his back. And he wasn't scared of the crazy man's message. The notion that God had created zombies to save humanity was as likely as Mead waking up tomorrow with a second cock.

What scared Mead was how easily the others bought into the man's fire and brimstone bullshit. How someone like Owen, who had seen some bad shit and had been given a safe place to live, was so willing to give it up because this nut job said it was God's will.

Mead couldn't understand how people could be such sheep. He didn't know much about the bible, but he was pretty sure that in Revelation, it didn't say anything about the zombie apocalypse. So why would men and women who seemed so normal and reasonable buy into that line of happy horse shit?

He thought about that for the next several days and never did come up with a good reason.

CHAPTER NINE

GRADY DRESSED IN SILENCE BEHIND THE TENT. THE FRESH BITE wounds on his arm had already stopped bleeding, the blood clotting to a deep crimson which rose up against his pale skin like globs of paint. He was careful to not disturb them as he pulled on a plain button-down shirt.

"You were inspiring today. As always." It was Juli's voice, and it was full of admiration.

At times, he felt her kindness bordered on uncomfortable fawning. "I only spoke the words God provided."

"But you delivered them with such passion, Grady. That's what brings them in. Why they stay."

Grady finished buttoning his shirt, then tucked it into his slacks. "Not all of them. We lost one."

Juli glanced toward the dirt path that led away from the tent. "I spoke with his friend, Owen. He said the man who left was vain and blasphemous. I doubt we ever had a chance for him."

Grady was shocked at the indifference, at her skepticism. "Surely you don't believe that. Even the greatest sinner isn't beyond redemption."

Her gazed dropped to the ground. "Grady, I--"

"Our flock is comprised entirely of sinners. Liars and thieves. Drug addicts and even murderers. And you and I, we certainly are not without sin."

"I only meant that he--"

"I failed today. I could have saved that man's soul. Instead, he left to wander in the wind without God's protection."

Juli eased her hand onto his forearm. "You can't save everyone, Grady. A person has to want to be saved."

Grady sometimes wondered if the woman listened, really listened, to his sermons or if she only placated him. Every day, in his prayers, he asked God to speak to her the way He spoke to him because he felt that even after these years, there was a part of Juli that didn't fully believe. That she was simply playing a role.

"It's my duty to make them want God as much as God wants them, Juli. That's why I've been given this mission. Ten men saved means nothing when the eleventh is lost."

"You're right. I'm sorry."

She turned away from him but not before he saw emotion in her eyes. It wasn't remorse, Grady thought. More a sadness. She slipped into the tent without giving him a chance to respond further, and Grady wondered if he was too hard on her.

She'd been at his side even before Grady himself understood his purpose. Before he understood God's plan. While he was lost in the darkness mourning the loss of his son, his Josiah, it was Juli who cared for him. Who protected him. And in the early days of his ministry, while others abandoned him and turned toward wicked lives, Juli remained. Of all his followers, she especially deserved his kindness and patience.

He grabbed the tent flap and began to open it when he caught sight of the friend of the man who had left. The fellow stared at the goings on around him with a mixture of awe and incredulity. Grady went to him.

When the man saw Grady coming, his body tensed, and his eyes grew so wide Grady thought he might spin on his heels and run. Instead, he knelt before him and bowed his head.

"Stand, please," Grady said.

The man glanced up as if trying to make sure he wasn't being tested or pranked. "Really?"

"Yes, yes."

The man stood.

"You can kneel before the cross, and you can kneel in prayer. But not to me. We are equals, my friend. Fellow servants of God. I'm Grady, and I'd like to know your name."

Grady extended his small, almost fragile hand, and the man swallowed it up between both of his own. "I'm Owen. Owen Varner."

"I'm so pleased to meet you, Owen Varner. And I'm even more pleased that you've decided to remain with us and help spread God's word through what's left of the world. Thank you."

Owen still clasped Grady's hand. "Thank me? Gosh, no. I was never one for church, or religion at all for that matter. When I was a kid, we went on Christmas and Easter, but that was the whole of it. And when I got older, well, I didn't bother with it. Last time I was even in a church was when my dad died, and that was more than thirty years ago."

He dropped Grady's hand and broke eye contact, ashamed. "So, I'm not sure if you really have much use for someone like me."

Grady put his hand on the man's shoulder. "I certainly do, Owen. And more importantly, God does too."

Owen looked up, a befuddled grin on his face. "You really think so?"

Grady gave his shoulder a light squeeze. "Yes, Owen. You're one of God's chosen ones, and, together, we're going to carry out his wishes, aren't we?"

The man nodded so hard his hair whipped around his head. "Yes, sir. I promise I'll do whatever's needed."

"That's good. That's all God asks from any of us." Grady motioned to a few folding chairs setting nearby. "Sit with me for a spell, Owen. I want to hear your story. And please, start by telling me about your friend who elected not to stay and where you came from."

Owen was more than happy to talk, and Grady was always willing to listen.

CHAPTER TEN

THE MAN WAS PERCHED ON A BICYCLE, RIDING DOWN THE middle of the highway. And from what Wim could tell, it was a girl's bike. He also appeared to be padded up like a football player, making him look far too large for his ride. It was an odd sight, but then Wim remembered that he was sitting in an old wagon, being hauled by a horse, and supposed he shouldn't judge. He set the binoculars aside, laid a shotgun across his lap, and waited for the approaching rider to close in.

His progress was slow, but he eventually closed the distance to a couple hundred yards, and Wim assumed the cyclist then saw him too because his forward progress came to a halt. They both sat there like that for several minutes, waiting for the other to make the first move. Wim had a feeling this could go on for a good long while if he didn't put an end to it and gave the reins a shake. Gypsy snorted, reluctant to continue on but grudgingly obliged.

It didn't take long to get within shouting distance, and Wim hoped the rider would take the opportunity to speak. But he did not. He supposed he was going to have to make all the first moves and cupped one hand beside his mouth.

"Hello, there. I mean you no harm." The words seemed silly once they came out of his mouth. As if a would-be assailant would confess to being a threat. Of course, they'd say something like "I mean you no harm." Sometimes, he wondered why he bothered speaking at all.

"Why should I believe you?" the rider queried.

Wim realized he had no good answer for that. "Well, I... I suppose I don't know. But it's the truth if that matters."

"It might."

The rider climbed off his bike and pushed it in Wim's direction. Wim noticed the man had something that looked like a spear strapped across his back and that the hand that wasn't holding the bike clutched that weapon. But seeing that he had a shotgun hidden on his lap, he felt the odds were in his favor should things go bad.

They were within twenty feet of one another when the rider stopped again. Wim saw his hand drop from the weapon and realized the man wasn't just looking at him - he was examining him. And he was smirking.

"I'll be shit," the man said.

That voice, it sounded like one he'd heard before, and Wim decided it was his time to take a better look past the girl's bike and padding and denim and to really see the man who was in his path. His hair was long and stringy, hanging far past his shoulders, and he had a poor excuse for a beard and mustache, but Wim thought he knew him.

"Mead?"

"The one and only."

While Mead stomped down the kickstand and let the bike sit, Wim climbed out of the wagon to meet him halfway. He couldn't believe his eyes. He'd last seen Mead more than four years ago while they hunkered down in a warehouse in West Virginia. There were many more of them then, and he tried not to think about that part.

"I saw that fucking plaid shirt and thought, 'That looks exactly like something Wim would wear,' and holy shit, it really is you. Dogs balls, man, what are the odds?"

Wim thought they were pretty extraordinary and leaned in to give the man an embrace, but Mead dodged that and went for a handshake instead. Wim grabbed Mead's palm between his own and pumped it. He'd assumed this man had died years earlier, and he'd never been so happy to be wrong. "I thought you were dead."

"Shit, man, I'm too good to die. Came close a couple times, but the devil doesn't want me just yet." Mead pulled his hand free of Wim's powerful grip and ran it through his hair, pushing it out of his face. "So, what the fuck are you doing in Alabama?"

"I guess I thought, if I wandered around long enough, I could talk myself out of murdering a man."

Mead's eyes grew wide. "No shit?"

They spent the next few hours discussing the events of the last few years. Wim was impressed with everything Mead had done and accomplished, even though it sounded like he, too, had dealt with his share of tragedy. He was glad Mead had found his note at the warehouse and even more glad that Mead hadn't been taken to the Ark with the rest of them.

When he told Mead about what had happened there, and what had happened later with Ramey, he thought the man's eyes misted over, but that might have been because his own grew bleary.

"Ramey's fucking father was the one who started all this shit? Brought this hell down on all of us?"

Wim nodded.

"I'm sorry, Wim. I was only with the two of you for a short while, but I could tell even then you had something special."

"We did."

"Something most of us aren't lucky enough to ever experience."

Mead looked away, and Wim suddenly realized why Mead had left them. He wondered how he could have been so dumb to not realize it at the time, but, in his defense, there had been a lot going on. Still, he couldn't help but feel a little guilty.

They were both silent for a moment until the emotions passed, then Mead turned his face back to Wim. "Do you think there's a good chance her father, Doc, is still alive?"

Wim thought about that a moment. "When we left, the Ark was on fire. There were zombies everywhere. But if anyone could survive that, it would be that weasel."

Mead nodded. "Okay then."

"Okay what?"

"Let's go kill him."

Wim was surprised. He hadn't expected this man, whom he hadn't seen in years, to be so willing to help. Especially since the trip back to West Virginia would take weeks, not days.

"You'd go with me?"

"Shit, Wim. If everything you said is true, and I've got no reason to believe it's not, I'll kill the bastard myself."

"Well, thank you."

"If you don't mind, though, there's someone I'd like to bring along."

"Anything you want, buddy."

MEAD HAD DEPOSITED the bicycle into the wagon and sat beside Wim as they headed west. As he told Wim about Brimley, the town he'd built, Wim realized it sounded familiar.

"I think an acquaintance of mine might have been there. Zeke?"

Mead thought about the name, then shook his head. "Maybe, but I don't remember the name."

"Older fellow, probably in the range of seventy. Blind in one eye with a cataract."

A slow smile crossed Mead's mouth. He dropped his voice a few octaves and tapped his helmet. "Wishum I had me a helmet like yours."

Wim couldn't hold back and laughed so loud that Gypsy glanced back to see what the ado was about. "That's him."

"Shit, yeah, I remember him now. Came and went like a fart in the wind. I think he just wanted food and anything else he could guilt us into giving him."

"I gave him my cabin."

"Holy shit, Wim! All I gave him were some cans of fruit and a few jugs of water."

Wim shrugged his shoulders. "Took a burden off my shoulders, though, so I shouldn't complain."

"Fucking Zeke, man. That old coot. What was his deal with green beans anyway?"

"He didn't appreciate the texture."

Now Mead laughed too. "Guess he never heard the saying about beggars and choosers."

It took them almost a week to get back to Arkansas via horse and wagon. Wim didn't mind the journey. He'd already been on the road for several weeks, but he thought Mead seemed anxious, maybe even nervous. He rarely slept and always surveyed the area around them. He remembered Mead to be high strung the last time they were together, but he seemed amped up by a factor of ten now. To say he was cautious was an extreme understatement.

As they rolled into Brimley, Wim was impressed. The town was fortified by metal shipping containers stacked two and three high. It was clearly a place meant to withstand the end of the world, but, at the same time, Wim could understand why Zeke likened it to a prison, and he doubted he could spend too much time confined within those walls either.

The man Mead wanted him to meet was named Aben, and upon their arrival, he came to them with a slight limp. Wim also noticed, upon first impression, that the man was minus his left hand. His face was scarred, but most of those old wounds were covered by a patchy beard. Wim wondered what the man had suffered through to obtain all those injuries but didn't dare ask. Most men of character tend to keep their pain hidden away inside and didn't care to have it brought up.

Aben was a big man. Taller and wider than Wim, although around fifteen years older. He looked like a rough character, the kind who wouldn't take gruff off anyone, and before the man had even said a word, Wim understood why Mead wanted to bring him along on their journey.

They stayed three days in Brimley, long enough for Mead to tell the residents about the traveling tent revival he'd found in Alabama and about how another man from town had elected to stay behind and join the show. Wim didn't mind the delay and thought it would be a good rest for the horse, but he didn't care to get to know anyone there on more than a superficial level. He supposed the last compound he'd found himself in had soured his opinion on other people to some extent, and while these seemed like good folks, he was fine with limiting his conversations with them to the 'How you doing' and 'Nice to meet you' variety.

Aben was the exception. He didn't say as much, but Wim got the feeling that the man was restless. Maybe it was the way he agreed to travel to West Virginia with them before Mead even got out a quarter of the story. Or maybe it was the way Wim caught him staring at the walls for long periods of time when he thought no one was watching him. Either way, Wim was glad they'd come back here and that they were bringing Aben along.

While Mead was busy making certain everything was secure in town and that they had enough supplies to last them through until they got back (and Wim, Mead, and Aben all knew *until* was really *if*), Wim had a chance to talk to Aben alone while the man gathered together the few belongings he wanted to take with.

"We're coming down on the time where it'll be too late for you to change your mind," Wim said.

Aben glanced up from the small bag he was packing. "That won't happen."

"I'm just saying, if you do, there won't be no hard feelings on my part. This is my fight, after all. Not yours."

Aben zippered the bag closed and took a seat on the edge of the bed beside his dog. "I wish that was true, but it's not." He scratched the dog's head absentmindedly.

"How's that?" Wim sat in a chair across from him.

"I didn't realize right away, but that island you mentioned and the men who attacked it that winter, I was hooked up with them for a while."

Wim leaned forward in his chair, intrigued. "You were?"

Aben nodded. "For a few months. It started out normal enough, just a bunch of hard cases surviving all this bullshit. But then it got mean. Or Saw did, anyway."

"Saw?"

"Solomon Baldwin. He's the one you talked about with the hole in his forehead. And the boy with the cut-up face. I can't be a hundred percent certain, but that must have been Mitch. Duplicitous little shit.

"Saw told us about his plan to take over the island, and that's when I decided I'd had enough. But before I cut ties, I made the mistake of telling Mitch, and Mitch told Saw, and..." He held up his foot to show the missing half. "Would have been a whole lot worse if Mead hadn't come along when he did."

Wim thought about this for a long moment. The events that brought down the Ark had all happened so fast and he'd been so caught up in mourning Emory and the shock of learning Ramey wasn't immune that he barely remembered much of it.

"I hope that doesn't sour your opinion of me too much."

Wim realized he'd stayed silent too long. "Oh, no. I'm just surprised, is all. You weren't there. You didn't do nothing wrong."

"That might be true, but I still feel partly responsible. Aiding and abetting, at the very least."

Wim shook his head. "Don't you fret about it. Everything at the Ark was bad. That place was like a poison. I'm not saying that Saw character was right in doing what he did, but the faster that all came to an end, the better."

Aben sighed, and Wim thought he seemed to sit up straighter. "Well, that's one less burden to carry anyway."

"You have others?" Wim meant it as a joke, something to lighten the mood, but it had the opposite effect.

"Hell, I got too many to keep an accurate count on all of them." Aben stopped petting his dog and glanced Wim's way. "Don't you?"

Wim only nodded in response. He supposed that was the price to pay for survival.

CHAPTER ELEVEN

MEAD LAID ON HIS BACK, SWEATED SOAKING WET AND OUT OF breath. So tired was he from the exertion that his eyes were slow to focus when the vaguely yellow shape came into view above him.

"Fuckeroo. That was incredible," Mead said between mouthfuls of air.

The woman who straddled him smiled. It was on the crooked side and revealed a gap where an incisor should have been, but the sight of her grin never failed to bring about one from him too. "Well, I'm pleased as punch to hear that. We could do this a hell of a lot more often if you'd stop leaving."

He grabbed her by the waist, his fingers sinking into her pudgy midsection. He liked all her soft curves almost as much as her lopsided grin. He pulled her down onto him, and she landed hard, pushing a happy *oof* from his lips. She giggled.

On one of the scouting missions, Mead had found Lydia Danville and two others traveling through Oklahoma. The man with them, Mead seemed to remember his name was maybe Frank, had a badly broken hip that had gone septic. The women, Lydia, and a middle-aged spinster type named Myrna were dragging him along on a homemade stretcher cobbled together from tree limbs, twine, and a ratty wool blanket.

Mead told them about Brimley, and they all agreed to return there with him, but Maybe Frank was delirious with fever, and less than a few days later, he died in the night. Mead awoke to Lydia's screams and found Maybe Frank grabbing hold of her shirt and leaning in for a mouthful of tit.

Even when sleeping, Mead never had a weapon more than a foot away, and that night was no different. He gripped a spear made of metal conduit and impaled the man from behind. The sharp end popped out Maybe Frank's right eyeball, which made Lydia scream even louder, but she was alive and her (in Mead's opinion) perfect tits were unmarred.

So, after that, it was just the three of them that finished the trip back to Brimley. Myrna wasn't much for chit chat, or common courtesy for that matter, and seemed to dislike Mead on general principle, but Lydia cozened up to him, and he wasn't about to push her away. She was in her mid-twenties with dirty blonde hair to go along with her curves. She'd been a school teacher before the plague, and Mead often thought teachers were a hell of a lot hotter now than when he went to school. That was well over a year ago, and, in Mead's opinion, she was just about the best damned thing left in the world.

As he looked at her body pressed against his, her wavy hair spilling across his chest, that opinion certainly didn't change.

"Believe me, I'd love nothing more than to do this every day. Multiple times a day, for that matter."

"Then why are you going? You don't even know this Will guy."

"Wim. And I know him. I saved his life four years ago as a matter of fact."

"You did?"

She looked up at him with her drab, hazel eyes, and he told her the story about finding Wim and the old man, Emory, trapped in a hotel surrounded by zombies. The way he told it, they were teetering on the precipice of death until he came along with his hockey stick swords and brought down hell on the undead horde. He might have embellished a bit here and there, but that was hard not to do with that beautiful woman looking at him in awe, and he felt he'd earned the right to be a bit of a braggart.

By the time the story was finished, Mead was recuperated and ready for round two. Lydia must have felt him rise to the occasion because she reached between his legs and took his hardness in her hand as a coy smile crossed her lips.

"Only way we do it again is if you make me a promise."

"What's that?"

She kissed his chin, then the corner of his mouth. "I want you to promise me..." She kissed him on the lips, her tongue pushing its way inside his mouth and tickling him.

Her hair fell into his face, and Mead put his hand behind her head and kissed her back. He was starting to think he really was crazy for even considering leaving this woman when she broke their kiss.

"Promise me you'll come back."

"You know I will, Lydia." He didn't want to outright lie to her. He cared for her too much to do that and hoped those words would suffice.

"You don't know what I know. I want a promise. I want the words, 'I promise'. No hedging."

Mead looked her direct in the eyes, steeling himself. "I'll come back when this mess is done. I promise you."

She grinned again, and Mead felt both relieved and guilty that she hadn't realized that he'd had his fingers crossed.

"I've never said this before because I take words serious. And I've never made a habit of saying something just for the sake of saying it. But I love you, Mead."

That made Mead feel even more guilty about the possible lie, but at the same time there came a tightness in his throat that stretched all the way down to his stomach.

He couldn't remember a woman ever saying she loved him. He

imagined his mother might have once or twice but couldn't pinpoint any particular memory of her actually speaking the words. And his blink and you miss it marriage started with "Oh shit, I'm pregnant" and ended with "I hope you rot in hell!" and there was little time for pleasantries in the middle.

As he looked at Lydia, he knew he wanted to spend his life with her, and he thought about telling her that in the moment. That he wanted to marry her. But he knew proposing the night before he went on a journey that had the very real possibility of leading to his death would have been a shitty thing to do.

He settled with, "I love you too."

That satisfied her, but Mead thought it seemed flippant. Four short words that did little to express his true feelings for this woman and his hopes for their future together. As they made love again, he told himself that, if he survived the trip to the Ark and back, he'd never leave her again. He owed her that. Shit, he owed himself that too.

CHAPTER TWELVE

ABEN TOSSED AND TURNED FOR HOURS, BUT SLEEP WOULDN'T come. He crawled out of bed and strolled to the window where he tried to guess the time, but the sky was full of clouds and all he could tell for certain was that it was still dark. He knew returning to bed for another try would lead to nothing but more restlessness and decided to save himself the trouble.

As he exited the cramped, three-room cottage that had been his home for the last few years, Prince glanced up at him with half-closed eyes. The dog didn't speak to him, but Aben answered him anyway.

"I'm just going out for a spell. You stay in bed."

The dog flopped its head down on the quilt, satisfied, and Aben stepped into the night.

He was glad to be leaving Brimley. He had no bad feelings against anyone here, but no matter how hard he tried, he couldn't find a way to feel comfortable. He was a round peg living in a square hole. If you tried hard enough, you could squeeze in, but it was never quite right.

The idea of the trip excited him. The road had been calling him since soon after his arrival in Brimley, and even semi-frequent scouting missions did little to satiate the need to be on the move because, no matter how big of a circle they made while out gathering supplies, he always knew he was going to end up back at the starting point again. He needed something open-ended, and this was the perfect fit.

He'd made it a third of the way through town when he smelled a familiar aroma. Baking bread. He didn't have to follow his nose to the source. He knew where it was coming from, and when he reached the porch of Coraline's house, the smell was so strong he was salivating.

Coraline's fresh-baked bread was one of the few things he'd miss about Brimley. And, to a lesser extent, Coraline herself.

"Only thing worse than a hungry dog is a hungry man."

He looked toward the voice and saw her silhouette in the kitchen window. "Morning, Coraline."

"For Christ's sake, Aben, it ain't even morning for another few hours. The smell of my bread woke you all the way from here to there?"

Aben shook his head, not that he was certain she could even see the gesture. "Can't sleep. Insomnia, I suppose. What's your excuse anyway?"

"Come inside and maybe I'll tell you."

He did.

Coraline was somewhere in the vicinity of sixty years old. Her black hair had gone mostly gray, and she kept it pulled up in a top knot so tight that it doubled as a face-lift. She was one of the first residents of Brimley, and although she was prone to cantankerous episodes when she didn't get her way, she was one of the more helpful members of town.

She'd pulled out a chair at the kitchen table and motioned for Aben to sit in it. He did. Then she sat across from him and picked up a pitcher.

"Coffee? I should forewarn you, I brewed it about lunchtime, so it's apt to be cold."

"Goes down the same regardless of the temperature."

She poured him a cup, and he took a swig. It was cold and bitter, but he wasn't about to complain. They sat there in silence for at least two full minutes with the orange glow of a kerosene lantern illuminating their wordless faces. Aben finished the coffee and had had just about enough of the scintillating conversation to last the rest of the night, but as he began to push his chair back from the table, Coraline finally broke the silence.

"Where are you in a rush off to?"

Somewhere less chatty, he thought. "Oh, nowhere in particular."

"Then sit and keep an old widow company for a bit."

Another long silence passed, and Aben cursed his nose for leading him to this house. He realized Coraline wasn't going to start a conversation and decided he'd give it a go. "So, you're baking bread."

She nodded. "We covered that already."

"How could I forget?"

She poured him another cup of coffee even though he didn't request nor desire it. Nevertheless, he drank it because it gave him something to do.

"You said you'd tell me why you were awake at this hour."

"I said I might."

Aben nodded. "You're quite specific, aren't you?"

"I'm baking bread--"

"As we've discussed."

Coraline gave a pinched smile. In his experience, that was about as good as it got from her. "Bread for you to take on the trip."

He liked that she called it a trip. Like they were going to Disney World or maybe Bar Harbor or Miami Beach. Just a few guys hitting the road for some fun in the sun and not three men heading to some deranged madman's island of misfit toys.

"You didn't have to do that."

"Course I didn't have to. I wanted to. There's a difference."

Aben finished off his second cup of coffee and turned it upside down on the saucer to prevent her from forcing upon him a third.

"I suspect you'll tire of canned goods in short order, and I never saw any great culinary talents from you or Mead, so unless that new fella can work magic over a campfire, your pickings are bound to be on the slim side."

"Well thank you for that. I appreciate it. I've always been fond of your bread."

"I know it."

That seemed to exhaust the potential conversation, and after a while, Aben stood. "Well, Coraline, I've got some packing to do, so I think I'll be getting on."

Coraline nodded and watched him move to the door. When his hand fell upon the knob, she spoke again. "Aben?"

He looked back, reluctant.

"You'll be careful out there, won't you?"

"I intend to be just that."

"Good. I occasionally get the sense that you feel out of your element here. But you're an important part of this town. People respect you."

"There's no reason to."

"Well, they do. Whether you want them to or not. And I'm one of them. So be careful and come back to us."

"Thanks again for the bread, Coraline." Aben opened the door and left the woman and the smell of her bread behind him.

CHAPTER THIRTEEN

It seemed to Wim as if every resident of Brimley had come to wish them well on their journey. Aben and Mead partook in the pleasantries, but Wim was eager to move. To get on with the getting on.

He watched as Mead said his farewells to the people for whom he'd provided a safe haven, and their admiration of him was obvious. He enjoyed seeing Mead get the credit he so deserved. He knew the man had been treated somewhat poorly the first time they were together, and that wasn't fair. He might be a bit of an odd duck, but he was almost certainly the best of all of them when it came to survival.

Wim noticed that Mead's goodbye handshakes had hugs shifted into slow motion when a buxom woman with blonde hair came along. He couldn't hear the words exchanged, but it was obvious to Wim that they were a couple. That made him glad too.

Wim was so busy watching them that he didn't see anyone approaching him until he felt a tugging at his shirt. He looked down and found a boy of about six or seven peering up at him, his eyes slits in the sunlight. He had skin the color of honey and wore a tattered Kentucky Wildcats ball cap that was a bit too large for his noggin.

"Hey, you," the boy said.

"Yeah?"

The boy pushed a skinny but long carrot Wim's way. "I got a carrot for your horse. In case he gets hungry."

Wim crouched down so that they were more or less at eye level. He saw a light mark on the boy's upper lip and realized it was a healed scar where he'd had surgery to repair a hare lip. "Well, that was nice of you. The horse is a she, though."

"What's her name?"

"Gypsy."

"Who named her that?"

"Someone I loved. Very much."

"Who was that?"

Wim had a sense this type of inquisition could drag on, and while he appreciated the boy's kind nature, he wasn't interested in drawing it out. "How about you give Gypsy the carrot? That way, she'll know it was from you."

"Really? I can feed her?"

Wim nodded, and the boy moved to Gypsy's front. The horse glanced down, mostly disinterested.

"Hey Gypsy. This young fellow--" It was his turn to ask a question. "What's your name anyway?"

"John Robert Hubbard. But everyone calls me JR. You can call me that too."

Lord, even his name was long, Wim thought. "JR brought you a carrot."

The boy pushed the carrot toward Gypsy's mouth. At first, she pulled back in a 'get that out of my face' gesture, but Wim stroked her mane, and she calmed a bit. As the boy wagged the carrot back and forth, the horse seemed to realize he wasn't going away unless she took it, so she grabbed it between her teeth. Wim could practically imagine she was thinking, why didn't the kid bring a sugar cube instead, but she chewed away on the root like it was cud, and JR audibly squealed with joy.

"She likes it!"

"She does," Wim fibbed. "I thank you. And I'm sure Gypsy would too if she could talk."

"Horses can't talk!"

Wim pondered making a *Mister Ed* reference but imagined it would go far over the boy's capped head, and he let the matter drop. With great relief, Wim watched JR skip away toward an elderly woman. "Mama Iris, I fed the horse!"

When the goodbyes and pleasantries were over, the men got to work loading up the wagon. They were nearly finished when a man, who Wim guessed to be on the downhill side of sixty, approached. He had a pistol on each hip and a rifle in his hands.

"You look like you're ready for the parade, Pablo," Mead said to him.

"I'm going with you."

Mead raised an eyebrow, and a smirk pulled at the corner of his mouth. "No. I appreciate that you're volunteering, but you stay here and keep an eye on things, okay?"

The man shook his head, and there was a steely look in his eyes that made Wim suspect he wasn't going to be deterred. "I heard where you're going and why. I lost my whole family to the plague. My wife and my three daughters. My grandson and son-in-law. They all died and turned into zombies, and I had to put them out of their miseries."

Pablo looked to Wim, and Wim thought the man's eyes might be the saddest things he'd ever seen. "You say that man started the plague. Then he is the one who is responsible for their deaths. So, I am going with you."

Mead looked to Aben, then to Wim. Wim shrugged his shoulders. Who was he to tell this man who'd lost maybe more than any of them that he couldn't be a part of this?

"Alright," Mead said. "You have anything to pack?"

Pablo motioned to his guns. "I have all I need."

"How about a bike? Because we're running low on transportation."

"I will retrieve one," Pablo said and jogged away.

Mead stepped to Wim's side. "Are you okay with this? I mean, it's kind of your show."

"I'm not in charge of anything or anyone. If he wants to go, I believe that's his decision."

Mead looked in the older man's direction. "I hope he doesn't slow us down, is all."

Wim could tell Pablo was a man with a mission, and he didn't expect him to be a hindrance of any kind. By the time Pablo returned with a bicycle, the wagon was loaded, and they were almost ready to go. There was only one horse in the town, a fact that made Wim smile and wonder if anyone else would get the humor. He rather doubted it. It was a young, black mare that made Gypsy look even older and more haggard. Aben had it by the reigns and walked it toward them.

"You do much riding?" Wim asked Aben.

"When I was in the Boy Scouts. I'm hoping it's like riding a bicycle," Aben said. "Or a little easier, preferably." He tapped his stump against his chest, then climbed into the saddle with surprising ease. The horse whinnied and took a few shuffling steps sideways, but Aben rested his hand on the mare's neck and stroked her mane, and she settled.

Wim looked toward Mead, who was locked in another embrace with the tearful, blonde woman. He was anxious to go but not to the point of interrupting their moment. He returned to the wagon where Prince meandered amongst the supplies and weapons, as excited as any dog to go for a ride.

That made Wim realize he was excited too. He knew that shouldn't be the case. That he shouldn't be looking forward to a trip that might turn him into a murderer, but having a purpose again, even a dark one, had reignited a fire inside him that had burned out several months ago.

CHAPTER FOURTEEN

THE MEN AVOIDED THE WORST OF THE MOUNTAINS AS BEST THEY could. It was three weeks into their trip, and they'd made it to Tennessee without issue. Travel was slow but steady, with Gypsy setting the pace. At times, Wim half thought the old girl might not survive the journey, but so far, she was plodding along. The new horse which Aben rode had no name, but its addition seemed to give Gypsy a renewed purpose, and Wim wondered if horses possessed something akin to pride.

Around the time the sun began to drop toward the horizon, they were on the east side of a middling city named Morristown. Aben spied a run-down log cabin at the bottom of a ravine and suggested they make it their home for the night. It looked as good a spot as any.

While Wim tied off the horses, Mead checked and cleared the cabin. It was small, only four rooms, but none of the men needed much space. Wim had worked up a good appetite, but even his hunger wasn't quite strong enough for the thought of cold canned food to activate his salivary glands. That was the worst part of being on the road, he'd found, the monotony of the food. When he noticed a rusty charcoal grill set ten or so yards from the cabin, he got an idea.

His hopes of hot food were temporarily dashed when he found the grill empty aside from some equally rusty grates. He almost gave up but then saw a dilapidated shed tucked into an overgrown honeysuckle bush. To Wim, that looked as good a spot to store charcoal as any, and he decided to go exploring.

The door opened hard. It took three strong yanks before giving way, and he couldn't understand why it had put up such a fight until he noticed the sharp end of three-inch nails poking out the back side. Before he could wonder who had nailed the door closed and why, a zombie stumbled out of the shed and into the waning light of day.

Wim had left his rifle inside the cabin and had already stripped off the pistol he typically had holstered on his hip and the knife that held residence in his belt. He was weaponless but not too concerned at the plight. The zombie was a boy old enough to count his age on two hands without doubling up. On top of being young, he was barely tall enough to come up to Wim's ribcage, and as the boy came at him, Wim simply reached out and grabbed a handful of his carrot-colored hair and held him at bay.

He glanced toward the cabin to see if any of the men might be taking this in but saw none of them. Even Prince was safely inside and unaware.

The boy gave a strange, high-pitched growl, and Wim returned his attention to the dead child that thrashed before him. His jaws clicked together as he bit in Wim's general direction but caught nothing but air.

Wim hated killing the children. Adults were bad enough, but at least they had had a chance at life. These poor wretches didn't even get that. But if Wim had learned anything in life, it was that it was far from fair.

He dragged the boy toward a good-sized rock that poked up from the overgrown crabgrass that grew in the clearing around the cabin. The dead child clawed and kicked but weighed less than a sack of feed and presented no challenge at all as Wim pushed his skull down on top of the stone.

The boy hissed up at him, and Wim had a moment to think that he should have laid him face down, but he saw no sense in turning him over now. Instead, he brought his boot-clad foot down on the child's face, and his head broke apart like a gruesome piñata.

As Wim wiped chunks of the mess from the sole of his boots, he heard the growling behind him, and it was so close that he could feel the creature's breath on his back.

He turned to see a second zombie, this one female and about his own age, he guessed. She, too, had carrot-red hair, and even though she was dead, he felt pretty bad for stomping her son in front of her.

The mom zombie swung at him, and he caught her upper arm, spinning her around so that her back was pressed into is chest. With her momentarily contained, his attention drifted away from her and to the shed where a dead teenage boy and an elderly male zombie had recently exited and were heading his way.

Wim sighed. All this for an attempt at some hot food.

The two newest arrivals were about five yards from him, and Wim decided it was time to call in reinforcements.

"Hey fellas. I've got myself in a spot of trouble out here."

The mom zombie strained, trying to break free, and he jerked her arm upward, so it pinched her neck. It would have been strangling her if she still needed to breathe.

The teenager was making better time than his undead gramps. Almost close enough to bite. Wim decided to use what he had in hand and shoved mom his way. The two collided with enough force to send them to the ground, and about that time, Aben emerged from the cabin with his homemade war club in hand.

"I suspect these were the homeowners," Wim said to him. "And they're not taking kindly to our presence."

The two fallen zombies were back on their feet and moving Wim's way again. Gramps still lagged behind but continued slow and steady like the tortoise.

Aben moved toward the scene. He slowed as he passed Wim. "There's a knife in my belt."

Wim grabbed hold of it as Aben passed him, but there wasn't much need. The big man swung his club at the mom zombie, and the ground down maul hit her behind the left ear with so much force that it tore through her skull, gouging a channel that started at the side of her head and ended at her right eye. It was like a small missile had been shot through her face, and, Wim supposed, that wasn't far off.

The dead woman's teenage son was next in the line of fire. That time, Aben went with an overhead swing and connected with the top of the boy's skull. As the bones shattered under the force of the blow, Wim thought it looked like his face was melting, and his flesh, loosened from the destroyed bone underneath, sagged down in a way that reminded Wim of a discarded Halloween mask.

Wim thought about joining in, but Aben needed no assistance. He looked over to gramps and shook his head. "Hell, old timer, if I wait for you to come to me, it's liable to be dark before you get here."

He strode toward the old, dead man and finished him with a less forceful hit to the temple. Even at a distance, Wim could hear the bones breaking like someone had dropped a sack full of china. It was a stomach-turning noise and some of his appetite fled.

Aben looked to him, and Wim saw a grisly hunk of flesh caught in the man's beard. "That all of 'em?" Aben asked.

"I'd imagine so." Wim motioned to the shed. "But we might ought to check just to be sure."

They checked, and the shed was empty of zombies and charcoal. There was a bright, red chainsaw that Wim thought might have made a good weapon in the years before the gasoline had expired, but aside from a few shovels and garden tools, the shed was now bare.

When he and Aben vacated the small building, they saw Mead and Pablo sitting on a wooden swing on the porch.

"Thanks for the hand," Wim said.

"Looked like you had a handle on it," Mead grinned.

As he walked toward them, Wim realized his boot was still sticky with preteen zombie skull, and he scraped it against the porch step.

"Took out just about the whole family. No pa, though. You check the cabin good?"

Mead nodded. "Wasn't much to check."

"Well, someone put 'em in there. Best to keep our eyes open, just in case."

Mead nodded. "I always do. But let's multitask and eat while we do it."

Even with his hunger halved, the thought of food brought a greedy rumble in Wim's belly.

"I saw a little grill over there." Mead turned to Pablo. "Pablo, you mind fetching that charcoal?"

"Not at all."

Pablo disappeared into the cabin, and Wim raised an eyebrow at Mead. "Where'd you find charcoal?"

"Under the sink. With the tongs and spatulas."

Wim supposed that made sense.

THEY COOKED the beans and spaghetti in the cans. The grill heated up quicker than expected and all were slightly charred, but the burned flavor was something new, and Wim appreciated the variety.

As usual, the men agreed to sleep in shifts. So far, the nights had been uneventful, but that was no reason to get careless. Wim had seen far too often what happened to careless people. Mead and Aben slept first, leaving Wim and Pablo to sit on the porch and listen to the mosquitos buzz. After a couple hours, Wim decided he'd rather hear human conversation.

"Were you from Arkansas originally?"

Pablo nodded. "My entire life. However, I lived further south, close to the Texas border."

Wim struggled to think of what to ask next. His previous conversations with Pablo hadn't gone far beyond the superficial, and he still wasn't sure what to make of the quiet, private man. All he really knew of him was that Pablo had been a high school economics teacher before the plague.

Mead told Wim the story of finding Pablo holed up inside his house, the bodies of his dead family members rotting in the hot sun outside. After killing them, he'd piled them up, and Mead said it looked like a mound of crash test dummies, except for the flies. And the smell. He'd intended to bury them, but the ground was too hard, and he'd been waiting for rain that never came.

The man didn't want to go with Mead. He said he owed it to his family members to give them a proper burial, so Mead offered to help dig. It took them two full days, and even then, they only made it down four feet and created a hole barely wide enough to fit them all, but with some careful placement, they made it work.

Mead shared a particularly detailed memory about how the stomach of one of Pablo's daughters broke open as he was moving it. He said that what came out made him think of a restaurant dumpster after a week in the summer heat and told Wim that there were so many maggots that it looked like someone had emptied a twenty-pound bag of rice into the hole in her midsection where her organs had once been. Only this rice moved.

That was more detail than Wim needed to hear, but it made him feel even more sorry for the man who was so quiet that it bordered on shyness. Even as they traveled, while Wim spent the days and nights bonding with Mead and Aben, Pablo kept to himself and rarely spoke unless one of them spoke to him first. He often wondered if that was an aftereffect of everything the man had been through, or if it had been his manner even beforehand.

Much to Wim's surprise, Pablo broke the silence.

"The place we are going. The Ark. Do you think we will have to fight the other survivors when we arrive? I do not mind killing zombies, but I am unsure whether I could do the same to another human unless I had good cause."

Wim took a swallow of beyond flat soda from a bottle. "I don't believe so. When we left, there weren't many people left. It was mostly zombies. And if I had to put money on it, I'd say the zombies got most of them. They were an isolated bunch and on the soft side. They never had to learn how to do what's needed to survive, and I suspect they went down without much of a fight."

"That is good."

"Mmm hmm."

"Did the Doctor say why he did this?"

Wim thought about that before answering. Over the years, he'd tried to block out most of Doc's ravings. "He was a cruel man. And angry. And intelligent. Those qualities don't blend well. Personally, I don't believe he had any reason beyond general meanness."

Silence fell between them for a while, their words replaced by the drone of the nighttime insects, until Pablo spoke up again. This must be a record, Wim thought.

"The woman you loved, she was his daughter?"

"My wife was his daughter. Yes. But she was nothing like him. She had no idea what kind of man he was."

"I hope I did not offend you."

"You didn't."

"Good. Because I did not mean to infer that she was in some way complicit. Children do not see their parents as they are but rather as they wish them to be."

Wim supposed that was true. He certainly had idealized versions of his own.

"My daughters were not perfect children, but then I was not a perfect father either. I was hard on them. Demanding. Because I wanted them to make good lives for themselves. I hope they understood my reasons."

"I suspect they did."

"I oftentimes wonder about their deaths, if there was any shred of consciousness remaining inside and alert when I had to destroy them. And if there was, what they must have thought of me then."

It was a horrible thought and similar to ones Wim had pondered over the years. Thinking it again now made him thankful that Ramey had left him before the end. That she'd spared him the agonized worries that haunted Pablo.

"I don't think there's anything human left in them at that point. I believe, I hope, that whatever made them who they were, that part goes away when they die. What gets back up and walks and fights and eats, that's just the brain misfiring and doing what comes from instinct. Like a rabid dog."

Both men looked to Prince, who was sprawled on his side, asleep. That seemed to bring the conversation to an end, and Wim was grateful. With these thoughts in his mind, he suspected that when it was his turn to rest, sleep would be hard to find.

CHAPTER FIFTEEN

ABEN WATCHED, SILENT, AS PRINCE LAID IN FRONT OF WIM'S feet, staring up at him and panting. Wim, however, seemed to be in his own world. He sat on a fallen tree and stared into the forested abyss, looking but not seeing. Aben was all too familiar with that blankness, and, after another thirty seconds passed, decided to interject.

"For a farmer, you sure can't read animals."

Wim came back to the land of the living and looked Aben's way. "What?"

Aben strolled his way, extra careful on the uneven terrain. Getting around without half a foot could be a bitch if he wasn't careful. "My dog. He wants your attention."

Wim realized the dog was at his feet and reached down to pet him. Prince rolled onto his back, and Wim ruffled the mottled fur on his undercarriage.

"You ever have a dog?" Aben found a tree stump close enough to Wim to have a conversation and used it as a seat.

"Folks would drop them off at the farm occasionally. Sometimes, they'd stick around for a spell, long enough to fill their bellies, but most drifted off soon enough. And the ones that decided to stay longer, soon enough killed a chicken or got into the pig manure, and Pa would end up chasing them off."

"So that's a no."

Wim flashed a weak smile. "I suppose. We had cats, though."

"A cat's not a dog. To a cat, you're at best a landlord. And they're surly tenants. Now, a dog, to him, you're his whole world."

"I always liked pigs."

Aben sighed. Wim gave Prince another quick pat which did little to satiate the mutt's need for attention. The dog rose up and went to Aben's side, and he petted him the way a dog deserved, and expected, to be petted.

"We're close now, aren't we?"

Wim's gaze drifted toward the road where the horses rested for a spell. "Mead's better with the map than me."

"But you've actually been there. And I can see it in you. We're close."

Wim nodded. "We are. I'd say less than a week out."

"You've grown quiet. You were never a Chatty Cathy, but you've been different. I can tell your mind's somewhere else."

"It might be."

Prince pawed at Aben's stump, wanting double the love. "I've only got one, you fool. That'll have to suffice." The dog whined but stopped begging. "I've got two ears, though, if you want to talk about anything."

Wim looked his way again, and Aben thought his eyes looked worried, or maybe haunted. "What if I made a mistake, deciding to go back to the Ark?"

"What's got you feeling that way?"

"I can't put a finger on it. I wonder if anyone's left there or if maybe they all died of the zombies or finally gave in to the flu. Doc included. That maybe I dragged you all this way for nothing."

"I doubt a one of us would complain if that ends up being true. We all had our reasons for joining you."

Wim opened his mouth to speak, then stopped himself. Aben despised the role of inquisitor, but the man before him looked as if he might burst if he didn't get out whatever he had dammed up inside.

"It's more than that. Is this about your wife?"

"No. Not directly but maybe in a roundabout way. When I found out that she wasn't really immune, when Doc fessed up about the virus, I promised him I'd come back and kill him if Ramey ever turned. I was so shocked and scared and angry."

"A perfectly reasonable response, if you ask me."

"Maybe. But that's the rub."

"What?"

Wim broke eye contact and stared at the ground. "I don't know if I can."

"Kill him, you mean?"

Wim nodded but still focused his gaze on the dirt floor. "I owe this to Ramey. He needs to be punished. I know that. But if he's still alive, still human..."

"Wim, look at me."

Grudgingly, he did. Aben thought his eyes looked wet, but no tears came.

"There's no shame in not wanting to kill a man. None whatsoever. So, don't you beat yourself up over it."

"Have you? Killed a man, I mean?"

Aben had figured the conversation would lead down this path. Reminiscing wasn't something he enjoyed, but he felt he owed Wim honesty. "I have."

"In the war?"

Aben nodded.

"More than one?"

Aben nodded again.

"How many?"

"As many as I needed to kill to stay alive, Wim."

Wim clenched his hands together, the knuckles turning white.

"If... When I kill Doc - I know he deserves it - but I don't know how I'll be able to forget about it after its done."

"You don't forget about it. You just move on."

Wim nodded and stood. Aben thought his eyes looked marginally less pained than before, and he took that small progress as a good thing.

"When the time comes, I have no doubts you'll do the right thing, Wim."

"Thanks."

"Welcome. I'm not good for a lot these days, but now and again, I manage to try."

Wim gave a small smile. More progress. Another minor victory. Aben watched him return to the road, then looked down at Prince, who had so enjoyed his belly rub that he'd fallen asleep.

He thought the life of a spoiled dog must be pretty damned good when compared to being a person. Dogs didn't have guilt and bad decisions that haunted them. He envied the dog.

CHAPTER SIXTEEN

WHEN THEY CROSSED THE BORDER INTO WEST VIRGINIA, WIM realized that they better start looking for a boat or canoe. Something they'd be able to use to cross the void between the shore and the Ark. Outside a small marina, they found an aluminum Jon Boat. The bottom and sides were covered in dents, but they could find no holes or rust, and Wim supposed that a motley crew like themselves didn't warrant a fancy ride anyway.

It was two more days of riding before they reached the dock Wim remembered so well. The place from which he was sent to neighboring towns to hunt and scavenge supplies. It looked much the same, only the sun had bleached the wood an even lighter shade of gray. The memories the sight conjured were not pleasant ones.

"We waiting for better weather or something?"

Mead's voice startled Wim out of his memories. "Sorry. Just thinking."

"Don't make a habit of that, big fella." Mead hopped down from the wagon and immediately began to grab weapons.

Wim joined him on the ground and tied Gypsy off to a tree. He made sure she was close enough to the water that she could drink and left the knot loose enough that she could break it if she tried hard. As old and cantankerous as she was, she didn't deserve to die of starvation should something happen on the Ark that prevented their return.

Prince had jumped free of the wagon and ran to Aben's side as he tied off his own mare. Wim wandered their way and told him about the rope and the knot, and Aben understood.

"What about your dog?" Wim asked as Prince ran loops around the horse's feet and just narrowly missed getting kicked.

"Him?" Aben looked down at the mutt as it grabbed hold of the horse's reigns and used them as a chew toy. "He can handle himself. I don't have a single doubt as far as that goes."

"All right then," Wim said. But before they left, he tore open a bag of dog food and left it for easy pickings in the rear of the wagon, just in case.

Pablo eased down the kickstand of his bicycle and stared out at the water. "I don't see your island, Wim"

"I doubt anyone moved it." Wim followed his gaze. "It's a big lake's all. And it's not my island."

Wim and Mead pulled the boat free from the wagon and carried it to the dock. The wind was strong and blowing their way, making whitecaps rise on the choppy water. Wim had little to no experience with boats, but he knew that wasn't going to make it any easier.

"Think we should take any food with us?" Mead asked.

"I don't plan to be there long. And if we are, then I suspect food won't be too high on our priority list."

Wim, Aben, and Pablo each had two guns. Wim had a machete, and Aben his war club. Wim didn't know exactly what Mead had strapped to his body, but he knew the man was more capable and prepared than any of them, even without a firearm.

Between the four of them and their weapons, the boat dipped low in the water when they climbed aboard. So low that, for the first few minutes, Wim thought there was at least a fifty-fifty chance it might founder. But once they settled in, it steadied itself out and they were afloat.

"If anyone wants to stay ashore..." Wim looked at them and no one volunteered.

"Well, hell, Wim. That would be like driving your family all the way to Disney World and waiting in the parking lot while they go inside to play with Mickey and Goofy." Aben grinned, and the wind whipped at his scraggly hair, revealing more of his scarred flesh than Wim had noticed prior.

"I was never at Disney World, but I've been to the Ark. And if I had a choice, I'd wait in the parking lot."

Mead clapped him on the shoulder. "Come on, farmer. This is your rodeo. May as well try to enjoy it."

Wim and Mead did the rowing. That seemed only fair since Aben was down a hand and Pablo was almost twice their ages. While Wim liked to think he was in good enough shape, half an hour into the voyage, he was bordering on exhaustion, and a glance Mead's way showed him that Mead was hurting too. The others had also noticed.

"Allow me to help," Pablo said. "I might be an old man, but I could provide one of you a temporary reprieve."

Aben dipped his stump into the lake. "I'd offer, boys, but I'm afraid I'd only row us in circles."

"I'm all right for a while longer." Wim wasn't sure if he believed himself, but this had been his idea - his rodeo as Mead had proclaimed - and he wasn't going to make others do the hard work on his behalf. Mead, too, insisted he could go on, and both men continued, pulling the oars through the choppy, gray water. Forward and back. Forward and back. The monotony of it was almost as bad as the fire that sizzled away in Wim's arms.

Another forty minutes in, and Wim was just about ready to give in when--

"Land ahoy," Aben said.

Wim scanned the distance, and after much searching, he saw a small, dark dot on the horizon. It was barely there, but it was all too familiar. He felt a mixture of dread and relief at the sight of it.

Fifteen minutes later, they arrived.

The wooden gate leading to the Ark hung open, just as it had when Wim and Ramey fled years earlier. As far as he could recall, it was in the exact same position, and the path through it, which had once been worn down to bare ruts, was now taken over by weeds and grass almost two feet high.

That gave Wim some hope. No one had been coming and going for a long time. He hoped that meant Doc had remained every bit the demented captain he'd always been and had decided to remain on the proverbial ship until the bitter end. And as far as any of them could see, the land ahead was empty.

"I have to admit, I'll be pretty fucking disappointed if we came all this way only to find the place vacant," Mead said. "I had myself all psyched up for a good fight."

Wim chewed on the inside of his lip. That was his biggest fear; that he'd led these men on a goose chase.

"I doubt they went all Roanoke, Mead. Don't be such a pessimist." Aben clapped Mead on the back.

Mead glanced Wim's way. "Sorry, I'm just tired. That was a fuck a lot of rowing."

"It was."

"Yeah." Mead pulled on his helmet and took out a conduit spear. Then the four men began the march into the Ark.

MEAD SAW the zombies before the others. Not that that surprised him. No matter how much he preached situational awareness, they all seemed to get distracted from time to time. At that moment, it was the first of the outbuildings which drew their attention. Wim had remarked that the trailer had been his home on the island, and Aben and Pablo fawned all over it like it was the Taj Mahal when, in fact, it was just a piece of shit mobile home little different from the one Mead had grown up in.

While they poked around inside and took the five-cent tour, Mead remained in the open, alert, watching. That's why he spotted the zombie when it was still forty yards away. A few others shuffled along behind it. Altogether, Mead counted eight. Not a lot, but more than they'd seen in one spot since passing through Tennessee. That was a little strange, he thought. Why weren't there more zombies? Almost every damned person in the country had turned into one, so where the fuck did they all go? They'd avoided the cities, of course, but still, it was weird.

Mead's definition of weird was redefined when the nearest zombie moved within fifteen feet of him. The creature had looked the same as any other undead bastard from a distance. Slow, stiff, gray. But upon closer inspection, he realized that it was anything but ordinary.

To start with, the motherfucker had four arms. The sight so surprised him that Mead jabbed his spear into the ground, flipped up the visor on his helmet, and rubbed his eyes to make sure he hadn't suddenly developed double-vision. He checked again. Still four arms. And then, he saw its lower jaw was gone, leaving only a gaping black hole and a gray tongue lolling to and fro like a metronome.

What kind of hopped up horse shit is this, Mead thought.

The other zombies were close enough for him to see in detail. They were like something a demented child would piece together from a box of GI Joe parts. One of the males was completely nude, and its extremities had been cut off and sewn back on. Another had its head on backwards. Two were missing an arm and a leg and had been somehow affixed together at the torso in an extra broad version of the undead. Further back, one of the zombies was almost nothing but tendons and bones as most of its meaty bits had been cut away. Each of the creatures had its own unique deformities, but they all shared one common trait. No lower jaw.

"So they can't bite... I'll be a son of a bitch," Mead said to himself.

Then he cocked his head toward the trailer. "Boys. You might want to take a look at this."

He heard rustling inside the abode, and even though the four-armed zombie was closing in, Mead saw no harm in waiting for them.

Aben was the first out of the trailer. As he pushed through the doorway, Wim and Pablo followed. Mead simply pointed in the direction of the zombies and smiled.

"What the..." Aben's words trailed off.

Pablo pulled a pistol from a holster, ready to shoot, but Mead held up his hand. "Easy now. This bunch looks harmless, but we don't know how many more are out there," he said as he motioned to the land beyond them. "That, we can't see. And for all we know, those might be able to bite. No need to call attention to ourselves just yet."

Mead looked to Wim. "This is like you were telling me. Only more fucked up."

Wim nodded. "These are new."

Pablo had moved toward the zombies. He was only feet away from a creature which had been vivisected. Its torso was open from neck to groin, and all its insides were missing. The loose flesh hung from its frame like oversized clothing on a wire hanger. The old man muttered something, but Mead couldn't make it out.

"What was that?"

Pablo had traded his pistol for a bowie knife. "This is unholy. An abomination."

He stabbed the zombie through the eye, the blade sinking in to the hilt. Then, he twisted the handle, jerking it back and forth and scrambling whatever brains were still inside its skull. The monster collapsed to the ground.

Mead wasn't about to let Pablo have all the fun. He grabbed the spear and finished off the rest of the zombies in less than a minute, then turned to the others. "I know you're a man of few words and all that, Wim, but you really underrepresented what a twisted son of a bitch your father-in-law is."

Wim grimaced, and Mead felt bad for the father-in-law jab.

"He's evil," Wim said. "No other way about it."

"Shit. He needs a word stronger than evil." Mead looked to the others. "What's worse than evil?"

Aben shrugged his shoulders, and Mead knew Wim was far from a walking thesaurus.

"El diablo," Pablo said.

Mead couldn't hold back a smirk and a comment. "Sorry, Pablo, but I don't believe in the devil."

Pablo wiped his blood-covered knife off on his jeans, then looked at Mead. "That is fine. But know that he believes in you."

Mead wasn't sure what to make of that but decided to take it as something akin to a compliment. Maybe the old man wasn't so bad after all.

"Well, we're done here. Are you all ready to head inland?"

They were. As they walked, Mead cozened up beside Pablo. "Can I ask you something?"

Pablo nodded.

"Why do Mexicans always throw out random words of Spanish like that? Even when everything else they say is in English? And it's always a word you know us white people know like 'diablo' or 'muerto' or 'pantalones.' You never just randomly interject the word for, I don't know, television, into a normal conversation."

Pablo stayed quiet as they walked for several yards, then said in his typical barely-above-a-whisper voice, "We do it to keep you confused. And I am not Mexican, you loco gringo."

He stared at Mead for a long moment, then a tight grin spread across his lips. Mead thought it might be the closest he'd ever seen the man come to smiling, and he couldn't hold back one of his own. The old man wasn't so bad after all.

CHAPTER SEVENTEEN

WIM LED THE WAY AS THEY ENTERED WHAT HAD ONCE BEEN something of a town square in the Ark. Only now all the buildings were either burned entirely to the ground or charred, black husks that stood out in stark contrast to the overgrown, green grass that had sprouted up everywhere.

They'd seen a few dozen more zombies on the way in. All were missing their bottom jaw, and most had been on the receiving end of what Wim assumed to be Doc's insane experiments. A great many of the creatures were also minus large chunks of their bodies.

They couldn't make sense of that when they passed them, but the puzzle came together when they found a fire pit with the remains of a leg strung across it like it had been roasted on a spit. The meaty parts of the thigh and calf were gone, but the foot remained intact. The toes were charred and looked a little like burned marshmallows, except for the toenails.

"It just keeps getting fucking weirder," Mead said from the sidelines. When they'd realized the zombies were harmless, he took his helmet off, and his stringy hair was plastered to his skull from the sweat. He pushed a few strands out of his eyes as he looked from the campfire to Wim. "You think this was your guy?"

"I was never much one for wagers, but I'd say that's as close to a sure bet as you can get."

"He's like that Nazi guy. Mangler or something."

"Mengele," Aben said. "Josef Mengele."

Mead nodded. "Yeah, him. This is all kinds of fucked up, man."

Wim wouldn't have used those exact words, but he agreed.

As the men searched what remained of the encampment, Wim headed toward the clinic underneath which Doc's laboratory had once lied. The building itself had been spared from the worst of the fire. Even the door remained, and Wim remembered with a pang of guilt Emory's plan to sneak inside and find out what Doc had been up to. The plan which had led to his death. Or the first one, anyway. Wim had taken care of the second.

The door was unlocked and hung partially ajar. Wim pushed it open with his foot and saw the clinic had been gutted, with only a few cots remaining behind. Past them was the doorway which led to Doc's lab. That was wide-open, and the dark cavern behind it practically called to Wim, even though he all too well remembered the evils at its end.

He was half-way down the tunnel when he heard Aben call out, "Wim."

Wim paused for a moment, staring into the abyss ahead. He wondered if anything was still down there. If any of those mutations - like the baby - were still alive. And he wondered what else the madman that had once been Douglas Younkin had conjured up.

"Wim. I think we found him."

That broke his trance, and he turned back.

Wim found the others near the burned-out building that had been the meeting hall. It seemed like every place here held a bad memory. This one was being sentenced to the box, of having everyone turn on him.

Now, it was only a shell, and a few yards beyond it, Aben, Mead, and Pablo stood with their weapons in hand, facing Wim's direction. Before them, the half-naked form of a man was turned away from him. When he got closer, he could see the man wore nothing but a pair of tattered briefs, which were a mustard-y shade of yellow-brown. His flesh was tanned almost mahogany in color, and his hair, which hung past his shoulders, was pulled back in a sloppy ponytail.

"Is this him?" Mead asked.

"I'm not sure."

Wim still couldn't see the man's face and circled around to get a frontal view, but before he could, the man spoke.

"My dear, William. Is that you? Come all this way to visit an old friend?"

Doc turned to face him. He was grayer and fatter than before. His purple, boot-shaped birthmark was almost black from sun exposure. But if Wim had any doubts, they were erased when he saw the man's maniacal cold eyes. They glinted in the sunlight as he smiled.

"I must say, William, I'm flattered. Welcome back to the Ark."

CHAPTER EIGHTEEN

They'd led Doc back to the fire pit, which, upon closer inspection, Wim realized could double for an altar. They tied his ankles together and bound his hands behind his back. In his dirty underwear, the man looked like an oversized toddler, but Wim knew better than to underestimate him.

He'd told them he was the last person alive on the island. That most had died in the days after the attack and that he'd killed the few who survived. He rambled and ranted and raved, and Wim wished they'd thought to gag him.

"The zombies aren't bad at all now," Doc said. "A little like house cats really. Always finding their way into places they shouldn't be and partaking in various shenanigans. It's amusing to watch, I must say." He grinned, watching one of the creatures try to climb over a fallen tree branch only to tumble face first into the ground. "However, in the early weeks, before I was able to capture and 'de-jaw' them, for lack of a better term..." He shook his head. "It was harrowing, to say the least. They're so hungry. Perfect eating machines really. A little like sharks in that respect."

"Shut up, already," Mead said and rocked his spear back in forth in a vaguely threatening manner.

"Apologies, gentlemen. You see, I've been alone for quite a while, and it's a refreshing change to have someone to converse with. Well, someone who can answer, I should say. The zombies, they're good listeners, but it ends there.

"Speaking of eating, I'm being an inconsiderate host. You've all traveled so far and must have worked up an appetite. You're more than welcome to help yourself to the leg of man." He nodded toward the cooked severed leg.

"You eat them?" Aben asked.

"I have to get protein from somewhere. And a man can only eat so many beans. The meat's rather tasty. I can see why they enjoy it so much. A tad gamey, like venison crossed with free range chicken. An exciting, new experience for the palate, I must say."

Mead wrinkled his nose. "You're a sick motherfucker."

"I understand the social stigma, but I think we can move beyond that now. After all, they eat us. How does the saying go, 'Turnabout's fair play?' Or maybe 'What's good for the goose is good for the gander' is more apropos?"

The sound of his voice, the cheerful exuberance, was making Wim's head throb. He wanted this man dead, but first, he needed answers. "Why are you alive even? Did you end up making a booster for the vaccine after all?"

Doc looked to the other men. "Booster. Vaccine. Listen to him tossing around medical jargon like he isn't nothing but a pig farmer from Pennsylvania. Oh, my daughter certainly did marry down."

Wim's hand fell to his pistol, and he had to fight the urge to draw it. As if sensing the rising tension, Aben stepped between them.

"How about you try answering the man's question? It's a simple enough one."

"Well, it was a multi-part question. 'Why am I alive?' Did you know there were one hundred and eighteen zombies here at one time? One hundred and eighteen versus one. I'd say most would have thought I didn't have the proverbial snowball's chance in hell. I'm alive because I'm resourceful."

"I don't care about that. I want to know--"

"Yes, yes, the booster. To answer that second part of your inquiry, no, I never created one."

"I thought you said it would wear off in a few years."

"Oh, it does. And it will. But science is imperfect in those regards. What might be effective for three years in one person could last ten in another. It's one of those fun, little mysteries, not that I ever took you as having a healthy interest in science or immunology, Wim. I didn't think your interests extended far beyond pig manure."

Doc cocked his head as if realizing something. "You're here because of Ramey, aren't you? Come to steal away the booster shot and play the hero yet again. Sorry to disappoint."

Wim looked away from the man. Between the headache, his building anger, and the grief that welled up at the mention of her name, he couldn't stand to look at him.

"Oh, William," Doc said, and even without seeing him, Wim could hear the smile in his voice. "I've committed a faux pas haven't I? It's too late for you to be a hero because she's already dead."

Wim forced himself to look at the man he'd traveled here to kill.

Doc's eyes blazed with mad excitement. "She turned. And you had to kill her. Just like you killed your friend, the old negro, after I turned him. What was his name? Erving?"

"Emory."

"Ah, yes, Emory. That was quite the sad little plan you two cooked up. He so expected you to come to his rescue. To save him. Right up until I infected him, he believed in you. What a fool."

Doc locked eyes with him, crazy hungry eyes. "But enough about him. Tell me about Ramey. How did she die? Spare me no details. I want to hear all about it."

Wim couldn't take it anymore. He knew he had to do this. For the billions who died because of the virus Doc had created. For Emory. For Ramey. And maybe most of all, for himself.

He drew his revolver, but before he could aim it, the right side of Doc's face imploded in a spray of blood and bone. His eye socket caved in while his eyeball popped out and dangled loosely at the end of the tendon, sagging down like a deflated balloon at the end of its string. His mouth opened, and his breath hitched. His lips moved as if trying to speak, but all that came out was a muffled "Uh... uh... uh..."

It went down so fast, so violently, that Wim didn't even know what had happened. It was like a bomb had gone off in the man's face.

"That's a man who didn't know when to stop flappin' his lips," Aben said.

Wim followed the sound of the voice and saw Aben holding his war club, the end of which dripped blood.

I should have been the one to do that, Wim thought. He was mine to kill.

But when he looked at Doc who still sat mostly upright, although tilting slightly to the side like a poorly-planted scarecrow, half his face dripping sinew and gore, he was relieved Aben had stepped in.

Only, Doc wasn't dead yet.

"Uh... uh..."

Wim saw dark wetness spread across his underwear as Doc pissed himself. He kept slipping further sideways but in slow barely discernible movements. And he kept on with the "Uh... Uh..."

Pablo stepped between Wim and Doc, and Wim saw he was holding his pistol.

"This is for my family. And if God curses me for murdering you, then I will see you in hell and, there, I will do even worse."

Pablo raised his gun and pressed the barrel against Doc's forehead. He squeezed the trigger, and Doc's head snapped backward in a motion so extreme that Wim could hear the madman's neck break. Doc's slow-motion tumble sideways turned into a hard and fast lunge backward, and he hit the ground with a thud.

Pablo returned his gun to its holster and turned to Wim. "I am sorry. Wim."

"What for?"

"For not giving you your chance at vengeance."

Wim looked at the dead man. Half his face was gone. Blood gushed from the bullet wound in his forehead, and brains leaked out the gaping wound in the back. His body was twisted on the ground, and Wim could smell shit and piss seeping from his groin.

"That's all right. I got what I needed. And he got what he deserved."

And it was done.

CHAPTER NINETEEN

No matter where she went in the big house, Mina couldn't escape the smell of puke. Even leaning out the window, trying to find fresh air, she still smelled it. When dealing with her daddy and his myriad if health issues, it was the smell of shit that haunted her day in and day out and she had thought nothing could be worse than that odor. She was wrong.

A light, dusty breeze kicked up, and she thought that should give her a break from the odor, but it didn't. The sickening sweet smell of vomit clung to her like dime store perfume.

She realized the smell might have permeated her clothes, maybe even the pores in her skin. She stripped off her blouse, not caring that she was naked underneath. It wasn't like she had anything of note to see, and besides, there was no one around to see her body anyway.

She balled up the shirt and tossed it onto a pile of garbage on the bathroom floor. The house was more of a hovel, and there had been a time in her life when living in such filth would have made her ashamed. But Mina had spent her whole life cleaning up other people's messes, and she'd reached the point where she no longer gave a shit about dirt or garbage or even the bugs that now shared their quarters and outnumbered them a few thousand to two.

"Gettin lazy, Birdie," her father's voice said. "That's what happens when you ain't got a man keeping you in line."

She tried to block him out.

Saw had been vomiting every few hours for going on four days now. She wondered what his body kept finding to eject because she refused to feed him, but that hadn't stopped it. And almost like clockwork, a pained retching noise echoed off the walls a few rooms over.

How can he be so damn loud, she wondered. Everything about the man was over the top and offensive, even his puking.

"Mina!" his voice boomed. "This goddamn bucket's full!"

She stared out the window, onto the bland beige world and wondered if she'd die if she jumped out. It was only two stories, so she doubted it. She'd probably only break her legs or maybe she'd cripple herself. As if life wasn't awful enough already.

Despite that, she turned away from the open window, afraid the darker part of her mind would win out and force her to take a swan dive, even though she knew it wasn't really a way out. There was no way out. Not for her. If Mina's life was a road sign, it would be "No Exit."

"Are you fingering yourself in there or what?"

She threw a glance down the hallway. She wished she'd have gone outside. Gone to town even. Then he could empty his own barf bucket. But she knew that he knew she was home, and if she ignored him much longer, she'd have more to worry about than spilling Saw's puke onto her shoes.

"I'm coming!"

She stomped out of the bathroom, toward the sound of his voice.

"Haven't heard that in ages." He cackled. "Good on you, love."

How could that bastard be laughing? She wanted him to be miserable, to suffer. But he was laughing like a schoolboy who just heard an exceptionally dirty joke.

It had been Mina who had introduced Saw to opioids. First was Oxy, which she assured him would stop the headaches that had plagued him since being shot in the head years earlier. The truth of it was that Mina didn't give a single shit about Saw's pain. His head could have rotted off, and she'd have been happy as a jaybird.

But when the headaches came, Saw grew even meaner than usual. And even on a good day, Solomon Baldwin was a fair share to the right of a junkyard dog. Anything worse bordered on sadistic, and some of the things she saw him do when he was in pain haunted her to this day.

The Oxy mellowed him. He was still a son of a bitch, but he was a slow-witted, less creative son of a bitch. The reaction to the drugs was so pleasant that Mina had asked Boyd to bring her heroin. The man protested at first. He knew the rules. But she assured him it was for Saw, that it was what Saw wanted. And if anything here was above the rules, it was Saw.

Saw wouldn't shoot up, said that was junkie bullshit, but smoking it was just as good. When he took that first hit, Mina watched his pupils expand and thought she could practically see the cruelty pour out of him as the drugs took effect. She knew she was onto something.

It was all going so well until that little prick Mitch had to get involved. She had never liked the boy, with his ratty, scarred face. While Saw held the title of the meanest man she'd ever met, easily toppling her father from that gold medal podium spot he'd held for so long, there was something about Mitch that was worse. She'd never been able to pinpoint exactly what it was she found so offensive, but she tried to keep her distance.

Her grand plan was that Saw would get so hooked on the heroin that he'd overdose. And if that didn't work, she'd ask Boyd for some Fentanyl, and she'd mix up her own toxic concoction. A high her husband would never forget. But that all came crashing down about the time Boyd was having his face eaten off by zombies.

"Poor stupid, Birdie. Can't even kill a druggie. Never could do nothing right."

She gritted her teeth and pushed away her daddy's voice, moving toward her and Saw's bedroom. The door was two thirds closed, and Mina didn't knock before opening it. She regretted that decision.

Saw sat on the bed with his finger two knuckles deep into the hole in his forehead. She watched his wrist twist and turn as he dug at the wound. At his brain. She didn't realize it, but she must have gasped because Saw snapped her way.

"Fookin thing won't stop itching." He pulled his finger free, and she thought she heard a *pop*. Blood coated his finger, and he stuck it in his mouth and sucked on it like it was strawberry jam.

The sight made her feel like puking, but that was the last thing this house needed more of. Besides the bed, a plastic pail filled with Saw's chunky, milk-colored vomit was on the verge of overflowing. What a horror show her life had become. Every time she thought it couldn't get much worse, it did.

"You've got to stop that. You'll get an infection. And I'm pretty sure all the antibiotics are a long-time expired."

Saw stared at her, and it took Mina a moment to realize he was looking at her chest. That's when she remembered she was still naked from the waist up. Her hands instinctively went to her mosquito bite breasts.

"Don't get modest for me, love. I was enjoying the show, unexpected though it was."

"I spilled some..." She couldn't conjure up a lie quick enough.

Saw didn't seem to care. He pointed to the puke pail. "Can you empty that for me? I'd do it me self but--" He held up his hands, which shook like he had Parkinson's.

Mina wondered how long it would take for him to detox. So far, the bad part of him, the cruel part, hadn't returned, but she knew it was a monster lurking somewhere deeper inside him, biding its time before clawing itself free.

She reached for the bucket and realized some vomit had dribbled down the side and clung to the handle. She felt her stomach do a summersault and closed her eyes as she reached for it.

Her fingers squished through the puke, which was thick and still warm.

Oatmeal, she told herself. It's only oatmeal. Don't think anything else.

"That ain't no oatmeal I ever saw," her daddy's voice said. "Less someone ate it and refunded it."

She knew she'd never make it to the bathroom even though it was only twenty feet away. That was too long to feel his barf in her hand. She realized the bedroom window was open and moved toward it as quick as possible without sloshing more vomit out of the pail.

She couldn't believe the weight of it. It must be five pounds of puke, she thought. How's that even possible? Not puke, she told herself. Oatmeal. Oatmeal. Extra chunky oatmeal.

Only this oatmeal had gone rancid. She didn't dare look in the bucket. The smell was bad enough. The sight would push her over the edge. She didn't bother upending and dumping the pail. She pushed - no, launched - the entire horrid mess of it out the window. She heard it hit the ground below, a heavy wet splat, but she kept her eyes averted and tried to catch her breath.

"You dropped me bucket," Saw said.

"I'll get you another."

The bed squeaked, and she heard his footsteps moving toward her.

Don't come to me. Don't touch me. "Stay in bed, Saw. You need to keep your strength."

But he was on her. She felt his bare chest press into her back. His flesh was hot and clammy at the same time, and it seemed to meld into her own, adhering to her naked back like an oversized suction cup.

"I'm starting to feel more like me old self."

His lips pressed against her shoulder. One hand wrapped around her waist. The other groped at her barely-there breasts.

Why'd I take off my shirt, she thought.

Despite months on heroin, despite losing more than fifty pounds from the addiction, his arms were still so strong as they wrapped around her. *He could break me.* She knew that was true. And as scared as that knowledge made her, the power in his embrace also reminded her why she had gone with him in the first place.

Safety.

With Saw, she was safe. He'd never harmed her physically and rarely said a cross word to her. His cruelty was always directed at others. She hated him, loathed the way he treated people, despised so many of the things he'd done, but through it all, he'd kept her safe.

As his hands caressed her, Mina felt wetness at her crotch, and a low groan slipped from her mouth.

At the sound, Saw held her tighter, and she felt his hardness pressing into her buttocks. When he reached around and unzipped her pants, slipping them down her slender thighs, she didn't protest, even though the smell of vomit seeped from his gaping mouth.

Four years ago, Mina made a deal with the devil. He'd held up his end of the bargain. It was her time to do the same.

CHAPTER TWENTY

Even though summer was coming to an end, it was still hot and dry, and Wim could see a zombie walking through the hazy mirage of purple and pink flames that rose up from the asphalt.

"You see that?" he asked Mead, who sat beside him in the wagon.

"I do. You going to shoot it?"

Wim pondered that for a moment, then shook his head. "Can't see wasting a bullet."

"Smart man."

Aben was ahead of them, riding the black mare. Pablo pedaled along in the rear. They were all at least a hundred yards from the zombie, and with the slow pace of each party, it would be a spell before they met.

The attitude on the return trip was far lighter than it had been on the way to the Ark. It was as if the cloud that had hung over their heads dissipated with Doc's death and their lives could begin anew.

Even Pablo was marginally more talkative and outgoing and partook in meals more regularly. On that day, for lunch, the older man had shared with them his culinary skills, adding some canned tomatoes with jalapeño peppers to their bean and corn stew. The result, to Wim's bland palate, was about as hot as a firecracker, and he drank two canteens of water all while Pablo laughed hysterically. Wim was glad to see him laugh, but even now, two hours later, his tongue still burned.

The distance between the men and the zombie had grown close enough to see the creature in detail now. It was a young man, probably in his twenties. Its jeans were filled with ragged holes, the kind that had been fashionable once upon a time, and it wore a t-shirt with an upside down American flag. When they got a bit closer, Wim saw text above the stars and stripes reading, "Fuck the flag!" That annoyed Wim, and he reconsidered whether it would actually be a waste of a bullet.

He reached behind and took hold of his rifle, leveling the scope and examining the zombie in more detail. Its face was a chewed-upon lump of mangled flesh, and Wim saw its earlobes were of the stretched-out variety. The rings that had once filled them were long gone, and they jiggled with each lumbering step. Wim estimated he could fit three fingers through the holes if he was so inclined, but he was not.

His finger danced around the trigger. It wasn't hard getting an aim, even with the bumps and bounces of the wagon, but he still debated whether he should take a shot or just let Aben bash its skull in with his war club when he was close enough. Wim took another look at the zombie, then decided he was worth a bullet after all.

As his finger curled around the trigger, he squeezed one pound, then two. He was almost at three when a flurry of black and white filled his scope, obscuring the dead man.

"What the..."

"Son of a bitch!" Mead yelled out, excited, almost gleeful.

Wim lowered the rifle to get a broader view of what was happening. When he did, he saw a bald eagle attacking the zombie. Its talons sunk deep into the zombie's chest, shredding the flesh like it was tissue paper. Black blood oozed from the wounds.

The eagle's wings flapped as its head darted forward, striking at the zombie's face. First, a wide divot was carved into its cheek, then its left eye was ripped out as the bird attacked.

The zombie clumsily waved its arms, trying to knock the bird loose, but it was no match. The eagle's head struck like a snake, and its yellow beak came away with a mouthful of stretched earlobe. The next bite took off two thirds of the zombie's nose.

"Pablo, are you seeing this shit?" Mead screamed as he bounced up and down in the wagon. "Get up here!"

Wim caught Pablo's approach from the rear out of the corner of his eye.

The man looked panicked. "What is going on?"

Wim pointed ahead. "Bald eagle versus zombie."

The zombie landed a glancing blow, striking the eagle in the side of the head, and the bird released the dead man and flew backward a foot. But the pause in the attack was brief, and it was back on the zombie in an instant.

That time, it grabbed hold of the zombie's head, its claws digging into the dead man's skull. Its remaining eye popped as a talon sunk deep into the socket. The bird flapped its wings once, twice. The zombie's body stretched upward, and it appeared to get four inches taller.

The eagle flapped again, harder, more forceful. The tendons in the dead man's neck pressed taut against its flesh, every muscle and fiber visible under the strain. The zombie's arms swung side to side, its feet tap danced on the pavement like some bizarre dance club move.

Wim could barely believe what he was seeing when the eagle's enormous wings flapped again, harder, stronger. And then the dead man's neck burst in a spray of black, semi-coagulated liquid. The flesh gave way first, tearing almost as if it was perforated paper. Then the veins and muscles and tendons underneath carried the weight of the zombie. Those stretched like taffy before snapping under the force.

And then, the head was severed from the body. The bald eagle soared upward, unleashing a triumphant scream as it flew through the air, soaring over Wim and the others. Droplets of black blood fell like rain.

Wim turned his attention back to the zombie's body, which took one more staggering step forward before crashing to the ground.

"That's the most American thing I've ever seen!" Mead screamed, then beat Wim on the shoulder with excitement.

"You didn't slip some peyote into that stew, did you Pablo?" Aben asked.

Pablo shook his head, a broad smile on his face. It was the most emotion Wim had seen from the man so far. "No. I cannot say I did."

Mead shook Wim again, and Wim found the man's excitement contagious. "That was fucking awesome, man! Wasn't it?"

"It sure was."

THEY WERE STILL HALF-DRUNK with excitement over the eagle attack when they came to an old bridge about half an hour later. The frame was metal, but the base was wooden slats that had gone gray and rough through weather and time. A hand-painted sign hung at the edge. "Weight Limit - 2 Tons."

"How much do you weigh, Wim?" Aben asked.

"Been a while since I checked, but back then, I was two ten."

"Two and a half bills here," Aben said.

"You two are fat asses." Mead pinched his waist, where there was little extra flab. "One fifty-five tops."

"But how much with all your armor?"

Mead shrugged his shoulders. "Another thirty or forty."

They looked Pablo's way.

"One hundred and sixty."

Wim did the math in his head. "I'd say between us and the wagon, supplies, and dog, we're looking at thirteen hundred pounds. Gypsy's mostly skin and bones. I doubt she hits nine hundred. Aben, your girl's solid, though. I'm thinking twelve hundred. That's around a ton and a half. Leaves us a fair bit of room to spare, but I think we should cross in pairs, just to be safe."

"Sounds like a plan." Aben waved Pablo toward him. "Let's be the Guinea pigs, professor."

Pablo didn't protest and, together, the men moved onto the bridge. Wim moved the wagon as close as possible without getting onto the wood, and he and Mead watched.

The bridge was about twenty yards across. A mostly dry creek trickled along underneath. The steep decline on both sides was lined with generic scrubby brush.

Aben and Pablo crossed the expanse in under a minute. "You're up!" Aben called from the other side.

Wim gave Gypsy's reigns a shake, and the horse trotted forward. Once on the bridge, Wim was less certain that the decision to cross was wise. The wood wasn't just old and weathered, but it was also knotty and cracked in places. They were a third of the way across, and he still hadn't taken a breath.

"Everything okay?" Mead asked, and his voice caused Wim to flinch.

"Yep," Wim said through tight lips.

They crossed the half-way point and were nearing in on the two thirds mark when he heard the snap. That was immediately followed by the wagon lurching sideways and sinking to the left.

"What's going on?" Aben called out.

Wim looked behind him and saw the wagon wheel had crashed through one of the wood slats. It was balanced between the boards and hadn't fallen all the way in. He turned back to Aben. "We'll know soon enough."

He shook the reigns again. Gypsy took a step forward, but the wagon didn't move, and she wasn't about to put any extra effort into it.

He turned to Mead. "We're gonna have to push."

"Whatever you say."

The two of them retreated to the back of the wagon and gave it their best try, but the wheel was further in than Wim had thought. They pushed again, but it made no difference. From the back of the wagon, Prince watched them, tail wagging.

"Darn it," Wim sighed. He still thought there was a way out of this, but it would take more than the two of them.

"Aben? Pablo? Care to lend your muscles?"

Aben tied off his horse, and the men came to them.

"If you can lift a little, we'll push," Wim said.

"I think I got this." Aben crouched down and put his shoulder under the rear of the wagon. "On three?"

Wim counted off. Aben pushed up, using his whole body. The wagon's back end came up a full inch, but the wheel was still caught.

"Push harder!" Aben grunted and used all his strength to lift the wagon further.

Wim, Mead, and Pablo dug their feet in and shoved with everything they had. The wagon began to move. Then, the wheel popped over the hole and onto the next board.

"I think we got it," Wim said.

"Bout damn time!" Aben fell to his knee, and the wagon came down with him. Hard.

It slammed into the bridge, and when Wim heard the crack, he thought a piece of the wagon had broken. Maybe the axel or something in the frame. But Mead changed his mind.

"Oh, fuck."

As soon as the words spilled from his mouth, the board which the wagon had been set down upon splintered, breaking off in large chunks that tumbled free and disappeared below them. Both wheels dropped into the hole and the frame smashed into the bridge. That brought forth a reverberating groan that Wim could feel in the soles of his feet. He knew this was all kinds of bad.

"Mead, untie Gypsy and get her across the bridge!" Mead raced to the front of the wagon and worked on the ropes.

Wim grabbed hold of the scruff of Prince's neck and threw the dog off the wagon. It bounced onto the bridge with a startled and pained *Yip* that made Wim feel bad, but there was no time for remorse. "Take your dog and get off here!" Aben wasted no time.

The wood underfoot creaked and cracked as Wim grabbed as many guns as he could carry. Pablo was on the opposite side of the wagon, doing the same. "Go, Pablo!"

"I will help. We need these!"

"Leave it!" Aben yelled from the end of the bridge.

Wim looked up and saw that he, Mead, the horses, and dog were all safe. Another board snapped, then two more. The wagon sagged toward the hole that was opening underneath, and Wim knew there was no more time.

He turned to Pablo. "Let's go."

Pablo struggled to free a rifle strap which was caught under some supplies, pulling at it with no results.

"Come on!"

The wood groaned again. Then, the painful sounding groan turned into an explosion. Dust and debris filled the air, and Wim thought it was rising and assaulting his face. It took him a moment to realize he was falling.

He dropped through the hole in the bridge but managed to grab onto a jagged shard of planking before plunging into the abyss. He only had hold with one hand and dug his fingernails as far into the wood as possible. Anything he could do to hold on.

As he dangled there, everything seemed to shift into slow motion, allowing him to get a better look at the goings on than he needed or wanted.

He locked eyes with Pablo an instant before the man plummeted through the hole. The man's face was filled with shock or fear or maybe just confusion as he fell. Then, the wagon tumbled through the bridge, back end first, somersaulting through the air, their supplies scattering into the wind.

Wim stared below, where Pablo fell twenty feet before hitting the ground. He tried to decide whether the man had survived the impact, but a moment later, the wagon landed on top of him. Wim saw a spray of blood burst from the pile, and he hoped the man had died on impact.

"Wim! Wim, hold on!"

It was Mead's voice, and Wim turned his attention from below to above. All he could see was the open sky and the metal bridge rafters. No faces.

His hand was numb, like his fingers had gone missing, and he couldn't even tell if he still had a good grip or not. He only knew he was almost out of time.

Footsteps pounded against the wood. They were close and getting even closer.

Hang on, Wim, he told himself. You only need to last a few more seconds.

Dust rained on his face as the footsteps came nearer.

He's almost here. You can do this.

"I've got you, Wim!"

His head swiveled, trying to find Mead, trying to find his rescuer. And then he fell.

CHAPTER TWENTY-ONE

GRADY'S BIBLE HAD LONG AGO GROWN TATTERED. THE SPINE WAS cracked, allowing pages to slip free if he wasn't careful enough. It wasn't that he needed the pages. He'd read the good book so many times, not dozens but hundreds, that he had virtually every word burned into his mind. He could quote entire books without so much as a glance. Yet, to him, the bible wasn't just a text. It was a sacred object.

That was why when a gust of wind ripped free a half dozen pages from the book of Ruth, he spent nearly half an hour chasing them through the empty plains of Kansas. He caught the last one moments before it drifted into a puddle, and he held the recovered pages tight to his chest as his heart pounded with relief.

He turned back, moving toward the small hill that overlooked their encampment. Grady stared down at his followers and felt pride in his heart. He'd accomplished so much over only a few years, and he knew that he could wander for another forty if that's what it took. He could be this new world's Moses, leading his people to the promised land.

Just as a satisfied smile pulled at his thin lips, he was attacked by a stabbing fire deep inside his skull. His hand flew to his eyes, the bible and the recovered pages falling, forgotten. All he could see was bright light so intense that it felt like his eyes were being deep fried in their sockets.

The white-hot agony sent him to his knees as tears streamed, carving thin tracks through the grime that had built up since his last bath. And then the fiery pain was joined by a deafening roar, like a tornado whirling and ripping and tearing through his ear canals. Grady had experienced this before but on a smaller, less miserable scale. This was the voice of God, only now God wasn't sharing his love or wisdom. God was punishing him.

The slender, almost waifish man who wanted nothing more than to please God collapsed face forward into the dirt, his entire body shaking and spasming as God's wrath went off inside him like an atomic bomb.

GRADY EMERGED from the blinding whiteness disoriented. He felt hands on him. In his confused delirium, he thought he was back in the first days of the plague and that zombies were attacking him. He flailed and lashed out with his arms, trying to push them away.

"Grady! Stop, it's me!"

The voice was soft, gentle. Unlike the sonic boom of God's commands that still had his head ringing. He risked opening his eyes, gradual, tentative, afraid he'd be again blinded by the white. As the world came into focus before him, he instead saw Juli. She knelt over him, her hands holding his own.

"Grady? Are you okay?"

He tried to remember where he was, but the visions God had put in his head had filled it up like a pitcher too full of water, yet more kept pouring in, and it had nowhere to go except to splash over the sides. He could barely think.

Beyond Juli, he saw many of his other followers, staring at him, gawking at him. Their faces clouded with confusion and worry. He knew he needed to compose himself and calm them, but his limbs still trembled from the onslaught of God's latest message.

"Can you say something, Grady? Anything?" Juli said.

"We found you on the bluff."

Grady's head swiveled to the new voice, and he saw Owen. "You had a convulsion or something."

"No," Grady said. "It wasn't a convulsion or a seizure. I was listening to God."

"Looked painful," Owen said under his breath, but Grady heard him nonetheless.

"It was, God's message for me." He turned to the others. "For all of us. It was hard to hear. To see. But now I know what we need to do and what travails we'll experience along the way. God is pleased with our work thus far, but we've been moving too slowly. We're running out of time. We must move on."

"But why? It's nice here," Phyllis, a woman in the crowd asked.

"That's exactly why. We must abandon all of the comforts of civilization because it was those very comforts that made us lazy and complicit to sit idly by while Evil took over the Earth. Every minute we sat on overstuffed chairs watching vain and immoral people on our enormous television sets, we drifted further from God.

"Every night we spent on our ergonomic mattresses, we fell asleep not praying to and thanking God but dreaming about our own hedonistic desires. God demanded a clean start, and now we must start anew."

"Where are we going, Grady?" Juli asked.

"To the desert. And along the way, we need to save more souls. God has commanded it. He said we don't have enough. We haven't brought enough into our flock. We need more. He needs more."

"How many?" Juli asked.

Grady turned to her. He knew what they needed to do, and he

knew it was going to be the greatest challenge of his life. Of all their lives. But they didn't need to know the details. Not yet.

"All of them," Grady said. Then, he turned to Owen. "Take us to Brimley."

CHAPTER TWENTY-TWO

"Wim! We're coming!"

Wim's arm felt like it was burning, and his first thought was that he was still holding onto the bridge. But he couldn't understand why everything was black. He squeezed his eyelids tight, then opened them.

He realized he was no longer dangling in midair but instead sprawled sideways on the ground. His face was pressed into a bristly clump of weeds, their jagged edges scraping at his eyes, and he tried pushing himself out of it. That was when the burning sensation in his arm turned into a full-on inferno.

Wim collapsed, again landing face first in the bush, which he was growing more than a little irritated with. He thought about trying to move again, but the pain in his arm and all of his left side really made him reconsider.

"Stay where you are."

That was Mead's voice. It sounded fairly close, and Wim looked skyward, assuming the man was shouting at him from the bridge. But when he looked up, all he saw was the gaping hole through which he, Pablo, and the wagon had fallen.

The next thing he knew, his face was getting wet and slimy. A sideways glance revealed a mound of fur that could only be Aben's dog.

"Oh, heck, Prince. Stop with the licking."

The dog didn't stop, and Wim couldn't push him off, so he laid back and accepted the wet fate until Mead arrived on the scene.

"Prince, that's enough." Mead gave the mutt a gentle shove back, and Wim enjoyed the break from the onslaught of slobber and dog breath.

"Are you okay?" Mead asked.

"Define *okay*."

"Well, on a scale of one to ten with ten being riding on the wagon without a worry in the world and one being Pablo, where are you?"

Wim looked down the ravine, where the wagon was shattered and blood seeped out from underneath it. "Well, in that case, I'm about a six."

"Poor Pablo, man. Dude's flatter than a tortilla."

"I wouldn't have thought of it quite that way, but yeah." Wim tried to work his way to a sitting position but was met with the same pained results. He grimaced. "Help me up."

"No, don't move him."

The new voice was Aben's, and Wim cocked his head in its direction. He saw the big man almost crab crawling down the bank.

"You stay still, Wim."

Wim didn't like being told what to do, especially when it came to something as simple as moving. But when he remained motionless, the pain shifted from torturous to bearable, so he resigned himself to being lazy.

Aben worked his way down, turning their duo into a trio. He was out of breath, and Wim thought that was more panic than from the exertion. "You took a long fall, buddy. You could have done some serious damage." Aben knelt at his side. "What all hurts?"

"Only my left arm. I think maybe I broke it. The rest, I can deal with."

"What about your legs? Can you feel everything? Can you wiggle your feet for me?"

Wim rocked them to and fro. "Nothing the matter with my feet or legs. It's my arm."

Despite the assurance, Aben ran his hands up and down Wim's legs, checking for injuries. Then he moved to his pelvis and waist.

When he started unbuttoning Wim's shirt, Wim managed a smile. "I'm not sure we know each other well enough for this."

"Just wait till I check your prostate."

"That's not even funny."

Aben pulled his shirt apart, but any time he got close his left side, Wim lost his sense of humor. Instead of trying to remove the shirt the usual way, Aben took out a knife and cut it away from Wim's left arm.

"I liked that shirt."

"Oh, shut up," Mead said. "You've got another dozen just like it."

Wim knew that was close to the truth.

"Can you bend your arm for me, Wim?" Aben held onto his wrist, providing surprisingly gentle support for being such a rough character.

Wim gave it his best shot, but before he'd moved it an inch, his head was swimming. Aben must have seen the pain on his face. "That's okay."

"Is it broke?"

Aben stared at Wim's shoulder, and Wim turned his head sideways to see what was so interesting. He saw a large fist-shaped ball a few inches below his shoulder joint. That certainly didn't look good.

"Not broken. But you definitely dislocated it."

"So how do we re-locate it?"

Aben turned his eyes from Wim's shoulder to his face. "Well, it won't be fun."

A few minutes later, Aben had managed to straighten his arm, an act which caused more pain and more woozy floating feelings in his noggin. The big man sat on the ground perpendicular to him, one foot in Wim's armpit and the other against his neck. In his meaty hand, he held Wim's wrist.

"Ready to give this a spin?"

Wim kept his gaze turned skyward. "I don't reckon I have much choice."

"Not if you want to use that arm again any time soon."

"Well, then, get on with it. Are you gonna do a three count or--"

Aben didn't count. He leaned back, using his body weight to pull Wim's arm taught. Wim felt like his upper arm was filled with broken glass which was shredding his muscles and tissue and whatever gooey bits were under his skin. He fought against fainting as the pain rocketed from a six to an easy nine.

Aben pulled and leaned, easing back slowly, millimeters at a time.

"You're gonna pull his arm off," Mead said from the sidelines.

"I don't plan on it."

Further. Further. Wim almost wished his arm was gone. He thought about telling Mead to give him a machete and cut the sucker off, but he couldn't squeeze out any words through the pain.

"I think we're getting close, buddy."

Some curse words passed through Wim's thoughts, but he kept them inside and gritted his teeth together as if that would somehow dull the pain.

And then it popped. It wasn't audible, but Wim felt it through his whole body.

"Son of a bitch!" Mead yelled, and that made Prince bark.

"Is it done?" Wim dared look. He found the fist-sized bulge was gone, and his arm looked normal enough. "Can I move it?"

"You tell me," Aben said.

Wim tried bending it. There was a bit of pain, but it was a raindrop in the ocean compared to what he'd been dealing with. Then he raised it up and across his chest.

"Take it a little easy," Aben said. "It's back in place, but everything in that joint's going to be stretched out and inflamed. You go too crazy and it's liable to pop out of place again."

"Then I won't go crazy." Wim sat up, ignoring the ache that lingered.

"I'd even consider a sling for a week or so," Aben said.

"I wouldn't go that far." Wim climbed to his feet, careful not to use his left arm. He looked down at himself and saw a variety of cuts and scrapes, but when he glanced at the bridge twenty feet above, he felt himself more than a little lucky.

"Well, boys, I'm sorry about all this. I really thought the bridge would hold."

"The bridge did," Mead said. "Some rotten boards was all it was. No one's fault. Just bad luck."

"Worse for some than others," Wim said as he looked at the wagon. "I'd say we bury him, but I didn't bring a shovel."

"Probably not much to bury anyway," Mead said. Aben threw a scowl his way, and Mead shook his head. "What? It's the truth."

"I feel like we should say something, at least. A few words on his behalf. You both knew him better than me."

Aben and Mead exchanged a glance that, to Wim, made it clear neither wanted to take the reins on this, and it became a staring contest for a good half a minute.

"Okay," Mead said. "I'll do it."

The three men turned toward Pablo's resting spot. Mead pushed his hair out of his face before starting. "Pablo was one of the best men in Brimley. He worked hard and would take on any chore assigned to him, even though before all this shit he was an educated man. He enjoyed hot peppers and playing the harmonica, and he even sang a little when he had a few drinks in him. He loved his family, and, in the end, was able to get some closure on that whole mess. He was a good man. And he'll be missed."

Mead looked to them. "Anyone else?"

Wim and Aben kept silent.

"Well, then. Pablo deserved a less shitty end than getting crushed by a wagon, but I guess we don't get to choose our grand finale. So, with that, goodbye and God speed."

"To Pablo," Aben said.

"To Pablo," Wim repeated.

"Is that good enough?" Mead asked.

"That was fine, Mead. Just fine. Thank you."

Mead nodded. "Now I want to get the fuck home."

CHAPTER TWENTY-THREE

AFTER MORE THAN TWO WEEKS CLEAN, SAW WOKE UP AND realized he'd slept through the night without the need to puke into the bucket or on the bed, or on himself for that matter. When it came to regurgitating his stomach contents, where they ended up tended to be a mystery.

As he sat up in bed, his head went for a swim, and he closed his eyes to regroup. The feeling passed soon enough, and, when he opened them again, he was surprised at how good he felt. His head ached, of course. That dull throb, like someone tapping on his skull with a ball peen hammer every three seconds was never-ending, except when the opiates drowned it out. But in a way, the familiar feeling of pain reinvigorated him.

He rose to his feet, stretched, and ripped a loud fart all at the same time. That made him grin, and when the rank smell of it hit his nostrils, the grin turned to a full-on smile. It was pure sulfur and made him hungry for eggs. Sunny side up if possible, but scrambled would do just as well.

Saw was naked as the day he was born, and when he looked down at himself, he was surprised to see his pecker swaying lazily in the morning light. He couldn't remember getting such a good look at his prick in years, and he went to the bathroom to see what else had changed.

He pushed his way past stacks of garbage, moving through the maze of trash that had overtaken the hallway. When did the house get so bad, he wondered. They'd had a girl come and clean once a week, but the lass clearly hadn't been up to task. He added that to his mental 'to do' list.

When he got to the bathroom and caught his reflection, he might have thought he was looking at a stranger if it wasn't for the hole in his head. His jowls were gone, his spare tire had vanished. He'd always been a fire hydrant of a man, but now he was well on his way to being a bean pole. He couldn't recall any point in his life when he'd been so slender, and he didn't like it one bit. Yet another thing he'd need to fix. But first he needed to get dressed and eat, in either order.

The trash-filled hallway was a harbinger of the rest of the mansion he and Mina had called home for a few years. It looked well on its way to being a garbage dump complete with flies dive-bombing him as he descended the staircase and moved toward the kitchen.

He almost lost his appetite when the smell of rotten food hit him. The flies in the rest of the house were only the first wave. The bulk of their forces had taken residence in the kitchen, and when Saw saw maggots writhing amongst half-eaten food on dirty dishes, he was tempted to look for a match and light the whole place up. Maybe a fresh start was what they needed.

He abandoned the kitchen, heading to the dining room, when he saw Mina in the backyard. She sat on a wooden lawn chair and held a liquor bottle in her hand, occasionally raising it to her lips and taking a drink before going back to staring at nothing.

Is this my fault, he wondered. He'd always been quick to fall in love - or lust - or obsession - or however he wanted to label it, and Mina was no different.

He liked her moxie from the time she walked up to his truck, after he'd killed several of her friends on the Ark and asked him to take her with him. The broad had guts. And while he never got the feeling that she loved him back, he was fiercely protective of her.

When they found this house, she'd commented that it looked like something out of a show on the telly she used to watch, something about rich housewives of California, and he could see the awe in her face, the want in her eyes. That look was the reason he'd stopped his violent march across the continent and settled there on the Texas/Mexico border, even though the land was shit and the climate was worse. He did it to make her happy, even though he knew that happiness and Mina were like oil and water.

He crossed the dirt and weeds that passed for a yard and was a few feet from her when he spoke. "Morning, Love."

Mina jumped in her seat like someone had fired a starter's pistol. The liquor bottle tumbled from her hand and landed on the ground. "Son of a whore!"

"Me mum had her issues, but whoring wasn't one of them."

Mina stared at him, still wide-eyed with fright and anger, but now confusion seeped into the mélange.

"What?"

"Did I ever tell you about the rabbits?"

"What?" she repeated.

"No matter. Anyway, I didn't intend to cause you a fright."

She grabbed for the bottle, but most of its contents were already in the ground. "Well, you still did."

"My apologies."

She squinted into the bottle. There was barely a swallow left, and she put quick work to that. Saw took the now drained bottle from her and set it on the table. Then he grabbed her hand.

"We're going to town."

"What for?" Her eyes were wary.

"Well, first and foremost, to get some food. I feel like my stomach's going to swallow me arsehole if I don't get something to eat soon. And after that, we're bringing a group of men back here to empty out the house and clean it up right good."

She turned her gaze toward the ground. "I suppose I fell behind a bit."

That was the understatement of the millennia, but Saw wasn't about to scold her. He took his rough fingers and lifted her chin so that she had no choice but to look him in the face. "Don't you fret about that, Love. You know why?"

She shook her head.

"Because even though I haven't been acting the part of late, I'm still the king around here. King Solomon. Wasn't he in the bible or something?"

"Yes. He was very wise."

"Well, I don't know how wise I am, but I'm still the fookin' king. And that makes you the queen. And last I checked, the queen don't got to do her own housekeeping."

He thought something close to a smile pulled at her lips, and he took that opportunity to lean in for a kiss. He could taste the whiskey in her mouth as he explored it with his tongue. He didn't like that she was half-way to drunk before noon, but he decided that nothing was going to ruin his good mood.

CHAPTER TWENTY-FOUR

MEAD'S FEET FELT LIKE TWO SAUSAGES SQUEEZED INTO HEAVY leather casings. His steel-toed work boots weren't meant for walking twenty miles a day, and he was half-afraid his little piggies would be destroyed by the time they got back to Brimley.

After the mess at the bridge, Wim rode Gypsy, and Aben continued riding the younger unnamed mare. Mead utilized Pablo's bicycle until he got a flat tire a few days later. Ever since, he'd been walking. And he grew more pissed off with each passing mile.

Almost as bad as the throbbing pain was the fact that their already plodding pace had been slowed down further. The other men needed to keep the horses at a slow trot so that Mead didn't fall too far behind. The fact that he was bringing up the rear, constantly smelling horse farts and avoiding piles of steaming horse shit didn't do a thing to better his sour mood.

So, when he heard rustling in a thicket of brush off the side of the road, he was more than willing to take a detour into the weeds and kill whatever was making the racket. It would do him well to take his frustrations out on something.

He stuck his middle and index fingers in his mouth and let loose a shrill whistle to get the attention of the men who were ten yards ahead. They looked back to see what the ado was about.

Mead pointed at the scraggly brush that lined the road. "Something in there."

"Need some help?" Wim asked.

Mead shrugged his shoulders. He imagined he could handle it on his own, but he'd seen plenty of overconfident men and women die the last few years. "Up to you."

The men turned their horses in the road and trotted back to him, but Mead wasn't willing to wait. He looked down at Prince, who varied between walking beside him and the horses. He quite liked the dog, even if he thought Prince was just about the worst name ever, and he didn't want to put him at risk.

"Stay, Prince."

Prince flopped down on his hindquarters, his tail thudding back and forth, back and forth, back and forth.

Mead grabbed one of his conduit spears and held it at the ready as he pushed through the weeds. They were hard and dry and clawed at his clothing like skeletal fingers and so dense he couldn't see anything but the thicket scraping past the mask of his helmet.

He didn't like going in blind. He knew he should wait for the others. He often told himself that anyone who got killed by zombies more than a year into the apocalypse died from stupidity, not zombies, and he knew that what he was doing at the moment was stupid.

But he pushed on, confident that his protective gear - and the fact that he didn't have a single square inch of exposed flesh - would protect him even if something awful laid ahead.

Three strides in and the brush thinned out. He could see a small clearing ahead and a muddy pond in the midst of it.

Mead stopped moving, deciding to look and listen instead. To use his brains rather than his balls. He couldn't see anything moving, nothing that would have caused the noise he heard earlier. And now the noise, too, was gone. He waited, gripping the spear, but nothing came.

Behind him, he heard a muffled curse followed up with Aben growling, "Son of a bitching branches!"

Mead smiled behind his visor. He'd grown annoyed with his companions being able to ride while he walked. They didn't care that he was wearing forty pounds of safety gear while they got by in regular shirts and jeans that didn't weigh five pounds combined. And they certainly weren't concerned with the fact that he had the worst case of swamp ass in this side of Louisiana.

Aben emerged from the thicket first, his face angry and a three-inch long scratch trickling blood high on his forehead.

"You should watch where you're going," Mead said.

Aben didn't smile. Didn't respond at all. Wim came through on his heels.

"Must've been a false alarm." Mead lowered his spear and tilted up the visor. "Sorry, boys."

Wim looked past him toward the pond. "Shame that's not clean. I sure could use a cool down."

You could, Mead thought. It's fifteen degrees hotter under all this shit. He thought about saying that out loud, but before he could, something slammed into his back, pounding against his kidneys and dropping him to his knees.

What the fuck was that? He felt like he'd been shot with a canon. He reached behind himself, expecting to find blood or maybe his entire flank missing, but his glove came back dry.

He was so confused that he didn't even realize that Wim and Aben were standing by idly, not only not helping but laughing, until he rolled onto his back and saw their stupid, amused faces.

Mead was so pissed off that he almost forgot about whatever it was that had attacked him, but a stab of pain when he tried to sit up brought that back all too quick.

And they still laughed.

"What's so fucking funny?"

As soon as the words were out of his mouth, a broad gray shape appeared over him. His brain immediately associated *gray* with *zombie,* and he reached for the spear, all the while wondering why his friends weren't helping him. Had the world gone even crazier in the last thirty seconds?

"Don't!" Wim yelled, and there was panic in his voice, a foreign sound to Mead's ears. Wim was normally as monotone as could be. The oddness of it all made Mead slow down and put his eyes to use rather than rely on his instincts.

He stared at the gray figure and realized it wasn't a zombie. It was too big. And on four legs. And the gray wasn't undead skin but fur.

"Is that a goddamn donkey?" Mead asked.

Wim started laughing all over again. "It is."

Mead stared at the animal that loomed beside him, its nose twitching like it was trying to figure out what type of cologne he wore.

"I got tackled by a motherfucking donkey?" Mead climbed to his feet, trying to ignore the throbbing in his side. He pushed the animal's snout sideways. "You asshole."

The donkey pulled back its lips, revealing over-sized yellow teeth, and brayed.

Mead looked to the others. "Ready to go?"

"Not so fast," Wim said. "I know it's gotta be rough walking all the time."

Tell that to my bleeding feet, Mead thought.

"Well..." Wim looked from Mead to the donkey, then back to Mead.

Mead looked at Wim, then the donkey. "You're not suggesting..." He turned back to Wim. "Ride the donkey?"

"Why not? It's a big one. And I'd imagine it's pretty strong, considering how quickly it put you down."

"Is that even possible? I mean, do they let you?"

"Depends how feral it is. But it seems pretty calm to me."

Mead still wasn't sure he liked this idea. He moved to the

donkey's side and laid his hand on its neck. The donkey tilted its head back, enjoying being petted.

"Why do I have to ride the donkey? I think one of you should trade."

"Maybe you haven't noticed, Mead, but we're both a might bigger than you," Aben said.

"I don't know what that matters."

"I'm just saying, some men are cut out for horses. Some are more suited for donkeys." To demonstrate just how much bigger he was, Aben tapped Mead on top of the helmet.

"I hate you."

Aben wrapped his arm around his neck and pulled him in close. Mead's face was at the same level as the big man's sweaty stinking armpit. "You're my favorite too."

Despite his annoyance and pain and the heat and the embarrassment of getting taken down by a jackass, Mead couldn't hold back a smile of his own. "Let's get the hell out of here."

CHAPTER TWENTY-FIVE

JULI PUFFED AWAY ON A STALE CIGARETTE AS SHE WATCHED Grady move through his flock. They'd accumulated hundreds of followers since leaving the Signs Following Church two years ago. When Grady had originally shared with her his plan - no, it's God's plan, she reminded herself - she thought he was insane. That she should have left with Aben and Mitch after all. But as time passed and Grady took his ministry on the road, he was proven right over and over again. Every time doubt crept into her heart, something happened to prove Grady right.

She saw Grady looking her way and dropped the cigarette, smashing it underfoot, but she knew he saw. Juli waved him toward her, and his head dipped in a nod. She knew he hated leaving them, that he felt so at peace amid them, but he gradually moved through the crowd and to her. Even though she knew she'd been caught smoking, she moved a dozen yards to the right, so the aroma of smoke wouldn't be too obvious.

When he arrived, the peaceful exuberance in his face almost brought her to tears. She wished he was that happy in her presence. That she could bring him such joy, but the harder she tried, the further he pulled away. She had almost given up trying to figure out what she could do to bring him closer to her. Almost.

"I spoke with Owen," she said. "We're close. Less than two days out."

Grady nodded, knowing. "Tomorrow, we're going to set up the tent a few miles from Brimley. While we do that, you and Owen will go there. Tell them about us. Invite them."

Juli fought off a shocked gasp. "Me?"

"Yes. You're quite capable."

Juli wasn't so certain about that. She sometimes struggled to make sense of Grady's messages, and she had years' experience. How was she supposed to convince a bunch of strangers that the little man from Baltimore had a direct line to God and that they needed to join them to save the world, or their souls, or maybe both? She wasn't even sure, and there laid the rub.

"Grady, I don't--"

"You will. I've seen this already."

"Well, then tell me what I said because I haven't an idea." The remark came off more flippant than she had intended, and she saw Grady's body tense up. "I'm sorry."

He nodded curtly and turned away from her.

"Grady?"

He didn't look back, but he didn't flee either, and she supposed that was as good as it was going to get.

"What if they won't join us?"

Grady paused, still not looking her way. "They will."

"But what if they won't?"

"They will because they have no choice."

He left her there, alone, his words echoing through her head. Since his last vision, Grady had been more direct, more confident, than she'd ever seen him. And she realized that scared her.

CHAPTER TWENTY-SIX

FOR THE PAST THREE WEEKS, SAW RARELY LEFT MITCH'S SIDE. In many ways, it reminded Mitch of the way things used to be, of their lives on the road. Only now they weren't avoiding danger. Now they were seeking it out.

Saw had decided that the town had become too boring. Too ordinary. Mitch didn't entirely disagree with that opinion, but Saw's solutions were so extreme and so violent that Mitch could hardly believe this was reality.

Before laying out his plans, Saw caught Mitch inside his motorhome so early that Mitch hadn't even had his first piss of the day. He was still in bed when the man hammered at the door.

"Wakey, wakey. Eggs and bac-y."

Mitch was only half-awake, but annoyance pushed sleep away as he rolled out of bed. He wore only a pair of boxer briefs but didn't bother dressing before opening the door. Saw's voice was impossible to mistake.

"Just fooling, Mitchy. I got no eggs or bacon."

"Then you're unwelcome." Mitch turned away from him but left the door open in an unspoken invitation that Saw accepted.

Mitch opened a cooler and took out a jug of water. He grabbed a glass, then looked to Saw with a raised eyebrow. "Want some water? Or do you prefer something harder to start the day?"

"I'm a new man. Or me old self, depending on how you look at it." Saw gave him the finger, wagging it back and forth. "Look at it, Mitchy."

Mitch was still annoyed and didn't return Saw's grin.

"Ah, cheer up, mate. I gots us some fun planned if you're up for it."

Mitch sat down at a small table and drank half a glass of water without pausing for a break. "I don't think we have the same idea of fun anymore."

Saw flopped down across from him. As he sat, a booming fart ripped its way out of his asshole, and he cackled. Mitch did not.

"I know you're angry at me, Mitchy, and I can't blame you none. I cocked things up. Not just a little either. A whole lot. Like one of those giant whales, the really big ones. Grey whales?"

Mitch shrugged his shoulders, uninterested in species of whales.

"Anyway, a hell of a massive cock up. I could of ruined everything we worked for. Everything we built. And I'm sorry for that. I am."

He looked Mitch in the eyes when he said that, and there was a glint that made Mitch believe him, even though he didn't want to. He didn't want to fall under Saw's spell again and had to keep reminding himself over and over again that he couldn't trust this man.

"But I'm better now. Better than before, even. Because now I got it all figured out. I got complacent, and then I got lazy. I'm sure you saw it."

Mitch nodded. Affirmative. Saw slid his chair around so that he wasn't sitting across from Mitch but was instead sitting beside him.

"That's because I was bored. We got it good here, we do. Maybe too good, though. We need some spice, Mitchy."

"Spice?

"I had a dream, like that Luther Martin bloke," Saw said, wrapping his arm around Mitch's shoulders. "When I was getting off the heroin, I saw it plain as day. There's nothing to do here but drink and drug and fuck, and that's all fine and well, but there's only so much of each you can do before getting bored with it all. We need entertainment, Mitchy. And I got some good plans."

Mitch realized he was getting excited, and he hated himself for it. But if there was one thing he could always count on from Saw, it was that the man knew how to have a damned good time.

CHAPTER TWENTY-SEVEN

SAW STARTED THINGS OFF BY CONFISCATING ALL THE LIQUOR and drugs. That got everyone good and pissed off, but it also put control back in his hands. He had all the supply and was free to make demands.

His first orders were to send most of the men, and several of the rougher women, on missions to capture zombies. He didn't want them dead, or deader. He wanted them mobile.

Over the following two weeks, the residents of Shard End had returned with nearly forty of the monsters. The captured zombies were tossed into the pit, where they stumbled back and forth, smacking into the earthen walls and bouncing off each other with hisses or growls.

The residents who were either deemed incapable of hunting zombies or had already nabbed their quota were given the task of moving many of Shard End's now useless trucks and SUVs. They were pushed about fifty yards outside of town and then maneuvered into a rough circle thirty feet across.

When this initial work was finished, Saw threw a party to reward everyone for their hard work. It started off with a raging bonfire that stretched several stories into the night sky and turned the entire town orange as a pumpkin. Saw cobbled together speakers and stereos and music from bands like *AC/DC* and *Motorhead* blasted.

There was dancing, or what passed for it, and fighting, although nothing serious, and fucking, which took place in the open, bodies pressed against buildings or bent over railings. All of this was fueled mostly by alcohol, but there was ample cocaine to go around for anyone so inclined, and that was most of the rough bunch who called Shard End home. What there wasn't, of course, were opiates, but no one seemed to mind.

Saw, Mitch noticed, avoided anything harder than beer, but the lack of drugs didn't slow him down in the least. He roamed between the men and women, from group to group, telling jokes, talking them up, and, Mitch realized, acting as much the role of a glad-handing politician as Senator Son of a Bitch had done when he was still alive. Only Saw was even better at it. Mitch thought these people would have elected him President, given the chance. Hell, they'd probably offer him their first born while they were at it. Saw wasn't just the leader in Shard End, he was their God.

And like most gods, he required not only devotion but penance.

THAT CAME a few days later when almost everyone had recovered from their exhaustion and hangovers. Saw asked Mitch to put the word out that there was to be a town meeting at dusk and that everyone's presence was required. Mitch knocked on a few doors, but when he made the announcement at the Dry Snatch, he knew it would race through town fast enough.

He went to Saw's house, which still smelled vaguely of trash but had been emptied of the garbage and had undergone a deep cleaning that left it looking almost new. Mina laid on a lawn chair, her dark skin baking to a dark chocolate under the midday sun. When he closed in on her, he realized she was nude from the waist up and quickly averted his eyes.

"Don't be bashful, Mitch. I don't got nothing you ain't never seen before."

He didn't want to look. He thought that if Saw found him in the presence of his half-naked wife, he might be liable to bash his skull in. But offending Saw's wife wasn't a great choice either.

Mitch turned back to her, eyes darting rapidly and trying not to stare. Her black as coal nipples stood erect atop her barely-there breasts. Sweat glistened against her small waist, and below that, she wore only a pair of white, cotton panties that looked almost bright as the sun compared to her flesh. She tilted a bottle of beer his way.

"Thirsty?"

Mitch was. The walk here was long, and it was over one hundred degrees, but he also wanted out of this situation as quick as possible. "I'm good."

"If that's what you're selling, I ain't buying it."

She smiled. A rare expression in the time he'd known her. Matter of fact, as he thought about it, he wasn't sure he ever saw so much as a hint of happiness on her face. Her upturned lips revealed a chipped front tooth, but aside from that, the emotion brightened her face, and Mitch couldn't help but smile back.

"Putting the moves on my dame, are ya?"

Saw's voice caused Mitch's smile to vanish. He turned and found the man coming toward him. Saw's shirt was off too, and Mitch could see his bulk was already returning. He wasn't muscular in a body-builder kind of way - he was more of a gorilla. Wide and thick and strong enough to break the average man in half without even trying hard.

"I came looking for you, actually. But I found someone better."

Saw laughed. "You got that part right." He stepped between Mitch and Mina, leaning in to his wife and giving her a sloppy kiss on the mouth. Then, he flopped down in a chair beside her. "You spread the word?"

"Easy peasy."

"Lemon squeezy," Saw responded. He grabbed Mina's beer and took two swallows before returning it.

"So, what's the meeting about? Or do I have to wait to find out like the rest of the riffraff?"

"Aw, Mitch, you know you're my favorite. You held this place together when I was indisposed, after all. Such a smart one, you are. And I won't forget that. Got my word."

"Well, thank you, Saw."

"We've been safe here, you know. Not a single zombie attack since we settled in."

Mitch nodded. He was well aware.

"Most folk probably say that's a good thing. But a safe man is a lazy man more often than not. Just like a man who don't never have to worry about not having food in his belly never appreciates how good it is to feel hungry from time to time."

Mitch was used to Saw's rambles. At one point, he had even found them entertaining, the way a boy might listen to his wizened grandfather and think the old man had life all figured out. But he'd come to realize Saw was mostly full of shit. Still, he let him go on.

"People here, me self included, we got fat and happy. But at the same time, we got bored. Remember when I said we needed some spice here?"

Mitch nodded.

"I got it figured out, Mitchy. We need entertainment of the sporting variety. In Birmy, we had our football, or soccer as you blokes call it. And every week, we'd go to the stadium and get pissed with our lads and cheer on our team. God, I still miss that sometimes."

Mitch felt like he was roasting in the sun and wanted Saw to get to the point already.

"But that's all long gone now, ain't it? Anyway, like I said, I got it all figured out. And it'll be a hell of a lot more entertaining than kicking around a ball. Mitchy, we're gonna have battles."

"Battles?" Mitch asked.

Saw nodded, excited. "Every night. It's gonna be fookin amazing. You just wait. Just wait and see."

The look in Saw's eyes was a sort of frenzied glee that Mitch found terrifying and alluring at the same time. Anything that could make Saw this excited was bound to be horrific. And that made Mitch all the more excited.

CHAPTER TWENTY-EIGHT

THE SMALL TOWN BEFORE THEM WAS SURROUNDED BY STEEL shipping containers, just as Owen had told her it would be. It was fifty yards in the distance, and all she could see over that barricade were occasional rooftops.

"How do we get in?" Juli asked Owen, who stood beside her.

The rest of the group had remained far behind, as Grady had instructed. As Grady had assured her would be for the best. But now that Juli saw the fortifications that surrounded Brimley, she had her doubts.

"We knock." Owen passed her by and continued to the town.

Juli chased after, her feet kicking up dust in the dry August heat. "Do you have a secret knock? Like Morse code?"

Owen was at the containers, at one which was turned with the steel doors facing them. He rapped on it a couple of times with his knuckles. The hollow tap-tap-tap gave an almost musical quality. He glanced back at Juli.

"No, just a knock," he said.

They waited, but the doors didn't open. Instead, a voice came from above. "Owen?"

They looked up and saw a young man standing in a makeshift lookout tower. A rifle was slung over his shoulder, and the sun backlit him, preventing Juli from getting a good look at his face, and she couldn't tell whether it was friendly or not.

"Hey, Pete."

"Shit, man, it's been a while. Who's the broad?"

Owen cocked his head in Juli's direction. "Juli Villarreal. She's a friend. Let us in before we get heatstroke out here, will ya?"

"Yeah. Hold up."

Pete disappeared from the tower, and she heard footsteps against the metal as he descended. Juli raised her eyebrows at Owen. "That's all?"

Owen nodded. "They're good people. Just like us."

More footsteps sounded inside the trailer, and they got closer. She heard metal grate, then slide, and the double doors swung open.

Now that Juli could get a good look at Pete's face, she saw it was indeed friendly, and a toothy smile filled the bottom third of it. He gave Owen a rough hug that rocked them both on their feet.

"Thought you ran away from home and joined the circus," Pete said.

"Don't believe everything you hear."

They separated, and Owen turned to Juli. "Juli, this is Pete. Pete, Juli."

Pete extended his hand, and Juli shook it. It was dry and calloused, the grip firm. He had sandy blond hair, and freckles dotted his cheeks, nose, and forehead. "Nice to meet you, Ma'am. Sorry I called you a broad earlier. My mouth works faster than my brains sometimes."

"I've been called worse," Juli said with a smile that she hoped didn't look as nervous as she felt.

Pete's attention returned to Owen. "So where have you been, man? We thought you were lost in the wind."

"That's why I'm here, actually. Why we're both here."

Pete kept grinning, but his eyes belied confusion. Nevertheless, he beckoned them forward. "Well, come on in. I know everyone's going to be excited to see you."

Pete led the way, and Juli and Owen followed.

JULI HAD KNOWN her share of lying men. From her philandering husband to her father who beat her mother behind closed doors, only to assure Juli and her siblings that their mother was a clumsy drunk with a habit of walking into walls and falling down staircases.

Owen Varner was a humorless, bland man who had spent thirty-three years building highways in Nebraska, and, as he spoke, Juli thought he could lie as well as any man she'd ever known, maybe even a tad better. His steel gray eyes seemed almost transparent, his voice velvety smooth. If Juli hadn't known better, she'd have believed him herself. Hell, she almost did anyway.

He talked and laughed and commiserated with the men and women of the town he had helped found for over two hours, all the while promising them that, even though they had a good life in Brimley, there was a better one waiting outside the walls. All they had to do was keep an open mind. And at the end of it all, Juli was certain he'd convinced them.

So, the next day, when Grady stood in front of row after row of empty chairs, she was more surprised than anyone. Certainly, more surprised than Grady who went through with his sermon even though the only people close enough to hear his words were the people who were already devoted to him. No one from Brimley came within a mile of the revival and, when it was over, Juli expected Grady to be distraught, perhaps even angry.

Instead, when she approached him afterward, he seemed indifferent at worst, but more at peace than anything else.

"I'm so sorry, Grady. We let you down. I failed you."

"You did no such thing."

"We tried. We really did. And Owen gave the best sales pitch I'd ever heard, even better than Donald in the Kitchen when he was trying to sell me a new set of porcelain cookware. I don't know what happened. Why they wouldn't listen to us."

Grady, who had been folding and stacking chairs, turned to her. "It's fine, Juli. I knew this would happen. It was part of the vision."

She stared at him, struggling to find words. Did he really mean that or was it something he was saying to ease her guilt? "You what?"

"I knew the residents of Brimley wouldn't come to us. That they wouldn't leave the safety of their town. Those walls are their burning bull. They trust in them more than they trust in God. They're Heathens. And we have to save them from themselves."

Juli stared at him, curious and confused. She didn't know why he had sent them there in the first place if he knew they wouldn't come and half-believed he was making all of this up as he went along. But that wasn't the man she'd known for the last four years. That man couldn't tell a lie if his life was at stake.

"But Grady," she said. "How can we do that when they won't listen?"

Grady's eyes shined, and Juli realized he had a plan. That he'd had a plan all along. "Those men and women had a chance to come to us. To put their lives in the hand of God, yet they refused. And so, tomorrow, we go to them."

He turned away from her and recommenced folding and stacking chairs as if all of this was routine, mundane. Juli had no idea what Grady's - or God's - plan was, but seeing the peace that enveloped him, she had no doubt it would be a success.

CHAPTER TWENTY-NINE

Saw chose Diesel, the bartender at the Dry Snatch, to be the first participant in the battles. He accepted this fate grudgingly and tried to use the fact that he only had one eye to weasel out of it, but Saw assured him that it wasn't a bad thing. Hell, it was an honor, really. Diesel's chance to be a hero in front of every man and woman in Shard End.

As the sun set, fifty-gallon barrels were filled with trash and debris, then set ablaze, turning the makeshift arena of automobiles into a glowing orange stadium. Everyone in town came out to see what Saw had planned and none of them left disappointed.

For most, it was standing room only, but Saw and Mina sat in lawn chairs perched on a platform made of scaffolding, giving them a bird's eye view. He looked around, pleased with himself for coming up with this grand idea and proud of Mitchy for helping pull it together.

Saw found Mitch standing a few yards away, sidled up with one of the local slags, Violet or Petunia or Rose. Something flowery her name was. They seemed close and, even though Saw wouldn't have got his pecker within ten feet of a bint like that, he was happy for the boy.

Saw turned his attention to Diesel, who sat atop a rusted-out Ford Explorer, rocking back and forth. Saw thought that if they waited any longer, the man might tuck tail and run, and that certainly wasn't how he wanted his games to begin. So, he rose to his feet and cupped his hands around his mouth.

"I'd start off with 'ladies and gentlemen,' but we don't have any of either here in Shard End."

The crowd laughed, their noise rough and throaty. Even their joy was hard around the edges.

"So instead I'll say this. Welcome to all of you ugly sons of bitches!" The crowd applauded, stomped their feet, and smacked their hands on the vehicles that formed the arena. "What we've got planned tonight is the first contest in a tournament of sorts. And our first contestant is Diesel."

Diesel looked toward Saw as if waiting for stage directions.

"Stand up, man."

Diesel did. Some of the crowd gave muted applause but most watched with avid anticipation.

"Hop on down there."

Diesel climbed down from the Explorer and into the ring. He looked confused and terrified and stared up at Saw like he expected a last-minute reprieve.

Saw wasn't about to do that. "Good on ya. Now, boys, bring in his opponents."

From opposite ends of the arena, two men, an Asian Saw knew only as Kwon and a hulking mute everyone called Polo, each dragged a zombie over the cars and into the ring. They used catch poles to keep them at bay and to keep themselves safe. Once the zombies were inside the confines of the ring, they loosened the nooses and slipped off the tethers.

The zombies staggered about as if trying to get their bearings, sometimes homing in on a spectator outside the ring and outside their reach.

"Now you might be wondering about the rules," Saw shouted, and the zombies turned toward the sound of his voice. "There ain't none. Diesel's job's to kill these bastards without getting bit. If he succeeds, he gets to choose who goes in the ring tomorrow. If he fails, well, we know what happens. It won't be comely. Sound fair enough?"

The crowd yelled in the affirmative.

"Good. Now, Diesel, you give that bonnet a good bang and get this show started."

Diesel hit the hood of the car beside him, but not too hard. Saw glared at him, and he gave it another try. This one was harder, louder, and it drew the zombie's attention.

Saw sucked on his bottom lip, excited to see how this would play out.

At first, Diesel kept to the edges of the arena, like a boxer staying on the ropes and making his opponent come to him. The zombies followed, growling and hissing. Diesel looked more panicked with each passing moment and even tripped over a chunk of a fender, allowing the zombies to get close as he scrambled to his feet.

Mina leaned in close to Saw and spoke into his ear. "If they kill him this fast, those people," she motioned to the onlookers, "Are going to be awful disappointed."

Saw shook his head. "I think the lad'll put up a bit of a fight. I'm not counting him out just yet."

He gave her a quick smile, and she returned a weak one.

"Cheer up, love. It's better than being stuck in the house, isn't it?"

Mina didn't answer, instead looking to the ring where there was a zombie on each side of Diesel. The crowd was docile with only an occasional jeer breaking their silence.

Diesel must have realized staying on the defensive wasn't going to be a winning strategy, so he grabbed hold of the arm of the zombie closest to him. The creature was a middle-aged man in a cheap business suit. Diesel took a good grip on its jacket sleeve, then he swung the monster in a circle, slamming it into one of the vehicles lining the ring. It fell to the ground.

That move got the crowd more interested and several spectators began shouting, some even throwing out words of encouragement.

"Get the fuckers!"

"Kill 'em, D! You got this!"

Saw was pleased to see their growing excitement. And he had a feeling it would only get better.

Diesel stomped on the zombie on the ground, then turned to the other creature. It was close enough to grab him and almost did, but Diesel ducked sideways and avoided its grasp. He jogged a few yards away, to safety, but the move allowed the fallen zombie to regain its footing, and soon, both were coming for him again.

Saw watched as the man moved further away from the zombies, scanning the area around him, searching.

Diesel's eyes locked on a piece of brick lying on the ground. He snatched it up, gripping it in his hand. Zombie number two, a shirtless young man in athletic shorts whose six pack was evident even in death, was closer. It trudged toward Diesel, and as soon as it was close enough, Diesel swung with the brick and smashed it in the face.

The zombie's almost aristocratic nose folded sideways, and a large gash opened on its face, oozing black blood. Diesel swung again. This time, the brick hit the creature in the ear, and the blow sent it to the ground.

The crowd erupted in boisterous screaming as Diesel crouched over the zombie and used the brick to hit it again and again and again. The monster's head was nothing more than a pile of broken skull and destroyed brain by the time the man was finished.

When Diesel looked up, his face was tattooed with blood spatter, and his lone eye blazed. The crowd shouted in approval.

Saw grabbed Mina's narrow thigh. "Told ya, love. One down."

Mina looked toward the action, but Saw wondered if she was really seeing it. She'd been so aloof lately. He thought she'd be at least somewhat grateful that he was off the heroin. That she'd show her appreciation. But no matter what he did, she seemed like half of her was somewhere else. Her attitude had him wondering, and a curious Saw wasn't a good thing.

He tried to forget about that to focus on the battle happening below. Diesel had finished off the younger zombie and was focused on the suited creature. That man was taller and broader, and when Diesel swung the first time with the brick, he only hit it harmlessly in the shoulder.

The zombie grunted as if annoyed and reached for him, catching hold of Diesel's shirt, which ripped down the middle, allowing him to slip away. What Diesel lacked in size, he made up for in agility, and he ducked behind the zombie before it could react.

He took the zombie by the collar and shoved it toward the nearest car, pinning it against the vehicle. The creature flailed with its arms, but its clumsy, slow protestations were of little use. Diesel slammed the brick into the back of its head, and Saw thought he could hear the crack twenty feet away.

The zombie went limp, and its body slithered along the car before hitting the ground. Diesel stomped on the back of its skull for good measure, but it was done.

The spectators roared with approval, and Saw rose to his feet. "Well done! Very well done! A round of applause for our lad."

The noise as they screamed and stomped and clapped was so loud it made Saw's ears ring, but he didn't mind at all. He didn't care much whether Diesel won or lost. He only wanted blood to be spilled, and he got that. And that was only the beginning.

CHAPTER THIRTY

THE SUN HAD BARELY CRESTED THE HORIZON, ITS GOLDEN RAYS casting long shadows before every tree and shrub. And even longer ones from the settlement of Brimley where the town was little more than a series of dark angles, backlit by the morning glow.

Grady stared at the town from fifty yards away. It was as he'd seen it. As he knew it would be. He couldn't see any of the residents, but he knew most were still in their beds. He knew the few that were awake were in the process of getting dressed or eating breakfast, still fighting away the sleep from which they'd recently escaped. He knew they had not the slightest clue of their coming fate.

In his vision, God had explained his plan. He told Grady what needed to be done to save what remained behind of mankind. And Grady knew the next months would not be easy. He knew there would be pain and sadness. Loss and mourning. Death and destruction. And it all began here.

They were less than ten yards from the town when Grady looked back to his followers. There were so many of them, all eager to do whatever was needed to fulfill God's will. Even if Grady hadn't been shown the future, he would have had complete faith in this flock.

He watched a dark silhouette skirting the exterior walls, ducking into and out of the crevices and crannies. Soon, the person turned and came toward them.

Grady met Owen half way, now less than 100 feet from the town. "It's done?"

Owen nodded. In his hand, he held an oversized decades-old walkie-talkie. "Been a while since I did this, but it's the kind of thing you don't forget."

Owen kept stealing nervous glances toward the walled-off town. Grady placed his hand on his shoulder. "I understand that you know these people. Lived with them. But this is what must happen."

"I know. I believe in you, Grady." Owen pushed the radio his way. "Just push 'talk'."

The walkie talkie was so large that Grady almost needed to use two hands to hold it. His eyes settled on the button, and without any hesitation, he pressed it.

THE FRONT WALL to Brimley collapsed in an explosion of smoke and debris. The blasts were so loud that it shook the ground, and Grady could feel the tremble underfoot. Owen's years' experience had paid off and the devastation created a forty-foot wide hole. More than they needed.

In the minutes after the bombs went off, the men and women of Brimley emerged from their homes, many still in their pajamas and nightclothes, some so shocked they stumbled out half dressed. They carried nothing but fearful expressions. No weapons. When they saw what waited outside their walls, some ran but most stared on with abject horror.

Juli, as usual, was at Grady's side, and her hand closed into a fist as she grabbed on to his shirt sleeve.

"What now, Grady?"

Grady didn't look behind himself, but he waved his free arm overhead.

"Go forth!" he shouted.

He could feel them moving. His flock. There were so many they displaced the otherwise calm air, stirring up the dirt and creating a dust storm so heavy it made it hard to see.

Juli's hand squeezed Grady more tightly, and he felt her trembling like the ground had trembled, like she was experiencing some kind of aftershock. He turned to her, and in his peripheral vision, he saw his flock passing by them, to the right, marching toward Brimley.

More than one thousand zombies passed by the dozen or so human members of Grady's congregation. The creatures were loosely bound together with ropes and cords and twine, lashed to one another at their waists and forming something like an oversized chain gang.

The sight of them stole Grady's breath, but he managed a few words to Juli.

"Now, God shows his wrath."

The zombies breached the town, and the people inside screamed.

CHAPTER THIRTY-ONE

Lumpy, owner of the exploited wiggling and dancing zombies, was the first human to die in the arena. Mitch wasn't surprised. The man did little more than run in circles for four or five minutes, then tripped over a discarded bumper. The zombies made quick work of him after that, and Mitch supposed there was a certain amount of karma involved.

The creatures ate at Lumpy's fat carcass for a good half hour before losing interest. Mitch had noticed that in the past too. The zombies never treated humans like all you can eat buffets, gorging themselves until they burst. They only ate what they needed. That, of course, allowed enough left-over meat to come back to life and for the endless, vicious cycle to carry on.

Lumpy reanimated a few minutes after the zombies stopped dining. Mitch wasn't sure how that part worked. The timeline never seemed consistent, but the coming back to life part never changed. The sad excuse for a pimp started to shake, then made it back to his feet. When he peered at the onlookers, his eyes had taken on the undead, gray pallor.

Saw gave a thumbs up gesture, and Kwon and Polo climbed into the ring, each holding the catch poles they used to transport the undead. At first, Mitch thought they might simply corral Lumpy and add him to the storage container with the other zombies. But once they had the noose around his neck, a third man, a tall, lanky Mexican named Fernando, joined the fray.

Mitch looked toward Saw, who had climbed down from his scaffolding tower and was entering the ring. This was getting interesting.

"Strip him down," Saw ordered, and Fernando did just that, not stopping until Lumpy was completely nude. The sight of his fat rolls and a conglomeration of odd, assorted growths made it clear to Mitch how Lumpy had earned his nickname. It was not a pleasant view.

Saw held a twelve-feet long section of steel rebar and looked toward the crowd of onlookers.

"You've all been wondering what would happen to the losers. Well, here it is. If you've got a weak stomach, you might want to go now."

Sally Rose grabbed onto Mitch's arm and whispered to him, "What's he going to do, Mitch?"

"I'm not sure." That was the truth. Mitch knew Saw had something planned, but the man wouldn't give him the details. "Don't want to spoil the surprise, Mitchy," was all he'd say. So, Mitch was as eager to see what came next as the other clueless spectators.

It was worth the wait.

"Put him on the ground," Saw told Kwon, and the Asian man did as ordered. "Polo, Fernando, spread his legs."

Each of them grabbed a leg and pulled them so far apart that it reminded Mitch of trying to split the wishbone after Thanksgiving dinner.

Saw moved behind Lumpy, who flailed but couldn't break free of his three captors. He held the rebar in the middle and carefully lined it up with Lumpy's hairy, mud-brown asshole which was puckered tighter than lips that had just tasted their first lemon.

"Oh, Jesus," Sally Rose said and buried her face in Mitch's

shoulder. Part of Mitch wanted to look away too, but the other part of him had to see this. Needed to see this. He heard his heartbeat in his ears. He was so excited.

Saw rammed the rebar up Lumpy's ass. It sunk in a few inches, then a foot. The crowd gasped. A few gave pained yips like it was them getting a chunk of metal shoved up their poop chute. At the sound, Mitch saw Saw grin and lick his lips with excitement. The man was loving this. And so was Mitch.

With a grunt, Saw sent two more feet of rebar into Lumpy. The zombie's body writhed and rocked side to side, helpless.

Saw rammed more of the rebar into Lumpy, and Mitch thought there must be close five feet inside him. A low, steady groan rolled out of his mouth.

"Kwon, tilt his head back for me," Saw said.

Kwon looked at Saw, clearly skeptical about letting go of the catch pole and moving into biting radius.

"Don't be such a puff. He's not gonna get you."

"Okay." Kwon set the pole down and approached, wary. But Saw was right. Lumpy wasn't a threat any more. Kwon grabbed hold of what little hair the man had left and pulled his head back, stretching out his neck.

"Good on ya. Now hold him."

Saw took a deep breath, and Mitch saw his body tense. Then, Saw thrust the steel rebar further up Lumpy's ass and the opposite end popped free from his gaping mouth. Chunks of tissue and shards of shredded intestines clung to the metal, and several of the women and a few men in the crowd screamed.

Mitch realized Sally Rose wasn't watching, and he wrapped his arm around her waist. "It's okay. He's a zombie. Nothing but a meat suit."

She risked a glance toward the arena, saw the skewered version of Lumpy, and immediately turned away again. "How could he?" she asked.

Mitch couldn't understand why this bothered her. He thought it was pretty damned fantastic, but they could have that conversation later. Right now, his attention was on Saw, who stood over Lumpy, whose arms and legs twitched, but he wasn't going anywhere with a few feet of metal jutting from his asshole, a few more feet poking out of his mouth, and the rest filling him up in between.

Saw took a playful bow, then pretended to tip a hat that he wasn't actually wearing. "And that, people, is why you don't want to lose inside the ring." He turned back to the other men. "Take him to the east side of town. I gots me a plan for him."

Polo and Fernando quickly took the ass end of the rebar. The view might not have been the best, but at least their end hadn't travelled all the way through Lumpy's insides. That left the gore-covered piece for Kwon. Together, the men lifted and carried the zombified version of Lumpy like a pig on a spit. They took him out of the ring and out of sight.

Mitch locked eyes with Saw, and in that manic gleeful gaze, Mitch found the man to whom he'd entrusted his life four years ago. And that gave him renewed hope.

CHAPTER THIRTY-TWO

ALMOST TWO FULL MONTHS AFTER LEAVING BRIMLEY TO GO TO the Ark and kill Doc, the round trip was nearly finished. Wim had considered parting ways with Mead and Aben (and Pablo, before his demise) several times along the return trip, but he'd grown quite fond of the men, and he knew he had nowhere else to go. He knew his stay in Brimley would not be permanent, but he had to admit to himself that it would be nice to spend the coming winter with others rather than going it alone somewhere. After that, time would tell.

He'd had plenty of time to think during the ride. Sometimes too much. He wondered if killing Doc had been worth all the effort. Worth Pablo's life. Doc's death hadn't solved anything. It hadn't reversed the plague. And it certainly hadn't brought Ramey back. He didn't get an apology, nor a smattering of remorse. The only closure came in seeing the man's lifeless body lying in the grass with the blood that made him human spilling into the ground. He supposed that had to be enough.

Try as he might, Wim struggled to find a purpose now that Doc was dead. He kept hoping he'd somehow find one along the ride, but as they passed by the hand-painted sign that declared, "Ahead:

Brimley. A safe place," he realized he was still waiting. And he knew he might end up waiting for the rest of his life, however long or short that might be.

They were on the straightaway leading toward town when Wim thought something was amiss. He had better eyesight than Aben, who rode near his side while Mead and the donkey lagged a ways behind. The burro acquiesced to being ridden, but any time Mead tried to encourage it to pick up the pace, the beast only trudged along slower.

When they got another ten yards closer, Wim looked from Brimley to Aben, checking to see if the man had realized what laid ahead. He hadn't yet, but that changed soon enough.

"What in the grand hell..." Aben said when he saw it.

The front wall of Brimley was nothing more than a jumbled pile of fragmented metal and debris.

"This is bad," Wim said, stating the obvious. He pressed his heels against Gypsy's side, and she picked up the pace. Aben did the same with his mare.

For some reason, Wim's first thought was that a tornado had gone through. Maybe because his Mama watched *The Wizard of Oz* every time it played on the TV. That was the only thing that made sense to him. What else could have caused such destruction?

But when he was close enough to look past the place where the wall had been, he could see the charred remains of houses and buildings inside, standing like blackened skeletons.

Wim looked behind, searching for Mead at their rear and seeing the speck of him still nearly a hundred yards back.

Wim and Aben were close enough to town, or what had been a town, to smell the leftover acrid aroma of the fire. Its pungent, sulfur smell made Wim think of putting eggs on the stove to hard boil and forgetting about them until the pan had gone dry. It made his eyes water.

"Goddamn it, Wim. Goddamn it. What happened here?" They were within ten yards of the town, and Aben hopped down from his horse, trading it for an off-kilter jog toward his onetime home. Wim did the same.

Ahead of them, a wicker basket sat on the ground. Before either of them could see the contents, Wim realized the smoke smell had become mingled with another too familiar odor. Death.

The basket was covered with a white cloth that had taken on a puss-yellow color in the center. Flies buzzed around it, diving and swooping through the air, climbing under the cloth and slinking out from beneath it.

Wim and Aben stared at each other as if that would somehow solve or explain things.

"I've seen enough bad shit to know that whatever's in there's going to be fucking awful," Aben said.

All Wim could do was nod.

"Christ, I don't want to do this." Aben squatted down and reached toward the cloth. He did it slowly, like he was afraid something might jump out and bite him, but he muscled through whatever worries he had and took hold of it.

He ripped it away in one clean jerk, and when Wim saw the contents, he wished he'd parted ways with the men hundreds of miles ago just so he could have avoided seeing it.

Inside the basket was a woman's severed head. Wim didn't know her name, but he recognized her as the woman with whom Mead had shared an extra-long goodbye when leaving Brimley. Her curly blonde hair was rust colored with dried blood. Her eyes were gone, the sockets filled with hundreds of maggots that writhed in the vacated cavities. Her mouth hung agape, and inside, Wim saw flies and their white wormy offspring that had infested that orifice too.

Her forehead was covered with deep gashes which at first looked random because the skin was swollen and ragged from being eaten at by the maggots, but as Wim looked closer, he realized they were letters. He tried to make it out through the carnage, but Aben beat him to it.

"Repent."

Wim turned away from the dead woman's head, trading that view for Aben's pained face. "My God, who'd do this?"

Aben acted as if he had an answer in mind but—

"What's going on up there?"

They both spun around toward the sound of Mead's voice. He wasn't a speck now, but he was still seventy-five yards away.

"Oh, Christ," Aben said, and he threw the sheet over the basket. "He can't see this. It'll ruin him."

"Hey!" Mead yelled. He'd abandoned the donkey and was running full bore.

"Stop him," Aben said. "Do whatever you have to do but stop him, Wim."

Aben grabbed the basket and looked around at the flat land, his face awash in panic as he tried to find a place to hide the basket and its horrible contents.

Wim let him handle it and ran toward Mead, who was sprinting his way and screaming.

"What happened? Where is everyone?"

The two men met within seconds. Wim was bigger and used his body to block Mead's view as much as possible, but Mead's eyes were frantic as they looked past him.

"What the hell are you doing, Wim? What happened?"

"It's gone, Mead."

"What? What the fuck are you blabbing about?" He pushed past him, and Wim grabbed hold of his collar, trying to hold him back. Mead struggled, but Wim held tight, which only made Mead angrier. "Let go of me, you motherfucker!"

"Stop, Mead. Stay here, with me."

Mead stared at what was left of Brimley, and, Wim realized, Aben. "What's he got there? What's he carrying?"

Wim jerked him backward, and their bodies collided. He still held Mead's collar and used his free hand to grab the man's shoulder. "We've got to talk."

Mead stopped struggling, and Wim thought some of the fight

went out of him. As if he somehow realized it was too late to bother. "Then talk, Wim. What are you two trying to keep me from seeing?"

"I don't know what happened, but it was bad. The worst kind of bad. I don't know how to say this but--"

Before Wim could think about breaking the news as gently as possible, one of Mead's oversized steel-toed work boots collided with his groin. An explosion of pain sent him careening backward, and he landed in the dirt, on his rear. All he could do at that point was watch.

Mead dashed toward Aben and caught him. The two men were twenty yards away, and Wim couldn't hear their words. It was like watching some tragic silent movie, only without the subtitles. As he saw Mead rip the basket out of Aben's hand, Aben gestured wildly, but it was no use. Mead set the basket down and tore off the cover. Both men stood motionless for a moment. Then Mead's screams broke the silence.

It was the sound of a wounded, dying animal. Maybe the worst thing Wim had ever heard. And all he could do was cup his aching balls and wait for it to come to an end.

CHAPTER THIRTY-THREE

IF SHE'D HAVE EATEN BREAKFAST, MINA WOULD HAVE THROWN up. Saw stood at her side, holding her elbow and staring at her like a schoolboy showing off an elementary school art project and waiting for his mother's approval.

"Don't keep me waiting, love. What do you think?"

It was like he was encouraging her to stare at an eclipse. She didn't want to see it, but she knew he wouldn't give up until she did.

Before them was the naked zombie that had been skewed the night prior. The man with the metal bar all the way through his body had been planted in the ground, or more accurately, he'd been staked in it. The end of the bar that emerged from his ass was buried into the dirt, and the zombie had sunk onto its knees. It kept trying to stand up, but always failed. It looked like it was genuflecting to an unseen God. Or to its king.

Mina turned to Saw, eager to stop seeing that horrible sight. "How did you come up with something like this?"

Saw grinned, baring his rotting teeth. "Dreamed it up one night, I did. Thought it would send just the message we wanted to anyone apt to wander along."

She risked another look at the zombie, to its upper half where the metal jutted from its open mouth, extending several feet into the air and keeping its head tilted skyward in perpetuity. "It's... something."

Saw pulled her in tight against him. The heat came off his body, making her feel like she was being swallowed up by a blast furnace. She wanted to be free of him but didn't dare pull away. At times, Mina tolerated Saw. At times, she loathed him. But all the time, she was afraid of him. While Saw had never raised a hand against her, had never said a cross word to her, she knew he was only one perceived slight away from beating her senseless. Or maybe even impaling her on a stake and planting her beside Lumpy, here at the outskirts of town. Saw had kept her safe, but she'd never stopped feeling like his hostage.

Mina watched as the zombie on the metal stake worked its jaw, chewing against the steel. She saw one of its front teeth snap in half. The broken piece tumbled into its gaping maw, and she thought the creature gagged or choked and its body gave a quick shiver.

"I wanted you to see it first," Saw said.

Mina was relieved to have an excuse to look away from the zombie, but Saw's prideful face wasn't much better. "Why?"

"Because I love ya."

She knew he wanted to hear her say she loved him too. She'd never said those words, and she was damned if she ever would. Instead, she kissed him. When they broke apart, he grabbed her by the waist and slid his hand into her pants, cupping her groin, his fingers exploring her.

He knew what buttons to push, literally, and she found herself wanting him in her even though she hated almost everything about him. He pushed her pants and underwear down in one quick motion. She unzipped his jeans and let loose his ample manhood.

They fucked in the open, Mina's back in the dirt, dust rising as they thrust against each other. She stared up at the featureless, gray sky. Her eyes settled on the impaled zombie. She watched it as Saw grunted into her ear, breathed hot fowl breath into her face. As the sweat dripped off him and onto her.

She watched the zombie as it wiggled and struggled, helpless against the pole, where it might remain for the rest of eternity, for all she knew. And as Saw gasped and groaned and pounded his seed deep into her, Mina thought this place was Hell.

And she wanted the Devil dead.

CHAPTER THIRTY-FOUR

IT HAD BEEN WEEKS SINCE THEY FOUND BRIMLEY DESTROYED and the people who lived there gone. Wim thought, aside from the bombs and fires, it looked like some sort of stampede had gone by the town. The ground was trampled, every blade of grass, every weed, pummeled. It made tracking whoever or whatever was responsible easy, and he, Mead, and Aben had been doing just that.

Mead was certain that the pastor with the traveling tent revival was behind it, and, considering that "repent" had been carved into the forehead of Mead's lady friend, Wim tended to believe him. After they found what they found, Aben opened up about his experiences in the early days of the plague and the man, Grady O'Baker, who had seen his dead son destroyed before him, only to go catatonic and later reemerge thinking he was some sort of prophet. From there, it was easy to do the math.

Their travel, by horse and donkey, was slower than it needed to be. Almost as if none of them were in a hurry to get to where they were going and were only doing so because it was expected of them. Conversation was slim. Even Mead, who usually talked enough for a half dozen men, barely spoke more than a few words a day. Wim could see he was hurting because he'd been there before. Heck, he was still there. That kind of pain never goes away. At best, you acclimate to it and live with it for the rest of your life.

In some ways, Wim blamed himself. If he hadn't set out to kill Doc, these men wouldn't have followed him there. They'd have been at Brimley when hell rolled into their town, and maybe they would have had a chance of preventing it.

But Wim doubted that. Two more warm bodies (or three if you counted Pablo) wouldn't have made a bit of difference against what had happened. Still, he carried the guilt with him like a satchel on his back.

They hadn't seen a solitary zombie since leaving Brimley in the dust, a fact that seemed impossible to believe if Wim hadn't lived it. It didn't matter whether they passed through the countryside or through middling towns. Everything in their path was gone. Nothing but a trampled, dusty path in its wake.

Wim had his theory as to what might be brewing, and his thoughts were fueled by a story Aben had told about that pastor having a conniption fit when another man killed a zombie. He didn't mention his thoughts to the others as it seemed impossible to believe, but at the same time, it seemed almost horrifically possible.

They were somewhere in southwest Texas, where the land had made the transition from green to brown, when he got his answer.

Typically, they spent the nights in a house or a trailer, or even a barn when the pickings were slim. But they'd wandered far enough off the beaten path that, around the time the sun set, there wasn't a structure in sight, so they decided to camp out under the stars.

Wim didn't like the idea much. This land was as foreign to him as Mars, and he found the notion of spending the night on the ground unappealing. He worried about snakes and scorpions, plenty of which they'd seen as they rode. They'd even heard some coyotes a few days earlier.

That was why he set off looking for whatever passed for high ground in this rolling terrain. He found a little butte that wasn't anything to brag about, but as he looked at it from below, he thought it might suffice. For some reason, he felt safer higher up. As he scaled the steep hillside, his feet sent rivers of pebbles and dirt cascading downward as they slipped and dug for traction.

After struggling for a few minutes, he made it to the top, and all he wanted to do was sit down and catch his breath, but what he saw put a quick end to that. In the distance—it was hard to judge from that vantage point, but he supposed it must have been at least a mile to the west—he saw a dark mass that looked like a black pond against the sea of tan dirt and sand. At first, he thought maybe it *was* a body of water, or maybe a large copse of dead trees, but neither made any sense.

He took his rifle and pressed the stock against his shoulder. He hesitated before peering into the scope, as if trying to decide whether he really wanted to see what was out there, but he knew he couldn't ignore it, so he steeled himself and took a good look.

What Wim found gathered in the hollow west of him was Pastor Grady O'Baker's army of the undead. There were so many that he had to keep waving the rifle back and forth as he tried to take them all in. They appeared to be roped to one another and stood mostly in place, only occasionally shifting a foot or two in any direction.

As he watched, every now and again, one would seem to take issue with its nearest neighbor and swat or grab at it. But the scuffles died out fast, like they knew it was pointless and since they were all dead, there was no sense in fighting amongst themselves.

Somehow, this seemed familiar to Wim, but he couldn't fathom why that was. He'd never seen anything like this. Heck, he doubted anyone had. Hundreds, maybe thousands, of zombies, lassoed together to create some kind of invincible, unstoppable killing machine.

And then he remembered the rats. What had Emory called them? He tried so hard to recall that his brow furrowed and his eyes squinted. Think, Wim. Don't be so dumb. There was a word for it. A foreign one. But what was it?

Rattenkönig. A rat king.

That was it. It was like the jumble of rats he'd found in the barn in the days before the plague came to his little farm. They'd scurried and skittered about, eating anything in their path and, by God, this cluster of zombies that he saw in the distance must behave the same way.

Wim had killed the rat king in his barn, but that only took two shots from his Pa's old shotgun. How would it be possible to destroy that many zombies with anything short of a nuclear bomb?

He had two other men with him, and he hoped that one of them was smarter than him and might be able to come up with something. Because if not, he had little doubt that those zombies, and the man who controlled them, would destroy what remained of the world.

ABEN TOOK no pleasure in reliving his past, especially his years in the Marines and his time in the Middle East. He thought himself a barely adequate soldier, and his most memorable contribution to the war was getting several of his friends killed because he was a shitty driver. Such memories belonged in the past. Nonetheless, when coupled with a pig farmer and fry cook, he seemed to be the default go-to source of information on strategical planning for what would almost certainly end up as a suicide mission.

The fact that they were outnumbered by at least three or four hundred to one was not lost on any of them, but Aben thought he was the only one who grasped the extreme gravity of the situation.

"We'd do just as well strapping ourselves up with bombs, pushing as far into the mass of them as possible, and pressing the button." He meant that remark to be sarcastic and was a little alarmed when neither Wim nor Mead immediately put the kibosh on it. Instead, they stared at him as if giving it serious consideration.

"Where would we get the bombs?" Wim asked.

Sweet Caroline, Aben thought. This is going to be even worse than I expected. "That was not a serious plan," he said. "You boys might be the 'go out on a blaze of glory' types, but I am not. I rather enjoy life, such that it is. I didn't sign up to save the world."

Thus far, the only ideas the others had tendered were getting the zombies to the Grand Canyon and somehow dumping them over the cliff or getting them to the ocean and drowning them.

Both plans were so flawed Aben felt they bordered on absurd. They must be six hundred miles or more from the Grand Canyon, and, even if they did somehow lead the zombies there, it seemed illogical to believe they could convince them to commit mass suicide like a bunch of lemmings. The ocean hypothesis was equally short-sighted. Aben's experience at the boy scout camp years earlier had proved to him that, while zombies couldn't swim, they also did not drown.

He had considered fire. That seemed to be a comparably simple idea, but Mead put a quick end to that when he shared with them the story about LaRon and the guns and ammunition store. That really left to options. Ignore them and let them become someone else's problems, or find a way to blow them up. And not with suicide vests.

Between those two, Aben leaned toward the former. He knew that was the coward's way of dealing, and he was fine with that. However, the other men possessed moral character of a firmer quality, and he was reluctant to say that, in his opinion as a long-ago professional soldier, they should tuck tail and run.

That left explosives, but seeing as how they were in the middle of some God forsaken West Texas desert, finding them was apt to be difficult, a nearly-impossible-to-conquer scavenger hunt, so they decided to stop tracking the horde and find a few of the nearest towns, cross their fingers and toes, and hope something turned up.

As far as plans went, it wasn't much, but under the circumstances, it was as good as it got.

In towns like Big Lake, Texon, and Rankin, they had no luck. Fort Davis, too, turned up no place to find dynamite, but it did possess a gun shop large enough to give Charlton Heston a hard on, even from the grave. They had plenty of guns, and any more would be more than they could carry, but Mead demanded they stop anyway.

"An old acquaintance of mine had something called, I think, target right," he said.

"Never heard of it." Aben wanted to move on. Even though they hadn't seen the horde in days, he knew it likely wasn't far.

"He said people used it for target shooting. You shoot it, and it blows up."

Aben turned to Mead, suddenly less eager to get a move on. "Tannerite."

Mead smiled, a rare sight these days. "That's the one. We got ourselves in a pickle, and he used it to blow up a van. Made one hell of a mess."

Aben's wheels were turning. This was a good idea. Better than dynamite which, to be frank, he had little knowledge about how to use safely or effectively. "I think you might be on to something, kiddo."

The store carried no Tannerite, but Aben knew the same product could be made quite easily with nothing more than ammonium nitrate and aluminum powder. They found the ammonium nitrate at a feed and fertilizer milling company. There was so much that they had to rig up carts to Gypsy and Mead's donkey to haul it.

Mead was the one who suggested they find a paint store for the aluminum powder, insisting that they used it to create the metallic fleck look. He was right, and at the end of the day, they had what they needed. Whether it would actually work remained to be seen.

CHAPTER THIRTY-FIVE

EACH OF THE EIGHT MOST RECENT MEN TO FIGHT IN THE ARENA had died there. All eight were now impaled in an uneven row outside town. And while people still seemed to enjoy the blood sport, they watched the events not only with excitement but also with fear. Fear that they might be next.

It was getting harder to find volunteers. Not that anyone had a real choice. Mitch got the feeling that, if someone didn't win soon, the tide might turn completely, and, while he was dubious about whether they'd revolt against Saw (and by proxy, him) he thought it wasn't a risk worth taking.

He was inside his trailer, compiling the latest inventory, when there was a knock at the door. He set aside the logbook and went to the door, expecting, or maybe hoping, to find Sally Rose. The two had been spending more and more time together the last few weeks, and she'd stop servicing other men in town. He appreciated that, even though he never would have asked her.

When he opened the door, instead of finding Sally Rose's smiling face, he found Mina's scowling one. The sight so surprised him that he was speechless, a rare occurrence for him.

"Are you gonna stand there like an asshole or are you going to invite me in?"

Mitch stepped aside, and she pushed her way past him. He closed the door behind her.

"We need to talk about Saw." She sat on the couch and helped herself to an open bottle of beer without bothering to ask.

"What about him?"

"He's cheating on me."

Mitch was in the process of taking a seat of his own when she said that, and her declaration so surprised him that he almost missed. "He would never."

"He is. Not that I give half a shit. But it's who he's doing it with that matters." She sat down the bottle and stared at him, dead serious. "Matters to you."

Mitch didn't know why he should care who Saw stuck it to on the side and resented being brought into their domestic matters. He was ready to tell her when she spoke again.

"It's that whore you see. Sally."

Mitch went from annoyed to angry as if she'd flipped a light switch. He was pissed that Mina of all people would call Sally Rose a whore, and he was pissed at the accusation that there was something up between her and Saw. He didn't know which angered him more.

"Shut the fuck up. Where do you come up with this paranoid bullshit?"

"I've known it for a while but figured what did it matter? Saw's gonna do what he wants. Nothing I say or do will change that."

"Enough!" Mitch stood up so fast his chair toppled over backward, and he saw Mina flinch. She recovered quickly, though, and grabbed the beer. That time, she finished it off.

"Ask her if you don't believe me. She was the one giving Saw the heroin. Apparently, they shot up together."

"Bullshit, Mina. The heroin came from Boyd. He admitted that to my face."

"Boyd brought it in. Sally the whore delivered it. I suppose that's when they started up. No good junkies, the both of em. He's still using, you know?"

Mitch's mind was in overdrive. All this information seemed impossible but made a perverse kind of sense. Maybe that's why Sally Rose had been sticking so close to him of late, trying to keep him off the trail. He knew she liked nose candy, but then again so did he. He couldn't believe she'd do H but, when he thought about it, what did he really know about her?

"Why are you telling me this?"

"Saw's gone off the rails. The violence, the torture. He's losing the town, and if he catches on, he'll burn this place to the ground."

She stood and moved to him. He could smell the stale beer on her breath, but the look in her eyes said she was sober. Sober and truthful. "This place and everyone in it," she said. "Now are you the kind of man whose gonna stand by and do nothing? Fiddle while Rome burns, like the saying went?"

Mina slipped by him. He heard the door open but didn't turn to look as she exited. When he heard the door close again, he went to the cabinet where he kept his stash and grabbed a baggie of cocaine. He poured it onto the kitchen counter, then used a spatula to divide it into lines.

He bent at the waist to snort a line, then stopped himself. He wanted to numb the pain that he felt, but he needed to keep his head clear even more. So he swept the drugs into the sink and turned his back on it. He was going to find out the truth one way or another.

CHAPTER THIRTY-SIX

MINA WATCHED FROM A DISTANCE AS MITCH STORMED TOWARD Sally Rose's trailer. The door hung ajar, and he didn't knock before entering. As he barged inside, she hoped she'd made the right decision.

"You done screwed up this time, Birdie," her daddy's voice whispered inside her head. "That boy's too smart to fall for your little nappy-headed games. He gone see straight through your lies, and then you's gonna have hell to pay."

She'd stopped answering him out loud, at least most of the time. Although, in this horrible place, talking to yourself was one of the less unusual habits a person could possess. But in her mind, she told him to shut up. Not that that ever worked.

"That boy's gone know straight away what you up to. Then he's gone tell Saw and Lordy help you. You thought I was hard on your skinny ass? You in for a whole new world of pain."

Don't be right, she thought. For once, let the old bastard be wrong. All her life, Mina had felt like she'd been playing a supporting role. First to her younger sister, who was always prettier and smarter. Then she became her daddy's caregiver and punching bag. And now she was nothing more than Saw's woman, asking 'how high' when he said 'jump'.

She was tired of always being in the background. Always being a person to whom things happened and not someone who made things happen. She was going to be different now. She'd made her choice, and it was too late to go back. Today was the day Mina took hold of her own fate.

From inside the trailer, she heard Mitch scream. Confused, angry sounds. Then things breaking. She held her breath and hoped she'd got it all right.

There was no more heroin. She'd spent weeks trying to find some but had no luck, but she thought some burned molasses on a spoon would be close enough to fool Mitch. She'd left that, along with a needle and syringe, beside Sally Rose's body after she killed her.

That act was far easier than she'd expected. The whore was kind and trusting and had seemed a little flattered when Mina arrived at her doorstep. She invited her inside without a single question, and her only concern seemed to be tucking away dirty dishes so that Mina wouldn't realize her housekeeping skills weren't the best. She'd just sat a stack of plates in the sink when Mina hit her in the back of the head with a rubber mallet.

She'd gone with rubber because she didn't want to leave any obvious wounds, but it wasn't quite as powerful as a regular hammer, and while the blow sent Sally Rose tumbling into her ramshackle cabinets, it didn't kill her straight off. The woman hit the floor and managed to turn her way before Mina could get in a second blow. She stared up at her, dazed and wide-eyed.

"Why'd you do that?"

Mina didn't answer. Instead, she raised the mallet over her head and swung it with every bit of strength her scrawny arms could muster. That blow connected with the top of Sally Rose's skull, and the woman went limp. Mina checked for a pulse and couldn't find one, but her own heartbeat was pounding so loud she knew she might have missed it.

After waiting a minute to make sure there wasn't any blood, Mina tossed the spoon and needle near the body and headed straight for Mitch.

Inside the trailer, the screaming and the commotion had stopped, and, as the silence dragged on, Mina began to wonder if things had gone bad. Maybe Sally Rose wasn't dead. Or maybe she was and had managed to bite Mitch. Either scenario meant game over for her.

"If you smart, you'd get your skinny ass outta Dodge, Birdie. Before anyone finds out what you done."

"They won't find out." The words slipped from her mouth before she could stop herself, but she wasn't sure whether she was saying them to her daddy or to herself. "This is gonna work."

But was it? Nothing had happened yet and her confidence in her plan and in herself began to fade. She was just about ready to run when she saw movement at the trailer door. A moment later, Mitch stepped through, into the harsh midday sunlight. He carried Sally Rose's limp body in his arms, and Mina saw the handle of a kitchen knife poking out of her eye socket.

The first part of her plan had worked. Now she had to wait and bide her time for part two.

* * *

SAW LOVED THE IDEA. He'd grown weary of watching the battles from afar, so when Mina suggested he step into the ring to end the losing streak and help boost morale, he thought it was pretty much the most perfect plan he'd ever heard.

But like all things, Saw wasn't content with going into the arena to fight a zombie or two. He needed something more dramatic. More grandiose. Because then his victory would not only show all the wankers how it was done, but it would also sear his greatness into their minds for the rest of their miserable lives.

He went to Kwon to find out how many zombies they still had in storage, and the man sheepishly told him there were only fourteen.

Saw had known the numbers were dwindling and sent Fernando out a few days earlier to gather more, but on short notice, fourteen would have to do.

He was so excited for the fight that he shagged Mina three times leading up to it. Part of it was the adrenaline and testosterone coursing through him, but part was because he wanted to put a baby in that hollow of hers. The bird was pushing forty, and he knew the odds might be slim, but the way he figured it, the more pokes the better the odds.

Since getting off the heroin, Saw had never felt so alive. He loved this place, the people. He relished the rough edges and the sleaziness and the fighting. And above all, he found the power a far more pleasing addiction than opiates. He truly felt like their king, and he couldn't fathom a more perfect kingdom. He wanted to live out his days here, and he wanted to create a legacy.

As evening approached, he found Mitch sitting in the corner at the dry snatch, a half-drained bottle of whiskey his only company.

"Afternoon, Mitchy," Saw said as he sat down across from him. "I got something special planned for tonight."

Mitch stared at him from the opposite side of the table, and Saw found the look in his eyes odd, something foreign on the lad's face. Was it sadness? "You aw right, Mitchy?"

"I'm fine." Mitch grabbed the bottle and took a long swig.

"Don't seem it to me.'"

"Whatta you care?"

The lad was definitely off. Depressed with a side order of anger. Both were unwelcome in the presence of Saw's good mood, and he snatched the bottle out of Mitch's hand.

"Nope. You've had enough. I need you to have a clear head for tonight."

Mitch reached for the whiskey. Saw had no tolerance for playing keep-away, so he smashed the bottle on the floor. The day's bartender, some old-timer with an egg-shaped head and a mustache long enough to tickle his chin, glanced their way, but when he realized it was Saw who'd created the mess, he turned his attention to wiping the bar with a dirty rag.

"Whathefuck?" Mitch asked, his words slurred.

"Since when do you get pissed in the middle of the afternoon?"

"I do what I want."

"Aye, you do. And I've never stopped you, have I?" Mitch glowered at him, and Saw wondered who'd pissed in the lad's cereal. He'd never seen him so sullen. "Listen now. Tonight, we're having a battle."

"We do every night."

"No. We, Mitchy. You and me."

The boy, who really was no longer a boy, stared at him, and Saw thought some of the sober Mitch came through.

"What?"

"We're going to battle all the zombies. The two of us. There's fourteen left. I figure that's enough to put on a hell of a good show."

Mitch sat up straighter. He was coming back around.

"You and me, we're gonna show all these wankers how men fight. How men kill. And after we show em how it's done, I nary a doubt no one around here will ever think about fookin with us. We won't be kings, Mitchy. We'll be goddamn gods!"

Saw was so excited that he smacked his palm on the table, and now everyone in the bar looked. He turned to them.

"Don't no one think about missing tonight's battle. My boy Mitchy and me got something real special in mind. It's what you might call, a can't miss event."

He looked at Mitch, who now wore a smile that Saw thought didn't look entirely genuine, but he was so excited for the night's events that he didn't even care.

CHAPTER THIRTY-SEVEN

MITCH PACED OUTSIDE THE ARENA. HE FELT LIKE PUKING, BUT he'd already done that. All the booze he'd soaked up earlier in the day was on the ground behind the Dry Snatch, along with some half-digested eggs. Even though it was empty, his stomach fought him.

He couldn't comprehend how terrible the day had gone. Mina's news of Saw's betrayal. Sally Rose's overdose. He had to put a butter knife through her eye to destroy the monster she'd turned into. And now this battle where he and Saw had to take on fourteen zombies in front of every asshole in Shard End. Part of him thought he should just let one of the zombies get him, but Mitch had never been the suicidal type. Besides, even if he let that happen, he had little doubt that Saw would still somehow come out victorious, and the bastard wouldn't hesitate to hang him on a stake with the others.

Saw's braggadocio had worked, and everyone was there to see the battle. Everyone except Saw and Mina, who always had to play up their King and Queen roles and make a dramatic entrance. When Mitch saw all heads turn, he knew that was happening.

When they emerged through the crowd, Mitch saw that Saw had come in shirtless. He'd regained most of the weight he'd lost when he was in the throes of addiction, and for a fleeting moment, Mitch wondered how he'd bulked up so quick if he was still using. The man's hairy chest rippled with coarse muscles. Not the kind built in the gym, but the physique of a genuine hardass.

Mina gave Saw a kiss on the cheek as he climbed into the ring. As Mitch went to join him, Mina grabbed his wrist. Her long, skeletal fingers felt like talons. She leaned in close. "This is your chance, Mitch," she said. "Find a way to end him."

Mitch stared at her, not sure what to say or how to react. But he realized she was right. This was the best, maybe the only chance, he'd have to take Saw out. He only needed to figure out how.

"Good luck, Mitch," Mina said loud enough for everyone nearby to hear, then gave him a gentle push toward the ring.

Mitch joined Saw in the arena. The man threw his arm around his shoulders and pulled him in tight. "Can you feel it, Mitchy?"

"What?"

"The energy. It's coming off em like shockwaves. I've never seem em so excited."

Mitch hadn't paid much attention to the crowd, but he took that moment to examine them. Saw was right. These people were almost frantic. And he used their frenzied furor to steel himself for what was to come.

"Where's that girl of yours?" Saw asked. "Daisy Iris or whatever her name is?"

Mitch's head snapped toward Saw. How dare the bastard even mention her?

"She too worried about you to come out and watch you fight?"

Mitch clenched his teeth to stop himself from going off on Saw right then. "Yeah. I guess."

Saw laughed. "A shame. She should be here. See what her man's capable of. I tell you, Mitchy, nothing gets a girl's snatch wet faster than seeing her man bash a couple skulls in."

"If you say so."

Saw laughed again, a deep throaty chortle. "Good thing you got me around to teach you lessons like this. Someone's gotta be your dad and show you how to be a man."

At the opposite end of the arena, Kwon and Polo brought in the fourteen zombies. As they began to meander toward them, Mitch leaned in close to Saw.

"There's something I never told you about my parents," Mitch said.

"What's that, Mitchy?" Saw looked away from the coming zombies and to Mitch.

"I killed them."

Saw's eyes narrowed, and Mitch couldn't hold back a grin. Now, he was ready to fight.

CHAPTER THIRTY-EIGHT

SAW HAD KILLED FOUR ZOMBIES TO MITCH'S TWO. THAT LEFT eight of the creatures with them in the arena, and the crowd was roaring.

An undead black man was heading Saw's way, but Mitch grabbed him from behind, his fingers sinking into the zombie's dense kinky hair. He jerked the monster's head backward and threw the zombie to the ground. The man looked up at him and growled. Mitch's response was a kick to the jaw. Two large white teeth fell out of its mouth, along with a slimy string of black drool.

The creature started to get up, but Mitch kicked it again, another blow to the head. The creature fell face first into the mud, and Mitch stomped its skull again and again until his boot broke through the bone and sunk into the soft tissue inside. When he pulled his foot free, it came loose with a thick wet *shwock*.

Mitch looked over to see Saw bashing a female zombie's head against a car bumper. Most of her face was caved in, and she looked like a porcelain doll that some careless child had dropped, but her arms still fought and flailed. Another two hard hits into the metal, and she went limp.

Saw dropped her and grinned at Mitch. His face was spattered with black blood that painted streaks as it ran down his crazed face. "Over half way there, Mitchy."

Mitch knew the man was a sociopath, but he still struggled to believe Saw could put on such a friendly, unaffected act after the way he'd betrayed him. Did he think Mitch was so stupid that he wouldn't catch on, or did he not even care?

"Behind you. Three o'clock," Saw said.

Mitch turned and found a teenage boy, a head shorter than him and even skinnier, approaching. The boy's face had been gnawed on and most of the left side was gone, just an oozing black pit. Mitch thought he'd be doing the kid a favor to finish him off.

He'd noticed earlier that a straight section of metal was hanging loose by a Jeep's windshield, and now he grabbed it and jerked it free. He felt the steel cut into his palms, but he had so much adrenaline that he didn't care. He spun back to the boy, stabbing the metal into what was left of its face, and they were down to five.

The zombies were on three sides of them, and the border of cars was at their backs. Mitch was certain they could take them out together, but he knew that this was going to be his best chance. Saw was partially in front of him, his back turned. Mitch still clutched the two-foot-long chunk of metal, and all he needed to do was slash Saw in the knee or ankle during the fight. Put him to the ground where he'd be at the zombies' mercy. If he did it at the right moment, in the midst of the chaos, no one would even realize what had happened. The zombies were closing in, and Mitch knew he had to make his move soon or he might lose the chance altogether.

A middle-aged dead woman came in at Mitch's side. Her iron-gray hair swayed with every awkward, lurching step and obscured her face. He tried to make out the details, to see who she was, and didn't realize another zombie was almost on him. It was not until he heard its raspy growl that he became alerted to its presence, and by then it was close enough to grab him.

And it did just that. The zombie had hold of his upper arm, its fingers sinking into his flesh. He could smell the decay and death spilling from its open mouth. He could feel it on his neck.

Holy fuck, he thought as it fell into him. I'm going to die.

Mitch couldn't believe he'd been so careless. He'd escaped thousands of these fuckers in the Greenbriar's bunker, but now he was inches away from getting chomped.

He jerked, trying to pull his arm free, and, in the process, dropped the strip of metal. The gray-haired zombie was at his other side, and she took hold of his shirt. Mitch felt like the bologna in a zombie sandwich. The female zombie leaned in to take a bite, but Mitch caught her gray hair with his free arm and barely held her at bay. She was so close he could see hunks of decayed flesh caught in her teeth.

And then her right eye burst out of its socket and hit Mitch in the face. The thick orbital slime as it slithered down his face would have revolted him if he wasn't so shocked. The gray-haired zombie still stood in front of him, but she no longer fought to attack. She was limp, and a second later, her body collapsed to the ground.

Saw had used the metal to stab through the back of her head, and, when she fell, it came free. Mitch watched as Saw wasted no time and stabbed past him. Mitch couldn't see what happened, but he heard the crunch as the bar broke through the face of the zombie who'd had hold of Mitch's arm.

The two zombies were dead, and Mitch was free. He spun around, searching for the other three who should still be waiting to attack but realized that somehow Saw had killed them too. He tried to think, to make sense of it, but he struggled to clear his head over the thunderous roar of the crowd.

Then, Saw embraced him. "Good brawling, Mitchy!" he shouted into Mitch's ear.

Mitch realized he was on the verge of crying. He was so relieved to be alive but still so confused over Mina's accusations. "Thank you," was all he could get out.

Saw pulled back, grinning and bemused. "You don't gotta thank me. I'd never let nothing bad happen to you. You're like my son, Mitchy. I love you, you little bastard."

It seemed so sincere that Mitch couldn't help but believe him. He realized everything Mina had told him was a lie. That she must have been the one who killed Sally Rose. He looked to where she'd stood outside the arena and realized she was gone.

Mitch leaned in close to Saw, locking eyes with him. "There's something you need to know."

CHAPTER THIRTY-NINE

"Oooh, Birdie, you done fucked up real good. Thought you could outsmart a coupla men. Thought I taught you better than that, but you never did listen to your daddy."

"Rot in hell, you bastard. I killed you!" she screamed the words out loud, but her daddy only cackled hysterically in response.

Mina ran as fast as her skinny legs could carry her. That was not fast enough. She hadn't made it half a mile when the spotlight illuminated her from behind and turned her into a silhouette.

She ran another few yards, her pace slowing as the light behind her grew in intensity. Then, her pace became a plodding walk.

"No sense wasting your energy, love," Saw said. "Time for running's over. How 'bout you turn around?"

Mina did not. She was done taking orders. Done doing what men told her to do. She stood there, facing away from the light, away from Saw, until she felt hands on her shoulders. The grip was firm but not the strongman's strength she was used to.

"Why'd you do this, Mina?"

That was Mitch's voice. That little, ratty bastard had ruined everything. If only he'd have listened to her. Done what she'd told him. This could all have ended so much better. They could have lived their lives without being under Saw's thumb. Without his sadistic brutality always lurking on the edge of his personality and ready to strike. Damn that Mitch for being such a chickenshit.

Mina did turn, but not before she'd worked up a mouthful of spit. When she came face to face with Mitch's ugly scarred mug, she unleashed it, and the glob of it splattered against the bridge of his nose, into his eyes.

"Because I thought you were a man. Turns out, I was wrong."

She expected him to hit her, but instead, he only wiped at his face with the back of his hand and looked to Saw, who stood a couple yards away, holding the floodlight. He stared at her and shook his head but stayed silent.

That silence, coupled with the flat emotionless expression on his face, had her on the verge of breaking. She could have handled him screaming at her. Cursing at her. Beating her. But the silence, the disapproval like she was the one who'd done something wrong, that was too much. "What are you gonna do, Saw? Shoot me? Run me through with one of your spears?"

"I won't do none of that," Saw said, and he lowered the light a bit, giving her eyes a small break. "While that island was burning, you came to me and asked if I could keep you safe. I told you I would. And I always did, didn't I?"

"He got you there, Birdie! You never did know how good you had it!"

She resisted the urge to answer her daddy's voice. Didn't speak at all.

"When I told you I loved you, which I told you a lot, I meant it. Weren't nothing I wanted more than to grow old here in Shard End with you beside me. What else did you want from me?"

Mina had no answer for him because she didn't know. He'd given her a mansion and safety and loyalty. But she hated who he was. That he wasn't her true love, Bundy, and nothing could have changed that.

"Aren't you even going to give me the courtesy of an explanation?"

Mina considered telling Saw exactly what she thought of him. That he was pure evil. That he was repugnant. That everyone he loved would never love him because, at his core, he was completely rotten. But she decided not to give him the satisfaction of saying words that would allow him to hate her back. She wanted him to spend the rest of his days wondering why. So, she bit her tongue and kept her mouth closed.

"Have it your way then."

Saw raised the light back up. She couldn't see him anymore. She could see nothing but the fiery white ball of the halogen flood. It was like looking into the tunnel everyone talked about and seeing the light at the other end, but Mina suspected she wasn't destined to see that light. Not after the things she'd done.

"Get on with it, Mitchy. But do it carefully like we discussed."

Mina returned her attention to Mitch and realized he had a machete in his hand.

"I think I loved her," Mitch said, and she realized the wetness in his eyes wasn't remnants of her spit but tears.

A sliver of her thought about saying something kind. Maybe even apologizing. But being nice never got her anywhere in life. It was a hard world, one that ground up the good people and tossed them into the dirt when it had used up everything worth taking. That was just as true before the plague as it was now. And if she was heading toward the exit, she wasn't going to fake it any more.

"I doubt she loved you. I doubt anyone could."

Mitch's gaze switched from melancholy to fury.

"Yo coming home, Birdie. We gone be together fo'ever!" Her daddy laughed and laughed as Mitch swung the machete.

The blade hit her low in the neck, barely above her collar bones, and as her head tumbled free, she saw the man who had killed her and the man who'd ordered her death tumbling end for end.

Their movements, which weren't theirs at all, of course, ceased when her head came to a stop in the dirt. It was mostly upside down but still faced toward the men, and she watched Saw grab her decapitated head by the hair and lift it up, looking her in the eyes.

"Promised you I'd never hurt you, love. Shame you didn't do the same."

The men turned and walked back toward town, Mina's head swinging in Saw's hand. She watched it all as her life drained away and the night went from dim, to black, to winking out entirely.

CHAPTER FORTY

MEAD SPOTTED THE LOG CABIN BEFORE THE OTHERS. IT WAS THE old-fashioned kind with thick, white layers of chinking between the wood, and it looked like it had been empty for maybe fifty years.

The roof was partially caved in and no actual windows filled the holes where glass had once been, but it was the first structure they'd seen in hours, and he thought it would suffice, even if it was a piece of shit.

He was ready to claim it for the night when a man stepped through the doorway. He was tall, dark, and anything but handsome. "Help you?"

Mead gave him a quick up and down and saw he had a pistol holstered on his hip. "Maybe. We've been riding for a while. Just looking for a place to flop for the night."

"I could go along with that. If you can answer me something."

Mead tended to expect the worst from people, and although he was suited up for fighting zombies, he knew none of his gear would help him if the man decided to draw and shoot. "It's your rodeo. Ask away."

"Why the fuck are you dressed up like some kind of crash test dummy?"

From behind his helmet, Mead grinned.

The man's name was Fernando Mejias, and over the course of the evening and night, they told him their stories, and he shared his. What he lacked in looks, he made up for in personality. He was raw and crude and, while Wim visibly cringed at his language, Mead liked him despite that. Shit, maybe because of it.

Fernando told them about the town he'd called home for the last two years, a place called Shard End on the Texas/Mexico border. He was out on a supply run but hadn't found much luck. They told him about Brimley, about the army of zombies, and suggested that reinforcements would be an asset for any coming fight. At times, Mead thought Fernando wavered between shock and disbelief, but he never outright questioned their tale, and, when the talking was finished, he agreed to take them to his home.

Sleep had been hard coming for Mead ever since he found Brimley destroyed and the woman he loved dead. The rough wood floor of the cabin didn't help, and he spent much of the night tossing from one side to the other, tormented by memories and regrets. Going in to that summer, he'd thought he had the world at his feet. That he'd taken on the apocalypse head on and come out victorious. But he'd been humbled.

Despite all the horrible things he'd seen, what happened in Brimley shocked him. He couldn't comprehend that type of cruelty. The thought of new people, a new fight, energized him. He thought it could be a chance to redeem himself. To test himself once more and get his revenge.

CHAPTER FORTY-ONE

JULI WOKE, TERRIFIED AND ON THE VERGE OF SCREAMING, BUT by some miracle, she was able to keep quiet. She forced her eyes to stay open, to stare at the dawn sky, which was full of pinks and reds and a fingernail of the moon. She thought staring at that might keep the horrors of her dreams at bay, but that didn't work.

Every night since the massacre in Arkansas, she'd had similar dreams. People running and screaming and fighting and dying. In the daylight, she could push those memories away, convince herself that it was all a necessary part of God's plan, just like when he killed the people of Sodom and Gomorrah. But at night, the visions that filled her dreams were too real.

She knew going back to sleep would be a wasted effort, so she climbed off the rollup mattress and stretched out her aches and pains as she came fully awake. This land was cool in the mornings, not like it had been further East, and she grabbed her blanket and wrapped it around her shoulders like a shawl.

As she left the small encampment where the few dozen men and women of Grady's congregation—the ones who were still human— slept, she tiptoed so as not to wake them. She'd grown increasingly uncomfortable around them since Arkansas, with their fervor and devotion. She'd been with Grady the longest by a good spell, but these people, they didn't simply follow him, they worshipped him. Even after all this time, Juli wasn't extremely familiar with the Bible, but she was relatively certain it talked about false idols or prophets or something like that. One of these days, I'll have to actually read that book, she thought. But she knew she never would.

Watching Grady get bitten by zombies was something she could handle. Could even believe in. And watching him round up zombies, lassoing them like runaway cattle and forcing them into a herd was bizarre but harmless enough. Grady had a way with them and, in the year plus he'd been growing his zombie horde, no one had been bitten. Aside from him, of course. It was like they were under his spell, docile and subservient. She thought them harmless.

Until Arkansas.

That had changed everything. And the fact that she was the only person in the whole bunch of them who seemed to see the horror in what had happened scared her even more. Would God really support sending in zombies to eat women and children? Grady said they were purging them of their sins, but what sins did little boys not even old enough for Little League have that were worth dying over?

She spotted Grady sitting cross-legged and motionless in the middle of nothing. She knew he was praying. Or listening, maybe. Getting his orders from God.

It's funny, she thought. Before the plague, if people passed a dirty homeless man on the street corner, one who was shouting about how God told him this and God told him that, everyone thought he was insane or ignored him entirely. But now, that same type of character wasn't only listened to but believed. Was there a good reason for that change?

Although she'd been quiet as a mouse, Grady turned to her as if he knew he was being watched. He smiled, that pinched-lipped barely-there smirk that used to seem boyish but now seemed somehow malevolent. "Come. Sit with me, Juli."

She didn't want to, but she did, of course.

There was nothing but silence between them for the first minute. Nothing but sitting and staring into the desert where the cacti were being backlit by the rising sun. She wondered if he expected her to speak, but while she tried to come up with something worth saying, he broke the silence.

"It's close now."

Juli looked at him, but he didn't meet her gaze. "What's close?"

"The end. The rapture, some might call it."

"That's where we all turn into spirits and float up to Heaven?" She hoped that didn't come out as sarcastic as she thought it did.

"In a way. It won't happen just like that, but the final result will be the same. We'll get our rewards for doing God's work."

"Reward?" Juli thought it an odd comment. Grady cared about nothing. Certainly not rewards.

He finally looked her way, that same small smirk on his face. "You'll see. I promise."

It wasn't unusual for Grady to be vague on the details, and Juli was never sure if that was because he didn't want to share everything God supposedly showed him, or because he was making everything up as he went along. She thought the truth was a coin flip. "I hope I do see it, Grady. Because lately, I'm... I'm struggling."

"I know this has been a long and difficult journey. I don't tell you enough, but thank you for everything you've done. Everything you continue to do. You believed in me when no one else did, and I'll never be able to repay you for that."

"I don't want repaid. I just need to know that this has been worth something."

Grady laid his hand on her knee. His eyes were almost painfully earnest. "It has! Of course it has! We're doing what God demanded when no one else had the courage to stand up and say, 'Yes, Father, I will do as you command!' When everyone else was running or trying to restart that damned forsaken world, we were the ones who said, 'No, we know there's something better. We believe our Lord has a plan!" That's not something. That's everything. You have to believe that."

Juli wanted to believe. She wanted that more than anything, and inside, she prayed that God would speak to her the way he'd supposedly spoken to Grady. Because if there was ever a time in her life when she needed to know the truth, it was now.

CHAPTER FORTY-TWO

THE NIGHT PRIOR, FERNANDO HAD TOLD THE MEN ABOUT THE people who ran Shard End. Saw and Mitch. From their descriptions, Wim had been relatively certain he knew them from the attack on the Ark, and when Fernando gave their names, Aben confirmed this.

As a result, the men knew the town they were now approaching was not only hard, but also quite possibly deadly. Fernando had promised to vouch for them, and Wim believed he would, but he knew he'd never fully trust Mitch after his double-agent stunt on the Ark. And, if Saw was as insane as Aben had described him to be, they very well might be riding to their executions.

To say the plan was risky was an understatement.

The first thing Wim saw when they entered Shard End was Mina Costell's head impaled on a spike. It was not a good omen.

"Holy hell!" Mead yelled behind him. "Is that Mina?"

Wim hadn't seen her in a few years, but he was certain it was her. He didn't even need to double check it against the wedding photo he kept tucked into his back pocket. The woman he'd considered a friend stared at him with gray, glazed over eyes. Her mouth opened and shut with low rumbles escaping through her dried out, blackened lips.

Wim spun toward Fernando, hand on his revolver. "What's going on here?"

Fernando, who sat behind Aben, sharing his horse, thrust his hands in the air, and the look on his face showed that he was almost as surprised about this as Wim. "I don't know. That's Saw's wife. Or she was when I left."

"Then what's her head doing on a stick?" Wim asked.

"I have no idea. Honest to God."

"Fucking shit!" Mead hopped off the donkey. "If those zombie cult motherfuckers beat us here and killed everyone, I'm going to have an aneurysm."

"There's no sign of that."

Mead turned and saw Wim had also dismounted. "Another severed head isn't a sign?"

Wim pointed to the ground. "Down there, I mean. All the scrubby little weeds are still perked up, not flat on the ground. When that lot rolls through, everything in its way gets trampled. Besides, there's no way they could have beat us here."

"Then what happened to her?"

Wim stepped to Mina's undead head. He held his hand toward it and flinched when her jaws snapped shut. He looked to the other men. "Let's go in town and find out."

They all elected to walk in, leading the horses and donkey by their ropes. Prince trotted along with them like he was part of the gang, and Wim supposed he'd earned that right.

Along the way, they passed several more zombies impaled on metal shafts and still as alive as zombies could be, but Fernando provided an explanation for those. Wim thought it a gruesome one, but the Mexican had already forewarned them that this was a hard place. And Wim knew he would need hard men to fight beside him if they had any real chance of coming out victorious.

He was still shaken up about Mina as they entered town,

wondering how she'd come to such an end. All the while, though, he remembered how she had left the Ark, running off with their attackers. He supposed it shouldn't surprise him that such a path wouldn't lead anywhere good.

Ahead of them, they saw a few dozen house trailers, motorhomes, and RVs parked haphazardly. As far as towns went, it wasn't much. Men and women stared at them from the stoops and alleys, and as the men passed by, Wim felt like he was some sort of zoo exhibit, on display for all these people to gawk at. He felt like things could take a bad turn at any moment.

Fernando made a slight detour to a large motorhome, the kind that Wim thought Emory would have enjoyed if he was still alive, and tapped on the door. It opened, and a face Wim could never forget came into view.

The man Wim had known as Wayne, the man whose life he'd saved when he found him with a face full of infection back in West Virginia, didn't see him initially. He was too busy speaking to Fernando, but as they talked, he looked toward the other men.

Mitch pushed past Fernando and came toward them. The boy he'd been on the Ark was gone, replaced with several inches in height and a man's gravity in his eyes. Wim thought he was coming to him or maybe Aben, but instead, he crouched down and smacked his hips.

"Prince!" he called, and the dog's ears perked up. The dog stared at him a moment, then took a halting step forward. "Hey, Prince!"

Prince looked from Mitch, then up at Aben, who nodded. "Go ahead." The dog broke into a run and launched himself at Mitch, his front paws landing on his shoulders as he licked Mitch's scarred face.

Mitch ruffled the dog's fur, then put his arms around him and pulled him in even closer. "I missed you, buddy." The dog kept licking, his tail going back and forth rapid fire. Wim realized, with considerable surprise, that Mitch was crying.

Mitch seemed to realize that too and quickly stood and composed himself. He wiped dog slobber and tears from his face with his shirt sleeve, then pushed his mop of hair off his forehead. He looked to the others, from Aben to Wim, then back again. Aben was closer, and Mitch went to him.

"Mitch," Aben said with a slight nod.

Mitch extended his hand, but the look on his face said he didn't expect the gesture to be returned. "I've got to admit, I never expected to see you here."

"I'd suspect not since you and Saw sent me off, pretty near naked, to turn into a popsicle." Aben didn't take his hand, and Mitch eventually shoved it in his pocket.

"Yeah," Mitch said. "I know this doesn't mean shit, but I'm real glad you made it."

"As am I."

Leading up to this, Wim had thought the men might come to blows, but that didn't happen. They weren't more than cordial, but it fell far short of the anger and violence he'd fretted about.

Then Mitch came to him.

"Hey, Wim. How have you been?"

"Around," Wim said. "You?"

Mitch shrugged his shoulders. "We've got a nice set up here. Rough but everyone's out in the open about that. Not like on the Ark."

"I wouldn't use comparisons to the Ark if you're trying to say anything good."

"I'm not. I just mean..."

"I know." Wim could feel the man's nerves and wanted to get past this awkward phase as fast as possible. "You healed up nice."

Mitch subconsciously tucked his chin and tilted his face down, an angle that made the scars less noticeable. "Thanks."

Mead stepped into the mix. "I heard you were a real son of a bitch. But the past is the past, and we've got some crazy important shit to deal with. I'm Mead."

Mitch looked his way and took Mead's outstretched hand. "Mitch, but I guess you know that."

"I do. Now take us to your buddy Saw so that we can have ourselves a serious discussion."

Wim admired Mead's candor, and, apparently, Mitch did too because he smiled and nodded. "Follow me."

SAW LISTENED to the men's story but found it hard to focus. He'd been missing Mina something fierce. Even if she had been a lying murderous bint, he still loved her. Missed her too. Occasionally, he'd venture to the outskirts of town and stare at her head and talk to her. She'd hiss and growl and snap her jaws, and even though that wasn't that far off from their conversations when she was alive, it simply wasn't the same.

He was thinking about her when he realized the room had gone silent and all eyes were on him. He didn't know if they'd asked him a question or were waiting for his general opinion on matters but knew he needed to say something.

"Well, one things for damned sure, I ain't gonna sit here playing tiddlywinks while some religious loony bird sets off to conquer the world."

He watched them, examined them to see if his answer would belie his daydreaming, but it seemed to work.

"Then you'll join us?" Wim asked.

Saw grinned, part from relief that no one had caught on, but also because the notion of a war seemed like the perfect thing to take his mind off his lost lover. "Of course. I never did like that mousy little bastard and his pity me attitude."

The plans came together quickly after that. Saw thought the odds of it succeeding were slim, but he was never one to let common sense get in the way of violence. Besides, what good was living if you were going to behave like a cowed dog and run away from opposition? Better to take it head on and deal with the consequences.

After everything was settled, Saw pulled Aben aside while the others left his house. "A word, Aben? If you don't mind."

"It's never a word with you, Saw, but I'll listen nonetheless."

They sat on the front porch, something Saw could actually enjoy now that the days weren't a hundred degrees. It wasn't cool, damp Birmingham, but it was bearable. He offered Aben a stale beer, and Aben accepted.

They each drank for a spell before the conversation got started.

"I got to say, I don't think much of this plan," Saw said, breaking the silence. "You really think you got a chance with the little weirdo?" That was the first part of the plan. Mitch and Aben, who had spent a few months with Grady at the outset of the plague were to go to him and try the diplomatic tact before all hell broke loose.

"Not particularly."

"So why bother?"

"Because it's the only chance of avoiding a whole lot of people dying." Aben looked out toward the end of town where Saw's growing display of impaled dead stood out of sight. "Not that you'd concern yourself with such moral quandaries."

Saw chuckled. "Everyone dies sooner or later. Don't see why the date matters so much."

"Probably because most people want to live as long as possible."

"Most people never live in the first place. They're too fookin scared of everything. Of everyone. They exist and nothing more." Saw finished off his beer and chucked the bottle into the yard. It collided with a rock and shattered. "You think I give a fook when I die? I don't. Because I've really lived. I do it every day."

"That's a unique perspective."

"Words to live by," Saw said.

"Or die by."

"Either or."

Aben took a small sip, and Saw watched him swish the beer around in his mouth before spitting it onto the porch.

"I'm glad you're alive, you know."

"I rather doubt that," Aben said.

"It's true. When you walked in here, I about shat myself. I knew you were one tough bastard, but I didn't expect that."

"Oh, I'd cashed in my chips and was waiting to die when Mead came along. Another half hour, I'd have been an icy speed bump, all courtesy of you."

"I always liked you and still do. If I didn't, I wouldn't a given you no chance at all."

"It wasn't much of a chance."

"But you're still here, aren't you? If you need reminding what happens to people I'm really upset with, stop by the head of my most recently betrothed and introduce yourself."

Aben set his half empty beer to the side and stood. "I'd like to say it's been good chatting with you, Saw, but..." He stepped off the porch and started toward town.

"Aben?"

The big man turned back, reluctant.

"Be careful when you go to Grady. It's easy to underestimate a crazy man. Especially one who believes his own bullshit."

"You'd know."

"I'm not crazy. Just mean's all."

"I won't disagree with the latter."

Saw smiled, one so sincere it would have been charming if not for his decayed broken teeth.

"And take care of Mitchy for me if ya will. Don't let nuffin bad happen to him, aw right?"

Aben nodded slowly. "I'll try."

"He's a good lad."

"Let's agree to disagree on that. At least for now."

Saw thought that was fair enough. He watched Aben leave the property and head toward town, knowing that in the morning, he and Mitch would be gone. He hoped he hadn't seen the last of the both of them.

CHAPTER FORTY-THREE

"I CAN'T BELIEVE YOU'VE BEEN RIDING THAT HORSE FOR ALL THIS time and you never bothered to give her a name. It's like Prince all over again," Mitch said. "What is it with you and names anyway?"

They'd set off at dawn and were making good time, but conversation had been limited to the bare necessities until Mitch had asked about his horse. Aben glanced sideways, taking in Mitch, who was riding Mead's donkey, and shrugged his shoulders, telling him the horse had no name. That reminded him of some old song lyrics, and he smiled. Apparently, Mitch took that smile as an invitation to strike up a conversation, and while Aben wasn't overly interested in such trivialities, especially with Mitch, there was no sense in being rude.

"She knows 'whoa' and 'go'. Expanding her vocabulary further might be apt to confuse her," Aben said. "And to save you from asking, that donkey remains nameless too."

"Maybe I'll name it."

"I see no one standing in your way."

Mitch managed to keep his mouth shut for almost a whole minute before barking out, "Jack!"

Aben only shook his head. "That's a little on the nose, don't you think?"

"Better than not having a name at all."

"I can't recall one single time in my life when having a name made a bit of difference. And I'm a man, not an animal."

Mitch laughed.

"I didn't realize I was being humorous."

"That's from that old black and white movie, *The Elephant Man*." He gave his voice a lower tenor and a bad British accent. "I am not an animal! I am a human being!"

Aben stared at him blank-faced. "Never saw it." He lied. He didn't want to be Mitch's friend. Mitch had almost gotten him and his dog killed years earlier, and he had few doubts the boy would do the same again if it meant saving his own skin.

"It was good. A little sad, though."

Aben thought that was about as much empathy as the boy possessed. Then he needed to remind himself that Mitch wasn't a boy any more. He was twenty-one years old, older than Aben had been the first time he was shipped overseas with a gun and a uniform to fight in a war he still didn't understand.

They rode the next five hours in silence. Aben preferred that but it didn't last.

"If it makes any difference, I'm sorry," Mitch said.

"Why? Did you pass gas?"

Mitch smirked. "You know."

"I suppose."

Mitch broke eye contact, staring into the desert ahead. Aben could almost see the wheels turning inside the boy's head.

"I was scared, I guess. About leaving Saw."

"He's just a man," Aben said.

"I know. But he's... He believed in me. That's more than my parents ever did."

Aben saw genuine emotion on the boy's face, and as much as he'd have enjoyed dragging Saw's name through the mud for the rest of the day, he knew that would serve no purpose other than making himself feel good. Mitch and Saw were two sides of the same coin. And maybe that coin was a wooden nickel, but nevertheless, they were inseparable.

It was easier to stay quiet.

ABEN SAW Juli before she saw him. She was a hundred yards or more from Grady's encampment and even further from the zombies, all alone in the desert, sitting at the edge of a dry creek bed and staring into space. She looked small against the landscape, like a lost child. And although Aben couldn't read emotion from that distance, he imagined she was melancholy.

"Damn, that chick hasn't aged well," Mitch said over his shoulder.

Aben wished he was alone, but Mitch's assessment was true. Juli's once raven-black hair was over half gray and her tanned skin etched with wrinkles. It was like fourteen years had passed since he last saw her, not four. He scanned the area again, triple-checking to be certain no one else was around, then Aben and Mitch pushed toward her.

They'd halved the distance before Juli caught on to their presence. She flinched, then scrambled to her feet, almost falling in the loose soil before regaining her footing and balance. She was on the verge of running when something in her eyes shifted.

Aben held up his hands. "Hello there, old friend."

"Aben?"

"I'd hate to think someone else out there is as ugly as me."

"Oh my God." She started toward them, slow at first, then shifting to a quick jog. She mostly ignored Mitch but threw her arms around Aben's broad chest, burying her face in his beard. "I'm not dreaming this, am I?"

Aben wrapped an arm around her shoulders. "I could think of better dreams."

"Me too." She let him go, and when she pulled back, he saw she was crying. She looked toward Mitch, blank at first, then shocked and curious. "Mitch?"

He nodded.

"You're so tall. So grown up." She stared at him, unblinking.

"And I have a fucked-up face. You can say it. My feelings won't be hurt."

Her eyes dropped. "What happened?"

Mitch opened his mouth to answer, but Aben took over.

"That's a long story and not a relevant one at the moment. We need to talk about Grady. And his zombies."

Juli bit her lip, and the trickle of tears coming from her eyes turned into a river.

CHAPTER FORTY-FOUR

Juli refused to take them to see Grady. She knew that if she did, Grady would cast them in to the undead, where their sins and their flesh would be consumed, and they would then join his flock. She cared about them too much, even Mitch, to do that. They deserved better than becoming sacrificial lambs.

She told them as much as she could, but it was enough that she knew the men would return from where they came, filled with stories of past horrors and coming doom. In a way, she thought that might be for the best. Maybe it would keep everyone away so that Grady's long march to the promised land would be through vacant towns and no one else would need to die. But in her heart, she knew better.

As dusk came around, she asked Mitch if he'd mind giving her and Aben some time alone. Mitch obliged without protest, without even a lewd remark, and she found herself a little surprised at the man he'd grown into. She'd had such low expectations for him.

Once the two of the were alone, she decided it was time to plead her case.

"I know you came here with a plan in mind. I'm asking you to abandon it. Stay out of Grady's way. Tell everyone from here to the Rio Grande to do the same. If there's no one to get hurt, maybe this can all end... Less bad."

Aben swatted a gnat away from his face but never took his eyes off her. "That's not my call, Juli. This affects a whole lot more people than me."

"I know. But they sent you, so they must trust you. Tell them to go away. Go east or something. It wouldn't have to be forever either. It's going to happen soon. I can sense it when I'm around him. The... excitement, or whatever it is, it radiates off him like a heat lamp. Whatever Grady's visions have shown him will happen in a matter of days, not months."

"And what if it doesn't? What if it's just more insanity and nothing happens? Where is God going to send him next? How many more people will die to become his army of undead God warriors or whatever the hell he thinks they are?"

"He's saving them. The living and the dead."

"You don't buy into that horse shit. It's written on your face clear as glass."

"I do. I've seen so many things that would be impossible without God behind them."

"Like what?"

"Start off with dead people coming back to life!" Her voice was high, her frustration bleeding into anger. "Five years ago, would you have thought that possible?"

Aben scratched his beard, then combed it back in place with his fingers. "I don't see God in that at all."

"It goes as far back as the bible. Jesus resurrected Lazarus from the dead."

"And he came back as a man, not a monster."

Juli shook her head. "Then what about Grady getting bit and not turning? It's happened again and again. He's been chosen."

"He's got an extra immunity gene or something. That's all." Aben reached out and grabbed her hand, swallowing it up in his own. "A couple years back, I was a dead man. I was nine-tenths naked and three fourths froze on the middle of a snow-covered forest in Bumfuck Pennsylvania. And just after I laid down to die, a man came along and saved me. Now if you want to look for a miracle from God, that's your miracle. Not letting zombies bite you like some Hillbilly preacher drinking strychnine and taking up serpents and jumping around yelling that God is protecting you. That's not God. That's crazy."

Juli pulled her hand away. She couldn't find words to respond.

"If you really believe in Grady O'Baker, then look me in the eyes and say it."

Juli did look him in the eyes. "I..." Her own welled up with tears. "I have to believe in him, Aben."

"Why?"

"Because I killed my husband. Because I saw my children turn into zombies. Because I lost everything I ever had or cared about. There has to be a reason for that. For all this. I have to believe because that belief is all I have left."

He reached for her again, but she pulled away before he could catch her.

"Juli, come with me. Get away from this craziness for a couple days and see if you really think this is what you need and what you believe in."

Juli jumped to her feet and put a yard between them. She knew she needed to get away, that if she stayed near him for too long, she might lose herself. "Go now. Go catch up with Mitch and get out of here, and I won't tell Grady you've been around."

"Stop this." He took a limping step her way. "Don't act like this with me. I know you stayed with Grady because you pity him. He was like a wounded animal that you latched onto to try to heal because you needed to make yourself feel better. But that was a long time ago."

It was true. She'd stayed with Grady at the Signs Following Church because she couldn't bear to leave him all alone. He was too fragile, too innocent. And while he was neither of those anymore, he was still the only constant in her life. "I said go. Go right now or I'll run back to camp and send them after you."

"I know you wouldn't do that."

Juli pulled back her shoulders and straightened her spine. How dare he think he knows her mind? "I spent about four months of my life around you, Aben. Four months out of almost fifty years. You don't know me at all."

She expected him to get angry, but he only looked sad. That was much worse. She backed further away because she knew her resolve would fade if she was pushed much further. "Please, just go. And tell the others to keep away from us. If they don't, whatever wrath comes down on them will be of their own doing."

"Well then, I'll say the same to you." He turned halfway around and paused. "Goodbye Juli."

She gave no response, and he didn't wait for one.

Juli watched until he was a speck in the moonlight, crying all the while. Then, she returned to camp. Most everyone was asleep, and that was good because she didn't want any of them to see her swollen red eyes, or hear her hoarse voice. She spread out her bedroll and wept herself to sleep.

IN THE MORNING, the sounds of the others packing up camp woke Juli. She was surprised she'd fallen asleep at all and assumed it must have been sheer exhaustion. The events of the previous evening weighed her down like a boulder on her back, and she avoided everyone as much as possible while she gathered together her own belongings.

Less than an hour later, all of them, the humans and the zombies, were on the move. It was a long, boring day of walking through the desert, but she needed that. The monotony of the trek allowed her to *space out*, as her twins would have said (not really) and not think about anything other than putting one foot in front of the other and not tripping over a rock or stepping in a hole.

By the time they stopped for the day, Aben coming to her seemed almost like a dream or a delusion. At least that's what she told herself. So, when Grady handed her a bowl of cold soup and a plate of beans and canned fruit, she was able to look him in the face with no shame. Well, almost none.

"Everything went as planned?" he asked.

"It did." Juli thought maybe she'd find something in his face, maybe remorse or close to it. But Grady's expression remained blank and doll-like.

"That's good."

"I still don't know why we can't simply go around them."

"Because that's not what needs to happen."

His tone was flat and matter-of-factly, and that made Juli want to smack him. "Then tell me everything, Grady. You talk about these visions and this grand plan God has for us, but it's like you're reading me every other page in a book. How am I supposed to make sense of any of it?"

Grady cocked his head, and Juli thought maybe there was something, not emotion per se, but an acknowledgment in his eyes. "It's not supposed to make sense. That's the point."

Juli gave an exaggerated sigh. "More riddles."

"This is our trial, Juli. It hasn't been easy, and it's not going to get any easier. God is testing us to see if, through it all, we can keep hold of our faith."

"I'm tired of being tested. And I'm tired of people dying."

"Without death, there is no rebirth."

"You have an answer for everything, don't you?"

"Not me. God."

Juli couldn't do anything but stare. Every once in a great while, she wondered if Grady was putting this all on, but most of the time, like now, when she looked at him, she saw nothing but innocent unquestioning belief. She wished she could believe in this mission completely, that her faith could be as strong as his. Maybe that would make this burden easier to bear. But she doubted it.

CHAPTER FORTY-FIVE

While Aben and Mitch ventured northeast, Wim spent the days mixing chemicals with Mead, creating their homemade explosives and pouring them into five gallon pails. It was simple enough, a task that any monkey could have accomplished, but Aben had asked them to do the work and they obliged.

The worst part about the tedium was how it allowed Wim's mind to wander. He thought too much about the past. About everything and everyone he'd lost. This foreign landscape didn't help matters any either. Everywhere he looked was flat and rocky and tan. He missed the color green. There was no green out here aside from a random cactus, and that was hardly the same.

He knew that, back home in Pennsylvania—even though he'd been gone from there for almost five years, it would always be home—the leaves would be changing, bursting with reds and yellows and oranges. His fields would be turning golden. And the wind would be crisp and cool, not dry and dusty like this piece of Mexico that was his current dwelling.

He tried to stop thinking at all, to just focus on mixing the right amounts of powder, but that was as impossible as turning back time.

"I don't know how much of this crap Bundy had in the van, but I'm sure we're beating it by a shit ton." Mead had become a bit more like his old self, and Wim hoped, for the man's sake, that acceptance was pushing aside some of the pain. But he suspected it was more likely that recent events had just taken Mead's mind off his loss. Even still, it was nice to see Mead less wounded.

"He certainly liked his bombs," Wim said.

"They never worked out quite right, though, did they?"

The memory of Bundy blowing up the ambulance, and saving them, wasn't one Wim cared to recall, but it came back anyway. "No, they did not."

"It's a shame about Mina. She never liked me much, and I guess that was mutual, but I didn't expect her to end up this way."

"Me neither." Wim desperately wanted to destroy the zombified head of the woman he'd once known. To put it out of its misery, but that wasn't in his place. And Saw's people never let them get far out of view, even if he was bold enough to try it. Which he wasn't. "But then, I wouldn't have expected her to take up with a character like Saw either."

Mead finished off a mixture and reached for a new bucket. But before he got back to work, he stared at Wim for so long Wim found himself getting uncomfortable.

"You all right, Mead?"

Mead paused, still staring. "I didn't picture it this way, you know."

"What's that?"

"The apocalypse. I thought it would be all mano y zombo action, at least for the first several years. Until the majority of the zombies were destroyed. I didn't think it would turn so fast."

"Uh huh."

"And don't get me wrong, I always thought the biggest extent of the population sucked ass. I guess I just hoped something this terrible might pull people together. Instead, it pushed them further apart." Mead grabbed some fertilizer and aluminum powder and started mixing. "You think there's any chance that Grady fellow's right? That he's really got God on the speed dial?"

That surprised Wim. He'd never heard Mead talk much about God, but when he did, it was usually in a derisive or disbelieving manner. "No. I don't. Not at all."

"Do you even believe in God, Wim?"

Wim thought about his answer before saying it aloud, but even with time to think, it was hard to find the right words. "I was never a church-going man, even when my Mama tried to make me. I didn't care much for the people there. They were all right outside of church, good folks the lot of them, but put 'em in side that box and they took on airs. They'd judge what you were wearing or gossip about you if you came in late or if you drifted off to sleep during one of Pastor Warren's long sermons."

"Speaking from personal experience there?"

Wim grinned. "They'd laugh, in a mean way, if you couldn't pronounce the words right when you were picked to read a verse or two. Or if you couldn't name all the descendants of Moses forwards and back. It was like they viewed piety as a contest."

Wim fell silent for a bit. Long enough for Mead to prod him. "That's interesting and all, but you ducked my question."

"I thought you might not notice."

"I'm too sharp for that."

"Well then, far as God goes, I always assumed he was there. I prayed, maybe not every day, but I tried to thank him when the notion came to mind. I did believe, in my own way."

"That's past tense, though."

These were thoughts Wim had been wrestling with for months, maybe even years, but he'd never verbalized them and had never intended to. He thought about brushing Mead's version of twenty questions to the side but felt he owed him honesty. "I haven't seen any evidence of God down here for a good long while now."

"Does that mean you've lost faith?"

"No. Not entirely. Maybe he's just taking one of those, what do you call them, sabbaticals?"

Mead laughed. "I never thought about that. I wonder how much vacation time God gets."

Wim shrugged his shoulders. "Or maybe he's the one who's lost faith in us."

Mead's smile faded, and Wim felt bad for possibly putting a damper on the man's good mood. "But what do I know? I'm nothing but a below-average farmer."

"You're a lot more than that, Wim. A whole lot more."

Wim thought he felt his face get hot and turned away in case a blush was coming. "How about you answer your own question? Do you believe?"

"I believe in myself. The man upstairs? Well, I guess I'll find out when my time runs out."

"Let's hope that's not soon."

Mead's smile returned, along with a spark in his eyes. "Yeah. Let's."

Wim decided that hoping wasn't quite enough. Instead, he said a silent prayer to a God he was no longer sure existed.

CHAPTER FORTY-SIX

ABEN KNELT ON THE FLOOR AND SLICED OPEN THE BAG OF DOG chow. After sifting through it for a few seconds to ensure there weren't any bugs or worms, he was relieved to find it was critter free, as locating a fifty-pound bag had been hard scrabbling. He'd already filled up the bathtub with water, along with several buckets and pails of varying sizes. It seemed like he should do more, but he was out of ideas.

He looked over at Prince, who laid on the tile floor in Saw's kitchen, his head resting on his paws. When Prince caught him looking, his tail began to thud.

Aben smiled. "I've got you set up about as good as possible. It's up to you to pace yourself."

Prince's tail turned into a whip at the sound of the man's gruff voice.

"Yeah, I like you too." He reached over and scratched Prince's right ear, then his left. The dog rose to its feet and climbed onto him, his front paws on Aben's shoulders.

"You're the best thing that's happened for me in a good long while. Maybe even forever. That's why I'll do my damnedest to come back here for you."

Prince cocked his head. Aben doubted the dog could understand what he was saying, but he did a good job of faking it.

"I think the term 'good boy' is overused when it comes to dogs, but you're the real deal, Prince. And I love ya." Aben put his hand behind the dog's neck and pulled him in close, tilting his forehead into the dog's face, not even minding how his fur tickled. He felt a little weepy but knew giving in to that would mean he was more skeptical about this coming battle than he was ready to admit, so he pushed them away.

He stood, because he never liked long goodbyes, and headed to the door. Prince moved to follow, but Aben pointed. "Stay." His voice was firm, and the dog plopped its hindquarters onto the floor. He remained that way when Aben stepped out of the house and was still sitting when Aben closed the door and locked the dog inside. He half expected the dog might be sitting that exact same way when he got back. Then he realized the situation to be much more a case of *if* than *when*.

CHAPTER FORTY-SEVEN

AFTER ABEN AND MITCH RETURNED, THEY SHARED ALL THE information they'd gathered. Grady was heading to the Rio Grande to baptize the members of his flock who were still human. They estimated there were about four or five dozens of them.

Once that was finished, they'd head to Shard End to *save* everyone who lived here. After that, no one knew, and Wim supposed that it didn't really matter. Either they'd stop Grady's army before then, or they'd all be dead. And if the latter became reality, the ultimate plan was none of their concern.

Some time ago, one of the men in Shard End had arrived with a mule and another had found a scraggly malnourished stallion that made Gypsy look spry. Still, when it came to transportation, they were of the begging, not choosing, variety, and both animals were enlisted for the coming journey. Saw took the Mule and Mitch the old horse, which he quickly named Rip Van Winkle. Wim thought that an even worse name than Gypsy.

As they were the only five with animals to ride, Wim, Mead, Aben, Mitch, and Saw chose to take the lead while the other couple dozen men and women followed on foot. One thing they weren't short on were weapons. There were more than enough to go around multiple times over. As Wim looked upon them, he thought they looked like a medieval army, ready to take on the world even though the odds were heavily stacked against them.

It took a day and a half of riding before the river came into view beyond them. Wim was surprised at how wide it was, but the water looked calm and on the shallow side. More like a long lake than any river he'd seen before.

"That should be the spot," Aben said from the side. He pointed to how the land on the opposite side seemed to funnel into the waterway. "That's how Juli described it, and this is pretty much a straight shot from the route they were taking."

"You think there's much of a chance their plans changed?" Wim asked.

"No. From as much as I could gather, they might as well have been carved in stone. I don't expect any deviation."

Mitch pushed his old horse into the fray. "I still don't like going all in based on what she told us. She could have been lying."

"I'd be surprised if she was."

"I wouldn't. How about me and Saw ride ahead, like a scouting mission?"

Wim thought the boy seemed too eager to play soldier, but on the flip side, it might not be a bad idea. He saw Aben looking at him.

"What are your thoughts?" Aben asked.

"I think I'll go along with whatever you decide."

Aben scratched his beard absentmindedly. "Well, I don't fancy being in charge. Especially of this lot."

"Aw right then," Saw said. "If none of you want to make a decision, I will. Like Mitchy said, we'll ride out and see what that goose has got cooking. While we're gone, you set the bombs--"

"They're not really bombs," Aben said.

"They go boom don't they?"

"That's the plan."

"Then they're bombs. You put em on that side of the river." He pointed to the opposite shore. "Stagger em out and try to hide em a little. Don't need a big fookin sign announcing what the fook's up, now do we?"

No one responded.

"If my people get here before we return, you tell em to wait back that way." He pointed again behind them. "Keep em outta sight." Saw looked each man in the eyes. "Everyone good with that?"

"What makes you the strategical mastermind?" Mead asked.

"I took on the Ark, didn't I?"

Wim raised an eyebrow. "And ran once the going got tough."

Saw gave a wide, nauseating grin. "Maybe I did. But is there anything worthwhile left of it?"

Wim didn't answer. Saw was right about that much.

"That's what I thought. So, unless anyone's got a better plan, let's get on with it."

He kicked his mule into action, trotting down the hillside toward the river, and Mitch followed.

The three others watched as they reached the water and pushed their four-legged beasts into the gentle currents. It was two to three feet deep, and they had no trouble crossing then starting up the opposite side.

Wim, Aben, and Mead exchanged glances.

"He talks too much," Mead finally said.

Aben rolled his eyes. "Talk about the pot and kettle."

Wim smiled as he watched them. Despite it all, he thought he was tremendously lucky to be surrounded by men such as these. He only hoped, by some miracle, they could all come out of it alive.

CHAPTER FORTY-EIGHT

ABEN HAD PLACED EIGHT FIVE-GALLON BUCKETS OF EXPLOSIVES, camouflaging them with debris and rocks, anything he could find to make their presence less obvious. It was all going well until bucket number nine.

He used a knife to dig about a foot into the loose soil and placed the bucket inside. For cover, he spotted a wiry, dead piece of sagebrush. It was almost the perfect size to conceal the pail, so he reached underneath it and grabbed hold of the trunk.

That's when he was bit. Then bit again. And again.

He jerked his hand back, thinking he'd stuck his hand into a nest of ground wasps. Or maybe a passel of scorpions. But a moment later, he heard the rattle and knew he'd made a terrible mistake.

Rather than doing the smart thing and getting away, Aben's temper took over, and he yanked the bush out of the ground. That gave him a perfect view of the rattlesnake nest. There was a big one, probably three and a half feet, and he guessed it was the matriarch. Two small ones curled at her side. They were somewhere between olive green and tan in color with a series of dark, multicolored blotches running down their backs. As they neared the tails, the blotches gradually morphed into cross bands.

Aben thought they might be a kind of beautiful, but he also suspected they were Mohave rattlesnakes which, if his memory was correct, were just about the most deadly snakes in North America. He considered killing them, mostly out of spite, but he knew they were just doing what came naturally and that he was the stupid one, so he let them be.

He took the sagebrush with him as he left. Might as well get something out of this mess. He covered the bucket with the bush, then took a reluctant look at his hand. There were three sets of bite marks. One in the fatty bit between his thumb and forefinger, one on the back of his hand, and the third on the underside of his wrist. His hand already looked a smidge larger than it had before, and he suspected this would go relatively quick from here on out.

"Wim! I need to chat a minute."

Wim was fifty feet away, placing buckets further down the river. Aben saw his head turn and watched as he jogged to him. Aben took a seat on the ground and waited.

It took him only a few moments, but by the time he arrived, Aben was already sweating, and unless his mind was playing tricks on him, the swelling had progressed a couple inches further up his arm.

"What do you need, Aben?"

"More than you can give, actually. But what's most important is that you pay real close attention while I point out where I put the last nine buckets."

Confusion clouded Wim's face, and Aben had the feeling he was going to start asking questions. He needed to stop that. "Just keep quiet and listen."

He pointed out the various hiding places, then asked Wim to do the same. The man did so without error and that took some of Aben's stress away.

"That's good."

"All right. But can you tell me why?"

Aben didn't want to tell him but knew trying to keep it secret would be pointless soon. He held up his wounded paw. "I got snakebit. Rattle snakes."

Wim's eyes grew wide and traveled from Aben's hand to his face, then back again. "Oh, damn."

That was the closest Wim had come to cursing in all the time Aben had known him, and, despite his predicament, that made him smile.

"Yeah. Damn would be a good starting point."

"You're sure they were rattlers?"

"Most definitely." Aben patted the ground beside him. "Sit with me a spell, will you?"

"We need to get you back across the river. Maybe Mead will know what--"

"Wim, my dog listens better than you. Now, sit."

Wim did, sending up a puff of dust as he flopped down.

"Saw's going to take the lead, but you need to keep him in check, if such a thing's possible. If he sends everyone in there all helter skelter, it's going to be a bloodbath, and we don't have the numbers for that. You'll have a bit of an advantage having the higher ground. Use that. You might think it's cruel, but take them by surprise and be quick about it. You have to be merciless if you want to come out of this mess on top."

Wim didn't respond. The color was gone from his face, and Aben thought he might be heading toward shock.

"Wim, you got me?"

"We could cut it off."

"What?" Aben asked.

Wim's hand dropped to the handle of his machete. "Your arm. I don't know if it really works but they do it in the movies all the time."

Aben appreciated his concern, but he didn't want to waste time on nonsense. "I'm already down a hand and half a foot. I'm not a puzzle, Wim. I can't stand to lose any more pieces. Especially my arm. Hell, I wouldn't even be able to wipe my own ass."

"But you'd be alive."

"The way my heart's beating, the poison's all through me. Cutting my arm off won't do any good. It'll just make a hell of a mess."

Wim sighed, but Aben thought he was accepting the reality of the situation. "I just can't believe this."

Aben licked at his lips and realized he couldn't feel them. "Yep. This sucks."

"It sure does."

They sat there in silence for a little while. Aben thought he should come up with something profound to say but had little luck. "I didn't expect this," he settled on. "Back when Mead saved me, I thought that meant my life was to serve some sort of purpose. That I was to do some good. Not die here, of a goddamn snake bite, before the fighting even gets going. It seems so damned pointless."

Wim shook his head. "If we stand any chance of stopping Grady, that's all because of you. Your ideas. That's not pointless."

"Mead could have done just as much, if not more. And with all that shit he wears, the snakes wouldn't have gotten him. Jesus Christ, my whole life depended on a pair of gloves. If that isn't something?"

Wim didn't respond but that was okay. Aben doubted it deserved an answer.

"I think you should be getting on now," Aben said.

"I can stay. I don't mind. I can even get some of the others if you want."

Aben shook his head. "I don't require a goodbye party. I'd just as soon be alone. No offense."

"I understand." Wim stood, but before he left, he reached down to shake hands.

Aben returned the gesture, even though his palm was fat and clumsy. "Can you do me a favor? Two, actually?"

"Anything."

"Don't forget about my dog, okay? You can have him if you want, but if you don't, see that someone kind takes him."

"I'll make sure he's cared for."

"I appreciate that. He's a real good dog." Aben swallowed hard and changed the subject. "And can you leave me your revolver? Take the bullets except one. That's all I'll need."

Wim withdrew the gun from its holster and emptied the ammunition into his palm. Then he put one back into the cylinder and handed it over.

"Thank you."

Wim stared at him, and Aben thought he could see gears turning inside his head. Then he spoke. "You've been a good friend, Aben. And I haven't had many of those in my life. It's been nice knowing you."

That made Aben smile. For the last few decades, he'd cherished his solitude and wore his outsider status like a medal. He'd forgotten that life could be any different but was glad it could be, even if only for a little while. "I'll say the same about you. I'm pleased we met and wish it could've lasted a spell longer." Aben tilted his head toward the river. "You get on now. Tell Mead I said goodbye. Saw and Mitch too, although I won't miss them quite as much."

"I will."

Wim left him, and Aben was relieved. His face felt like an invisible force had swallowed it up, and he could feel his heart pounding rapid fire in his chest. He suspected all this could go on for hours, but he didn't care to wait that long. All he wanted was to let Wim get out of sight.

CHAPTER FORTY-NINE

WIM FLINCHED WHEN THE GUN WENT OFF, BUT HE DIDN'T LOOK back. There wasn't any point in exploring the aftermath. As he crested the embankment, he found Mead running toward him.

"Did you shoot?" Mead asked.

Wim explained as best he could. Mead took it hard, but Wim also picked up on a sense of resignation that he could relate to. None of them expected this to end well. They'd known from when they first saw Grady's flock and, if anything, the odds had just gotten worse. There wasn't anything they could do now but wait.

It was almost two full days until the waiting was finally over.

Wim scratched at the dirt with a stick, drawing random shapes then erasing them with his foot and starting over. The anticipation, if you could call it that, was wearing on him. He wanted to get on with it already, good or bad.

He got his wish when Mitch and his old stallion galloped into the makeshift camp, kicking up a storm of dust in the process.

"They're coming! I'd say less than a mile out."

Any sense of calm disappeared with those nine words.

CHAPTER FIFTY

THERE WERE TWO FACTIONS TO GRADY'S FLOCK. THE FIRST group, comprised of a few dozen men and women who remained human, had the lead while the zombies, which numbered over one thousand, took up the rear. Grady held court in the middle.

"Friends, for some of you, this journey has taken years. For others, months. But I know, it has been a challenge for all. Thank you, for believing and trusting. For never losing faith."

He looked to Juli. Of all his flock, she was the one who seemed to suffer the most from doubt and worry, but today, even she appeared content.

"Ahead lies the river and the waters in which we will be reborn. Reborn without sin, without worry, without pain. So now, come with me." He said those words to the humans. To the zombies, he held his hand in a 'halt' motion. "Wait, children. Your time will come soon."

Over the previous months, there hadn't been the slightest deviation from what Grady was shown in his visions, and he had no doubt that the events to come would be no different. Fear was a foreign emotion to him now because he knew God's plan was coming to fruition. Soon, he would be reunited with Josiah. Soon, he would be with God. Soon, he would be home.

CHAPTER FIFTY-ONE

IT WAS ONLY FOUR OF THEM WHO LAID AT THE TOP OF THE HILL and watched Grady's people flow into the river. Wim took it in through the scope of his rifle while Saw, Mead, and Mitch viewed through binoculars or, in Mitch's case, nothing but his young eyes.

Soon, all the men and women were in the water, submerged to their waists. Grady stood at the opposite shoreline, and they all faced him. Which meant they faced away from Wim and the others.

"I say we start," Saw said. "Pick 'em off like the sitting ducks they are."

Mitch was quick to agree, but Wim's general curiosity preferred a slower approach. "Not just yet. Let's see what's up first."

"Aw, you're wasting time," Saw climbed to his feet and stomped away. Mitch followed, to the surprise of no one.

Wim watched them return to the Shard End group, which was about twenty yards further back and completely out of view from the river. "Don't you go starting anything just yet."

"Yeah, yeah," Saw said. "We ain't waiting around all day, though."

"I had no plans to." Wim turned back to the river where Grady had entered the water.

The day was calm, with not even the slightest breeze, and Wim could hear his words.

"As Peter said in the second book of Acts, 'Repent and be baptized, every one of you, in the name of Jesus Christ for the forgiveness of your sins. And you will receive the gift of the Holy Spirit."

Grady dipped his hands into the water and scooped up handfuls, tossing it over them as he moved down the line. "I baptize you in the name of the Father and of the Son and of the Holy Spirit. God's promise is for you and your children and for all who are far off—for all whom the Lord our God will call."

This went on for several minutes as the little man gave all his followers a good drenching. Too long.

The sound of dozens of footsteps on the dry ground gave Wim plenty of warning that his pleas for patience had run their course. He didn't expect to be listened to, not when he was a stranger and Saw was the blowhard who'd been leading them for years.

He pointed past the river where the undead army formed a black oasis against the sand and stone. "Let them get closer, so they're by the explosives."

Saw shook his head. "No, Wim. Those folks down in the water ain't got no weapons as far as I can see. We wait, they might go back the other way and load up with guns, and then we'll be fooked. We need to get em now and get em fast."

"I believe that's a mistake."

"Believe what you want." Saw turned to his people. "Are you all ready for this?"

Wim was surprised this lot had the sense not to respond with a thunderous roar of approval, giving away their location. Instead, they nodded and muttered affirmatives.

"Good. Now there's no sense wasting bullets on a bunch of unarmed, church-going ninnies. Save your ammunition for the zombies and let's do this the old-fashioned way!"

Saw raised a machete. Mitch carried Aben's war club. Others in the group had axes and knives, hammers and spears. Wim didn't know exactly how this was all going down, but he knew it would be bloody.

"Let's do it!"

The few dozen men and women poured past Wim and Mead and down the embankment, toward the river. And what followed was a massacre.

When Grady's people realized the type of hell coming their way, they tried to run, but Saw's army only gained momentum as they sprinted down the hillside and splashed into the water. His people were brutal, bloodthirsty, and merciless. They chopped off limbs. They cut throats.

"Holy fucknuggets," Mead said. "These fuckers are animals."

Wim saw a man with one eye use a spear to stab an elderly woman through the face. She fell into the river, and the man ripped his weapon free, bringing half her head along with it.

Saw chased Owen, the man who had helped betray Brimley and who now ran for the shore, taking big, galloping steps through the water. Just as he got a foot on dry land, Saw swung the blade and chopped off his leg below the knee. Owen tumbled backward into the water, where Saw caught him and stabbed the machete through the underside of his jaw, ramming the blade into his skull. Then, Saw dropped the lifeless body into the current.

Mitch smashed in the skull of an elderly man off whose bald pate the sunlight had been reflecting a second earlier. And as soon as that was done, Mitch found a young woman trying to flee and slammed the club into her face, shattering all the bones.

Wim had to look away. All the zombie-created carnage he'd seen the last few years paled compared to the bloodbath that was happening in the river. Even when he wasn't watching, their screams, coupled with the sounds of death and dying and hopelessness filled the air, and it all sickened him.

He wanted to leave, to head back to Gypsy and ride off and let these human monsters finish the fight on their own, but he couldn't bring himself to go. He was the one who knew where all the pails of explosives were hidden, and it was his job to shoot them and set off the bombs. Because even if Saw and his people could slaughter a few dozen defenseless zealots, they stood no chance against the real fight that was inevitable. The battle against the undead.

"Wim," Mead said. "I know you don't want to see this. Neither do I really, but check out the pastor."

When Wim looked down, he saw the river running red. The blood of the death staining the rocks and shore, the water so full of dead bodies that it looked on the verge of overflowing.

"Over there," Mead said, pointing. Wim followed his gaze and saw Grady not only alive but hurrying from his people as they died horribly in the waters of the Rio Grande. "That chickenshit's running away. I'll be motherfucked."

Juli was with him. If there hadn't been any context, Wim thought they might have looked like two lovers, out for a midday jog. But he knew better.

"He's not running away," Wim said. "He's going to the zombies."

They watched as Grady and Juli crossed the divide between the river and where the zombies waited. Wim lifted his rifle and peered through the scope to get a better look. He couldn't hear Grady's words from such a distance, but he saw the man's mouth moving, his arms gesticulating.

Then, Grady turned back to the river and walked. Juli kept pace at his side. And the zombies followed.

"Oh, shit," Mead said.

Wim thought that about summed it up.

MOST OF GRADY's followers were dead in the water, with only a few stragglers still fighting for their lives. Saw had hold of one of them, a man in his early twenties, who was taller and fitter, but Saw had him overmatched in meanness. He punched the man in the jaw and heard a loud crunch as it broke. He held his arms in front of his face protectively.

"Please, don't!" his words came out garbled through his injured maw, but Saw wasn't in the mood for mercy.

Saw grabbed hold of the young man's hair, then used a machete to scalp him, tearing away his curly brown locks along with the flesh underneath them. As the man's body sunk into the water, Saw waved his trophy in the air like a triumphant warrior.

"Saw!"

He heard his name but didn't know where the sound had come from. He looked around, mostly finding the dead or dying. Who's calling me name, he thought.

"Saw! Get your people up here!"

The 'up here' tipped him off to look at the hill, where he found Wim waving frantically. "Why?"

Wim didn't respond verbally. He only pointed. Saw followed the gesture and discovered the zombies pouring into the earthen funnel. That made him smile. This was the fight he'd been waiting for since the very beginning.

He turned to look up at Wim. "You start taking out the buckets. We'll finish off the ones that get through!"

"No! Come up here and fight!"

Saw wasn't in the mood to argue. He was too full of adrenaline and bloodlust. He waved the dumb farmer away. He could fight like a coward if he chose. Saw was going to war like a man, and so were all his people.

He cupped his hands around his mouth. "Listen up you bastards!" his voice boomed above the din of death and dying. "We're getting some company, and if any of you run, I'll kill you me self."

They all stared at him and not one dared disobey his orders. He was their leader, their King, and he knew they would be loyal to him until the end.

"Those religious puffs were just the warm up act. This is the main event. Now, take a deep breath and get ready to kill yourselves some zombies!"

Saw spotted Mitch nearby and went to him. "You ready for this, Mitchy?"

Mitch nodded. "I am."

"Right now, you think about every bit of hate you got inside yourself. Think about every person who ever let you down or disrespected you. Think about every rotten moment in your life. Do it for me now."

Mitch stayed silent, eyes narrowed, his breath quickening.

Saw grabbed a handful of Mitch's hair and pulled him in close, pressing their foreheads together. When Saw spoke, his spittle splashed against Mitch's face, but the boy didn't pull away. "That's my boy, Mitchy. Now harness that hate, every bit of it, and use it to fight. Because we can do this. I don't care if we're outnumbered thirty to one. Hells bells, it could be a hundred to one, and we can still win this. You believe that, don't you?"

"I do."

"Good on ya, son. Are you ready?"

"I am."

"So am I."

Saw released him and looked again to the others. "Let's end these fookers once and for all!"

The men and women roared.

CHAPTER FIFTY-TWO

"They're so fucking insane," Mead said.

All Wim could do was nod. As he looked onto the zombies, he was again reminded of the rats. It had taken only two blasts from his Pa's old shotgun to finish them off. This lot would be much harder. Maybe impossible. He felt like it all depended on him, and that wasn't a role he was comfortable playing.

He had his rifle shouldered and had slowed his breaths, so they came in shallow and steady. The sights on the scope were lined up with the bucket Aben had been hiding when the snakes got him. He could see specks of white through the cover of the sage brush, and it was now just waiting for the zombies to get close enough to maximize the damage.

They were five yards away. Then three. Then just a couple feet. Wim licked his lips, squinted, and squeezed the trigger.

The bucket full of fertilizer and aluminum powder disappeared in a cloud of smoke. Rocks, dirt, and debris sliced through the air. Mixed among the natural elements were bits and pieces of zombies. Most were too small to identify, just random hunks of flesh, but there were a few larger chunks that caught his eye. Part of a head. A lower leg. A lone hand. All of it blew up into the air and then rained down.

"Holy fucking shit!" Mead screamed, and out of the corner of his eye, Wim could see the man bouncing up and down. "That's better than anything! That's better than the Gatling gun! You just wasted a couple dozen of those motherfuckers!"

"It's a start," Wim said and sought out the next bucket.

He fired again with similar results. A third shot and a third bucket was even more dramatic, and he saw a zombie's head fly fifty feet into the air before rocketing back down to the ground.

The area was filling with dusty smoke, making it harder to find the other hiding places. It took him half a minute to lock in on the fourth, but he got a bull's eye, and it blew with spectacular results.

So far, Wim was pleased, and there were another ten buckets to go, but when he looked at the overall picture, he saw that blowing up the zombies had created an unintended consequence. The ties that bound the monsters together were now mostly obliterated. The zombies were now free to move on their own and, as individuals, their pace quickened.

It's not gonna work, Wim thought. There were simply too many of them. It seemed like the first four bombs had killed so many, but hundreds still remained, and they were coming.

They were hungry.

He shot the fifth bucket.

CHAPTER FIFTY-THREE

MITCH HAD TUCKED THE HANDLE OF ABEN'S WAR CLUB INTO HIS jeans, instead using his hands to hold a semiautomatic rifle. The zombies were pouring in, a dozen every few seconds. Most of the men and women from Shard End were shooting, but their aim was poor. Many shots missed entirely, and the ones that hit landed in chests, arms, torsos. The zombies kept coming.

Mitch's aim wasn't much better. He'd never shot a gun in his life before the plague and didn't spend much time on learning afterward. He was barely adequate and fired four times before he dropped the first zombie with a headshot.

He felt like his own head was wrapped in cotton. The unending gunfire had his ears ringing, muffling all sound and the smoke from the explosions, and shooting put a blue haze over everything and everyone. He saw motion to his right and spun in that direction, firing on instinct. The bullet ripped through one-eyed Diesel's throat and a spurt of blood, like water from an underground spring, jutted out.

Shocked at the misfire, Mitch lowered the rifle and took a step toward the dying man. Before he reached him, two zombies pounced on him from the rear. Mitch plunged into the water as he fell. He sucked in a mouthful of the blood-tinged water, fighting to free himself, but he was getting attacked from all sides and couldn't escape.

Then, he heard a light pop. A zombie fell into the water, blood streaming out of a hole in its face as it floated by him. Another pop and he felt the hands on him release.

Mitch burst to the surface, coughing and choking, puking up mouthfuls of the foul water and trying to get his breath. He heard two more shots and saw zombies in his peripheral vision fall. He turned and found Saw beside him, a pistol with smoke spilling from the barrel in his hand.

"Close one, eh, Mitchy?"

An explosion rang out, and they both looked to see another burst of smoke and bodies on the hillside. That was followed by yet another just seconds later. All around him, there was splashing in the water as body parts rained down. An upper arm landed just inches away. A falling ear smacked Saw in the face.

Mitch spun around, trying to gauge the situation. The zombies on the hill were almost gone, either blown to pieces or having escaped into the river. The creatures in the water were winning. He guessed there were less than twenty men and women left alive, and that number was falling fast. Meanwhile, there were more than a hundred zombies.

Saw ran through the waist-deep water, directly at the closest zombie. He shoved the pistol in its face and pulled the trigger. The back of its head blew off, and it dropped into the river. He moved on to the next and did the same.

Mitch thought that seemed like a splendid idea, especially since he couldn't shoot worth shit. He copied Saw's actions, killing three zombies in less than a minute.

He was on his way to a fourth when he saw an undead young boy coming in at Saw's back. He was too far away to reach them and didn't dare trying to shoot.

"Saw!" he screamed, trying to be heard over the cacophony of fighting and dying. Saw didn't react. He was too busy grappling with an extremely tall zombie who had over a foot on him in height.

"Saw!" Mitch tried again.

Saw managed to shove his pistol under the chin of the tall zombie. He shot, blowing its brains out the top of its head. Then he turned back to Mitch. "What you holler--"

The dead boy pushed its face into Saw's side. His shirt had been pulled askew in the struggle, and his love handle was exposed. It made the perfect spot to bite, and that's exactly what the boy did. His tiny teeth sunk into Saw's skin, and when his face came away, a mouthful of flesh came with it.

Mitch opened his mouth to scream but couldn't make a sound.

"Why you little bastard?" Saw said. He looked at the boy's face, a thin surgical scar stretched from his upper lip to his nose. He pointed the gun at the boy's face and pulled the trigger, only to discover his gun was empty. "Bollocks!"

Saw wouldn't be deterred that easily and used the butt end of the pistol to beat the dead boy's face into a mangled pulp, something unrecognizable as human.

Mitch got there just as the motionless corpse fell into the water.

"Little bugger got me, Mitchy."

Mitch reached for the wound. Blood seeped from it, running down Saw's side and into the river. He covered it with his hand, not even sure why. It wasn't the blood loss that was going to kill the man he so admired. It was the virus or bacteria or whatever it was that transferred the disease.

Saw grabbed him by the wrist and pulled his hand away. "Chin up, boy. I had a good run of it."

"But--"

"No buts. Let's finish this shite."

Saw turned away from him and returned to fighting. Mitch didn't see the point. He stood in the water, chaos reigning all around him, and wished it was all over.

CHAPTER FIFTY-FOUR

"I think Saw just got bit," Wim said. He only saw the tail end of it through the scope, but he saw the small bleeding oval wound and couldn't imagine anything else.

"Goddamn. I thought that fucker was too mean to die."

The zombies were gaining momentum and fast. Wim counted only nine people alive. Even if he had missed a few of them, there were several dozen of the undead. Many of the zombies had continued past the people and were climbing out of the river, onto the other side of the banks.

Wim turned to Mead. "Grab a couple of those extra buckets."

Mead did without question. While he was gone, Wim used the rifle to kill five zombies, their bodies dropping into the river and floating away in the current.

When Mead returned, waddling back and forth with two buckets in each hand, Wim set the rifle aside and grabbed two from him. "Roll them down the hill."

They did, the buckets gaining speed as they careened down the embankment. One hit a large rock and the pop topped free, making its contents useless, a second ended up in the river, bobbing along and drifting out of range, but the other two came to rest before the waters.

Several zombies were within the blast range of one of the pails. Wim waited until they were closer, counting to pass the time. There were eighteen of them, or was it seventeen, or nineteen? He counted three times but got different results with every effort and gave up, deciding to shoot instead.

The bullet hit the bucket dead on, and it blew. The roar was much louder on that side of the river, and Wim felt his ears ring. A *woosh* of air rushed past him, and there was so much dust and smoke that he couldn't see anything for a full thirty seconds. When it finally settled, he saw a hole in the ground and scattered bits of zombies.

The second bucket was further away from the undead and Wim saw little sense in using it just yet. He returned to using his rifle to shoot zombies, getting kills with most shots, but it wasn't long before he realized his ammo was running low. He checked, then looked to Mead.

"I'm down to two shots."

Mead had no gun, and, until this point, had been taking it all in from afar. But Wim knew the man was no coward, and when he heard this news, he was on his feet. "We're going down, then?"

Wim nodded. "I am. Whether or not you do is your call. No judgement from me either way."

Mead pulled on his helmet. "I just wanted to be fashionably late."

Wim was surprised he wasn't more scared. It wasn't that he thought he was impervious, or incapable of dying. In fact, as they started down the embankment, he thought that the most likely result. But he was tired. He was ready for this to end one way or another.

CHAPTER FIFTY-FIVE

MITCH WAS STILL IN A FOG WHEN HE FOUND JULI AT THE FAR end of the river. She sat on the shore, staring down at the water like she'd never seen anything wet before. And like there weren't hundreds of people and zombies dying all around her.

He splashed through the current, skirting the violence around him. When he reached her, his shadow fell over her body, and that finally drew her attention up.

"Mitch," she said, stating the obvious. Like they were meeting at the mall on a Sunday afternoon and not in the middle of a war.

"You could have stopped this," he said to her.

She shook her head slowly. "No. That was impossible. All of this was predestined."

"Fuck that bullshit!" She flinched at his tone.

An explosion down the river rocked the ground. Mitch didn't bother to look. The longer he stared at this woman, the woman who had helped Grady take his craziness to whole new levels, the more he hated her. "Aren't you even a little ashamed of what you played a part in?"

He stepped aside so she could see the carnage around her, but she either didn't look or didn't care, and her expression remained blank.

"Saw's gonna die. Aben's dead. All because of you."

He thought he saw some comprehension through her fog, but that might have been wishful thinking.

"Aben died?" she asked. "How?"

"Does it matter?"

"I guess not."

Juli looked at him, her eyes squinting in the bright midday sun. "I don't expect you to understand belief, Mitch. Not with your rich parents and spoiled upbringing. Did you ever have a trying incident in your life before this? Something worse than having your allowance withheld for a week?"

Mitch wanted to slap her face but held back.

"When everything is handed to you on a gold plate, you don't need to believe in anything. But some of us, we experienced life. We know it isn't all Bentley's and Rolex's. We need to know there's someone above us to get us through the hard times. But you wouldn't know that."

"You're just trying to make yourself feel better. At least, I cop to my actions. I don't blame all this shit on some made-up man in the sky to avoid responsibility."

"You know, Mitch, when I first met you, I thought you might be able to replace my son. Not really, of course, but in a way. Give me a second chance at being a mother. Boy, was I mistaken. You were an entitled asshole then, and you're a mean-spirited son of a bitch now. Nothing at all like my son. " She smiled a little. "See, I *can* admit when I'm wrong."

"Can I ask you something?" Mitch twirled his fingers around the handle of the war club.

"You don't need my permission."

Mitch slammed the metal end of the club into her mouth. Her bottom lip was torn in half, two ragged flaps of skin that sagged almost down to her chin. Most of her nicotine-stained teeth shattered and went flying through the air, accompanied by a spray of red saliva. Blood seeped from her gums and drained onto the ground.

She turned her face up to him. He loved the pained look in her eyes, the destruction that marred the bottom half of her face. He knew she deserved that and so much more. He'd make this last days if he had the time, but he'd caught sight of a half dozen zombies coming up behind him. His gun was out of bullets, and his only option was to run.

The younger Mitch, the spoiled son of Senator SOB (Juli wasn't far off the mark on that), would have ran. He would have done anything to save his own ass. But time had changed him. He didn't care about getting away any more. All he cared about was teaching this bitch a lesson.

"Do you still believe in God?" Mitch asked.

Juli spit out a mouthful of blood, and a few more chunks of teeth came with it. "Yes," she said.

Mitch reared back with the club. "I don't."

He swung again. Her skull went to pieces as the zombies grabbed him from behind and dragged him down. He could feel their teeth ripping into him, chunks of flesh being excised from his body.

One got a hold of his ear and took it off in a single chomp. Another bit into his neck, and Mitch could feel his hot blood coursing down his body. As far as ends went, he thought that was about as good as it got.

CHAPTER FIFTY-SIX

MEAD DIDN'T LIKE THE NUMBERS, BUT HE WAS CLAD FROM HEAD to toe in denim and armor and thought he'd be able to make it through all but the worst of attacks. The key, he believed, was not letting the motherfuckers surround him.

Using his conduit spear, he was able to kill the zombies from a distance. Over and over again, he jabbed the ends into their eyes and mouths and ears, destroying their brains with relative ease.

He'd put down all the ones in his immediate vicinity and looked around to see who else, if anyone, was still standing. He first saw Juli dead on the ground, and Mitch beside her as zombies gnawed away at him. Then, he found Saw in the river, fighting with his blades and destroying anything in his path.

Further down, Wim used a machete to chop off the head of one zombie, then the upraised arm of another. He finished the maimed one off a moment later.

There have to be more of us, Mead thought, but as he surveyed the area again, he couldn't find any survivors on their feet. Only him, Wim, and Saw. The only good thing about that was that there were less than twenty zombies up and moving. The majority of them had grouped together in the center of the river, with only a couple stragglers in Wim's and Saw's vicinities.

Mead thought, with more than a little surprise, they were going to win this after all. When Wim killed the two zombies remaining near him, and Saw dropped the four closest his position, all that remained was that huddled mass. And Mead had the perfect idea how to finish them.

He splashed through the water until he reached the last bucket, picking it up, and holding it above him to keep it dry.

"Wim!" he called out. "You still have any bullets?"

Wim looked to him. "Two."

"Well, that's one more than we need."

The men came together in the river, and Mead held up the bucket. It was heavy, and his arms were getting tired. "These buckets are waterproof, right?"

Wim shrugged his shoulders. "I reckon it'll stay dry for as long as we need."

"Good. Then I'll chuck it over, and you plunk it?"

Wim nodded, but Saw reached out with his hand. "Give it to me, lads."

"You want to throw it?" Mead asked. He was looking forward to that part, but he also realized Saw was stronger and probably had better aim.

The excitement and jubilation he felt faded when Saw turned sideways and lifted his shirt.

"I'm fooked," he said. "One of the little ones got me too. Never did much like kids. Maybe that was me penance."

Mead handed him the bucket. "You don't have to..."

"I know it. I want to." Saw looked at Wim. "Always did want to go out with a bang. Figure you can take care of that part, big boy."

"If that's what you want."

"Want's a little strong, but it'll do." Saw took a few steps away from them. A few steps closer to the zombies. "Let me ask you, though, if you head back to Shard End, do me a favor and tell Mina I really did love her."

"Tell that to her head, you mean?" Mead asked with a raised eyebrow.

"Sure. That'll do. Daft old cow, she was. Don't think she ever realized how much I cared."

Mead doubted a man who could put his lover's head on a spike was capable of genuine love, but then again, the world had gone hard, and traditional niceties had changed. "Okay then, we will."

"Thanks, for that." Saw moved another two yards closer to the zombies, but slower now. Like he wasn't quite ready for it all to end. "That was some hella good fighting today. One of you oughta write it down case there's a future after this. Hells bells, this was better than the Alamo. All of those fookers died, didn't they?"

"I believe so," Mead said.

"Aw, good then. We bested 'em in triplicate. Just be sure and get it right, though. My name's Solomon Baldwin, but all me friends called me Saw."

Saw was just a few feet from the zombies, and they now moved toward him, closing the distance quickly.

"It was good knowing you, boys!" he called out, then clutched the bucket against his chest, embracing it.

Mead and Wim rushed to the side of the river, getting as far as possible from the blast radius, but as soon as the zombies were on Saw, they stopped.

Wim raised the rifle, aimed, and pulled the trigger.

Saw went boom, and so did the last of Grady's zombie army.

CHAPTER FIFTY-SEVEN

WIM WAS SO EXHAUSTED HE BARELY MADE IT BACK UP THE embankment. They'd checked all the bodies, making sure no one who should have been alive wasn't somehow still clinging to life and ensuring that everything that should have been dead was. That took over an hour, slopping back and forth through the river, and it had sapped him of all his energy.

The day's events replayed over and over again through his mind, like a TV station stuck on the same program. In many ways, it was worse than his most dire predictions, but in others, he still couldn't believe they'd emerged victorious, even if it was just the two of them. Stopping Grady's mad march was worth all the death. At least, that's what he kept telling himself.

They were heading to the camp, where their supplies and animals had been left before the fighting, still a hundred feet away, when Wim saw movement.

He stopped in his tracks so abruptly that Mead almost plowed him over from behind.

"What the hell?"

"Someone's there."

Mead moved to his side and followed his gaze. He saw it too. Someone sat on the ground, rocking back and forth in a way that made Wim think of the way of monks doing chants.

He raised his rifle and peered through the scope to get a better look, but Mead had already taken out binoculars and beat him to it. "Fuck me sideways!" Mead said.

Grady O'Baker sat at their camp, swaying like tall grass in the breeze. He was unarmed and appeared uninjured.

"Just shoot the fucker," Mead said.

Wim thought the idea wasn't half bad, but first he wanted to talk to the man whose actions had brought them to this point.

They continued, and when they were close enough, Wim could hear Grady saying something. Repeating it over and over again. A little further and he realized the man wasn't speaking. He was singing.

"I see a Crimson stream of blood. It flows from Calvary. Its waves reach the throne of God, sweeping over me. Today no condemnation, abides to turn away. My soul from His Salvation. He's in my heart to—"

Their coming footsteps interrupted the hymn, and Grady looked their way.

"Is everyone dead?"

Wim nodded. "All except us."

Grady rose to his feet, his face peaceful or blank, Wim couldn't tell which. "As it was prophesized and shown to me."

"You fucknugget!" Mead shouted. "You're happy about this? About everyone dying?"

Wim held up his hand for silence, and Mead reluctantly relented.

"I need a minute. Do you got this?"

Wim nodded again, and Mead grabbed the reigns for the donkey and led it away, leaving just the two of them.

"You're Wim, aren't you?"

"I am."

"A farmer. A good man. Throughout these trials, you've saved many people."

"Not nearly enough."

"There's never enough, are there?"

Wim wasn't sure what the little man expected, but his very presence unnerved him. "You ran while your people died?"

Grady took a step toward him. "They didn't die. Their bodies may have, but today, their sins were washed away, and their spirits, their souls, have been called home."

The man moved closer to him, and Wim took an instinctive step back. He dwarfed the short slight supposed preacher, but he didn't trust anything about this situation.

"And now it's your turn," Grady said.

Wim's hand tightened around the stock of his rifle. "You want to kill me now? Kill me to save me?"

Grady tilted his head. Something close to a smile crossed his mouth. "Oh no. No, Wim. Not that at all."

"Then what are you going on about my 'turn'?"

"It's your turn to send me home." Grady held his arms out at his side as if he were strung up on an imaginary cross. "Now, you must kill me, Wim."

Wim let go of the rifle. All of this was crazy, but this was the cherry on the sundae. "I'm not gonna kill you."

"You are. Just as God showed me."

Wim turned away from him, leaving him and going to Gypsy, who grazed on the dry grass, uninterested in the goings on.

He heard Grady's footsteps behind him. He was running. "Stop, Wim! Stop right now!"

Wim didn't stop. A moment later, Grady was on his heels. The little man grabbed his shirt, trying to pull him away from the horse, but with no success.

"It was in the vision!"

Wim spun around, raising his elbow and catching Grady in the face. The man fell to the ground, a small trickle of blood seeping from his left nostril. "Keep away from me," Wim said.

Grady climbed to his knees and started to his feet when Wim raised his hand, which was balled into a fist.

"I mean it now. Keep away or I'll knock you silly."

Grady sagged back, his face full of panic, fear. "You have to kill me!"

"I don't got to do anything for you."

"Not for me, Wim. For God! This is his plan. It was all his plan. I was doing what he commanded of me. Now you have to do the same." Grady clasped his hands together, pleading.

Wim had never been so disgusted in another human being. "If God wants you dead, then let him do it himself."

Without another word, Wim hopped on Gypsy and gave her reigns a curt shake. He didn't care about taking any of the other provisions. He wanted away from Grady. Away from it all.

As he rode off, he could hear the man screaming, wailing. And Wim didn't feel the slightest bit guilty.

CHAPTER FIFTY-EIGHT

WIM RODE BACK TO SHARD END WITH MEAD. HE TOLD THE man about Aben's dog, and, when they reached town, Mead raced to Saw's house and thrust open the door. Wim thought he looked about as excited as a kid on Christmas morning. The dog ran straight past him, looking for his owner, and seemed disappointed when he was nowhere to be found. It took a couple of days, but Prince eventually seemed to realize that his old buddy wasn't coming back, and he accepted Mead as a suitable replacement. Wim enjoyed seeing how much the man cared about the dog. He thought they both deserved someone to love them.

It seemed like the smart thing would have been to stay in Shard End with Mead, at least for the winter, but Wim couldn't bear to spend another week in the West, let alone a season. Mead helped him fill a wagon with food and assorted tools, and a couple days later, they said their goodbyes. Wim knew he'd miss the man who had initially seemed to be such an odd duck but turned out to be one of the best men he'd ever known. And maybe the best friend he'd ever had. But home—his real home —in Pennsylvania, was calling. It wasn't God's voice, it was the sounds of his past. And even if nothing but memories remained, Wim needed to be with them.

CHAPTER FIFTY-NINE

THE JOURNEY FROM WEST TEXAS BACK TO PENNSYLVANIA WAS arduous, at times torturous, and constantly a pain in his rear end. He hit winter weather around the time he got to Oklahoma, and a blizzard in Missouri forced him to hole up in a stable for almost ten days.

He avoided the cities, and the few times he came close enough to them to get a good look, he saw they were overrun with zombies. The small towns weren't as bad. Most of the time, he was able to slip by them unnoticed. If they did catch on, a little extra prod made Gypsy trot faster, and he moved on with little ado.

On the entire trip, he was only forced to kill a few dozen zombies, and that was spread out over five months. That was still more than enough, though. He'd lost his desire to end them. Now, he just wanted to avoid them.

There were no adventures to be had—it was just mile after mile after mile of riding. One day bled into the next into the next. On many a day, he thought he'd lose his mind from the boredom. And truth be told, he thought maybe he'd lost it already. Why else would he subject himself, and this old horse, to such pointlessness?

But once winter passed and he began to see some of his beloved color green back in the world, his attitude and his optimism took a decidedly good turn for the better. When he crossed the Ohio/Pennsylvania border, the spring rains couldn't dampen his spirit. He thought that even Gypsy seemed more at home here, then realized that was only his mind playing tricks on him because he'd found the horse in North Carolina, and the odds that she'd ever been in Pennsylvania were about as likely as it was that he'd wake up and discover this had all been a wild dream.

He was two days out from his old farm, and they felt like the longest days of the entire journey. He tried to steel himself for something bad, like maybe a wildfire had gone through and razed his simple abode. Or that zombies had overrun the whole place and he'd be forced to go elsewhere. He told himself he could accept either, so long as he could have an hour or two to sit by his Mama's grave and tell her everything that had happened. Tell her everything her boy, who had never before been more than fifty miles away from home in all his life, had been through. Even though she wouldn't be able to respond, he wanted her to know.

Wim was so excited that he cut loose the wagon ten miles from home, abandoning the paved roads which were winding and roundabout, to instead ride Gypsy across the fields and pastures of his neighbors. That 'as the crow flies' tactic shaved an hour off the trip, and soon, he crested the little hill where his entire family was buried.

He climbed down from Gypsy, who appreciated the break, and walked the rest of the way to the family plot. He was relieved to see nothing had happened to their tombstones, although what exactly he'd been worried about, he did not know. They looked the same as when he'd left, unmarred in any way.

"I'm home, Mama." He dropped to his knees in front of her headstone, laying his arms on top of it and kissing the cold granite. I'm finally home."

He saw purple and yellow crocus flowers blooming in front of the stone and was so happy he almost lost his composure and broke down in tears. These were new, and he supposed a chipmunk or squirrel must have dragged some bulbs in from somewhere and left them lay there long enough to take root. They were a welcome addition.

The entire afternoon passed, and Wim didn't move from that spot. He told Mama just about everything that had happened but sugar-coated a few of the more disturbing parts. He told her about the friends he'd loved and lost. About the places he'd been to and seen. By the time he was finished, he was so hoarse that he couldn't get out any more words, and that was when he decided to see what condition the house and barn were in, if they were still standing at all.

He took his time walking to them, his stomach in knots over worry about what he might find. He told himself that, if they were fallen in or gone, he'd find a way to rebuild them. He was never much of a handy man, but he didn't need anything fancy. Just a couple rooms and a shed or barn big enough to keep a few animals. He was a simple man with simple needs.

To his relief, the farmhouse and barn both stood tall. Some of the siding had blown off the house, and the barn was missing some shingles, but those would be easy fixes. He didn't realize how much he'd missed all of this until he saw it.

As he passed by the barn, he heard the all too familiar sound of chickens, and he broke into a trot as he circled around to the source of the sound. He found over a dozen of them roaming around the back side of the building, pecking away at the ground for bugs and worms. The birds seemed unconcerned with his presence, but he was almost ecstatic over theirs. One wandered right up to his feet and didn't so much as flinch when he reached down and ruffled the feathers on its back. She just gave a contented cluck, cluck and went back to sourcing something to eat.

He'd barely gotten over the excitement of the chickens when he heard a whiny moo inside the barn. Chickens, he could understand. It seemed entirely possible that the smell of poultry's past had drawn them to his farm, and that explained their presence, but a cow was harder to write off as happenstance, and when he peeked inside the barn and saw three of them, his heart sank.

Wim supposed it shouldn't have been a surprise that some other survivor had stumbled upon his farm and made it their home, but the notion of it made him sick. He'd never thought himself to be a selfish man, but this was the only thing he had left in the entire world, and he didn't want to share it with anyone. If he'd wanted a roommate, he could have returned to Zeke and the cabin in North Carolina.

Then he realized that the person who'd taken over his farm might not be interested in roommates either. So uninterested that they might not only share his disappointment, but that they might also shoot him on sight or, at best, send him away. After all, there were no more laws. No deeds to say, 'This is mine, not yours.' Whoever had been living here had just as much right to the farm as he did. Maybe more.

Wim considered leaving at that very moment. He could turn on his heels and head off somewhere else and never have to deal with the awkwardness of confronting this new resident. But before he could do that, he heard a shotgun shell being racked into the chamber. He swallowed hard.

"I am unarmed and not a threat. I promise you that," he said and hoped that would be good enough to keep himself from getting shot in the back.

No response came.

"This was my farm a while back. That's the only reason I'm here now. I've been away for a long time, though, and I guess things change."

Still no answer. He risked swiveling his head a slight amount, trying to look behind himself and see who held him at gunpoint, but he couldn't make anything out without risking a more dramatic movement.

"I'm going to turn around now, but I'll do it real slow, and I'll keep my hands in the air. Please, don't shoot me."

"Jesus Christ, Wim. I won't shoot you."

The voice. It was so familiar to his ears. He knew it the second he heard it, but he had to be wrong. It was his mind playing a mean prank on him, nothing more. That wasn't her voice. It couldn't be.

"What the hell are you waiting for?"

His heart kicked into overdrive, and he felt his stomach tie itself up in a knot. It's not her, he kept telling himself. It's impossible. He knew he was going to hate himself for it, but he was so excited he could barely stand still. Then he stopped trying.

Wim spun around, dropping his arms and not caring if he got shot because if the person with the gun wasn't Ramey, he'd just as soon be dead anyway.

But it was her.

She dropped the gun, and it clattered on the floor, making her flinch as if she expected it to go off, and, in some horrible twist of fate, kill one of them. Only the shotgun didn't go off, and she ran past it and didn't stop running until she hit him in the chest so hard he lost his balance.

He tried to regain it, but it was too late, and they fell onto the dirt floor, getting tangled up in the old straw and moldy feed and not caring in the slightest. She grabbed his hair, which had grown so long he was almost embarrassed by it, and pulled their faces together and kissed him. He kissed her back, and they stayed locked in that embrace, afraid to let the other go, for so long that Wim's arms started to go numb.

"How?" he asked. He knew there should have been more words in that question but could only get out the one. That one was enough.

"I guess I just had the flu. I realized that about a week later when I was still alive. I tried going back to the cabin, but you know my sense of direction always sucked. I ended up in Georgia, and by the time I did get back, you were long gone."

It was all so much to take in. Wim didn't know what to say, but that was okay because Ramey, as always, talked enough for the both of them.

"I can't believe you gave our cabin to some old fart named Zeke."

"In my defense, I thought you were dead."

"I know but still. Zeke? I stayed with him for almost a month, just in case you came back. He kept feeding me green beans. And saying, 'I wishum you was my woman.' Ugh." Ramey stuck her finger in her mouth and faked a gag. "I'd rather be with Bobby Mack."

"Who's Bobby Mack?"

Ramey grinned, and Wim thought he saw some color rise in her cheeks. "Never mind." She kissed him again. "I thought about wandering around and looking for you, but I knew the odds of it were a billion to one. So, I came back here. I really didn't expect that you'd ever come home, but this place, just being here, it made me feel like part of you was still with me."

"I'm sorry," Wim said. His throat was tight, and he felt like crying but fought against that. "I never should have let you go."

"You didn't, you dummy. I saw you out there digging my grave. I took it upon myself to leave. I thought it would be easier for the both of us. Thank God I was too much of a coward to shoot myself."

Ramey put her hands on his face, her fingers entwined in his beard. "And you really need to shave." She laughed. He didn't know how much he'd missed that sound until he heard it again.

"I know."

"But I like the hair." She grabbed handfuls of it and pulled his face into hers, and they kissed, long and lazy and never wanting the moment to end. "My God, Wim. I'm so damn happy."

"I am too." And he was. Happier than he ever thought possible.

"Tell me where you've been all this time."

He knew he'd tell her all of it soon, but he didn't want to spoil the moment. There'd be time for stories later. For now, he just wanted to hold his wife, his love, in his arms. Even if the world was coming to an end around them, there was still happiness to be found. There was still something worth living for. A reason to go on.

THE END

AUTHOR'S NOTE

And there we have it, dear readers. I hope I managed to create a satisfying finale for you and remained faithful to the characters and the story. Writing this was an emotionally taxing experience, but I'm glad there was some light at the end.

And who knows, since there are some survivors, they might reappear down the road, but for the time being, let's pretend they lived happily ever after.

I'm going to take a break from zombies for a little while. I need to cleanse my palate, and I have a few thrilling horror story ideas I'm planning to write. I sincerely hope you'll follow me along this long and winding road.

I can never thank you enough for taking the time to read these books. The success of this series is because you took a chance on a mostly unknown writer from rural Pennsylvania and cared enough about these characters to keep on reading. And I love you for that!

I sincerely enjoy hearing from readers, so if you'd like to reach out, please visit my website or send me a friend request on Facebook. The links are:

http://www.tonyurbanauthor.com

http://Facebook.com/tonyurban

I also love giving my readers free stuff, so if you sign up for my mailing list, you'll get 3 free short horror stories.

http://www.tonyurbanauthor.com/signup

As always, Happy Reading! And thank you, from the bottom of my heart!

ABOUT THE AUTHOR

A professional photographer, writer, and fan of general weirdness (both real and imagined), Tony has traveled tens of thousands of miles, seeking out everything from haunted locations, UFO crash sites, and monsters like Bigfoot and the Mothman. In a previous life, he worked in the independent movie industry, but he finds his current career much more exciting.

Tony's first writing memory involves penning a short story about taking a road trip with his best friend and his dog (two different creatures) to watch KoKo B Ware in a professional wrestling event in Pittsburgh. He wrote that epic saga while in the 3rd grade, and it was all downhill from there.

His first books were a series of offbeat travelogues but recently, his zombie apocalypse series, "Life of the Dead" has been a bestseller online and grossed out readers all over the world.

His ultimate goal in life is to be killed by a monster thought by most to be imaginary. Sasquatch, werewolves, chupacabras, he's not picky.

If that fails, he'd enjoy making a living as a full time writer. Which of those two scenarios is more likely is up to the readers to decide.

For more information:
tonyurbanauthor.com
tony@tonyurbanauthor.com

Printed in Great Britain
by Amazon

35779023R00157